Julia

Queen Mab

Vol. I

SALZWASSER
VERLAG

Julia Kavanagh

Queen Mab

Vol. I

Reprint of the original, first published in 1863.

1st Edition 2022 | ISBN: 978-3-37500-164-3

Verlag (Publisher): Salzwasser Verlag GmbH, Zeilweg 44, 60439 Frankfurt, Deutschland
Vertretungsberechtigt (Authorized to represent): E. Roepke, Zeilweg 44, 60439 Frankfurt, Deutschland
Druck (Print): Books on Demand GmbH, In de Tarpen 42, 22848 Norderstedt, Deutschland

QUEEN MAB.

VOL. I.

QUEEN MAB.

BY

JULIA KAVANAGH,

AUTHOR OF

"NATHALIE," "ADELE,"

&c., &c.

IN THREE VOLUMES.

VOL. I.

LONDON:

1863.

PART THE FIRST.

JOHN FORD.

QUEEN MAB.

CHAPTER I.

QUEEN SQUARE, Bloomsbury, is a quiet place. Securely it sleeps within the shelter of the neighbouring Law and the shadow of a few old trees. It hears, indeed, the subdued roar of Holborn, and the distant hum of the city; but it hears them as in a dream, and, heeding neither, it slumbers and dozes on. Its lot is cast in peace and silence; rude carriages disturb it not, for it has but a few inconvenient outlets, and intruding feet seldom profane the grass that grows freely between its ancient flags. It has seen better days, that a glance will tell, but the ghost of departed greatness protects it from the last humiliation of decay: it is not populous. It has ceased to be fashionable, but, thank heaven, it is still "genteel."

The houses suit the place; they are old, brown, substantial burgher houses—they have never been palatial mansions. They deal little with the vanities of life, but mind their own concerns, and see to their little gardens behind, and look at their green and quiet square in front, with its damp stained statue of that Queen Anne who took and filled her father's throne, and was called "Good."

To persons of a speculative turn who see such a place for the first time, it is a perfect godsend. If they enter it from Gloucester Street, for instance, fresh from the turmoil of Holborn, they are struck with its quaint charm; for one it has, and quite its own. To be sure, it is neither picturesque, nor pretty, nor beautiful. It was never meant to answer any of these epithets, but then we do not look for beauty in great commercial cities; and who that is wise would wish to live in a pictureque neighbourhood, or would even indulge in conjectures concerning its inhabitants. But here the very absence of all that is brilliant or striking is a temptation. In that shady house beyond a student might roost and dream away a lifetime. In its sad looking neighbour an invalid, to whom country air was no necessity, might pass through querulous years, and not be affronted with the cheerfulness of places more favoured. In this a miser might hoard his gold, and contrive hiding-places of his own. Or a disappointed man might hide his head from the world's cold scorn, and sink unheeded into his grave. But whatever the tenant might be, that decorum which seems innate in Queen Square, would be expected to mark his habitation.

Now, it was precisely decorum that was wanting in Mr. Ford's house. It was that which made it look so singular and incongruous a dwelling. It had no business in Queen Square. It was as well built, as valuable a freehold as its neighbours on either hand, but they looked comfortable if not affluent, and Mr. Ford's house was decidedly shabby and poor. Their very plainness was suggestive of citizen comforts; they were homes where a hearty Christmas dinner could be served up, and whence a respectable funeral could issue, after gout and good living had done their work; but Mr. Ford's house, dingy and forlorn, suggested none but images of poverty or avarice. A miserly or a needy man alone could inhabit this desolate abode. Country poverty has its graceful aspect; weeds grow prettily amongst the loose stones, and moss does very well on a roof; we need not even trench upon ivy, which belongs to ruins, to make something nice and becoming of a dilapidated country mansion; but London decay is like London itself, rather grim, smoky, and dirty, and Mr. Ford's house was inconceivably dreary to look at. The doorsteps, that last stronghold of English cleanliness, were of a dull grey, and told of a negligent or overtasked maid-of-all-work. The paint on the door was worn away in frightful patches of scarred brown. The handle of the area bell was broken; and the bell itself, when put in motion by some mysterious piece of mechanism, uttered a faint and ghostlike squeak. The curtains of the kitchen windows were yellow rags torn and never mended. The faded blind of the parlour window was of a common printed pattern; poor and miserable looked its Gothic arches that nearly met a rusty iron screen, savingly substituted to the clear muslin of the neighbouring houses. The first floor, indeed, had a decent look. The yellow blinds were never raised—but, though yellow, they were whole; and everyone knew, moreover, that behind them there was a tale and a mystery; but the second and third storeys were even more conspicuous than the lower part of the house. Broken panes, mended with brown paper stuck on with wafers, were of common occurrence in those unfortunate regions; it was even said that sundry garments had there been hung out to dry. "But that must be a slander," as Mrs. Smith kindly remarked; "for had they not the garden and the back windows?" Mrs. Slater, who owned a house in Devonshire Street, took a less lenient view of the matter, and openly declared, "Mr. Ford's house was a disgrace to the Square, it was. And she did not care who heard her saying so. And she neither cared nor knew who Mr. Ford was."

Part of this declaration was very true. Mrs. Slater did not know who Mr. Ford was, and Queen Square was no wiser than Mrs. Slater. Some knowledge indeed it had, but of that broad delusive kind which is almost worse than complete ignorance. This at least leaves imagination free; now to know a little is to be fettered in a most unpleasant manner. It is in some sort to be compelled to the labour of distorting, and not to be allowed the delightful liberty of invention.

Mr. Ford's house was his own freehold property—that everyone knew; he had also chambers somewhere, but what he did there, none seemed able to decide. He led a dull, silent sort of life; his three boys, a grim servant-woman, and Mr. Ford himself, were the only persons on whom the shabby door ever opened and shut again. Visitors being unknown at Mr. Ford's, attention became all the keener: and Mr. Ford, a shabby-genteel man, with a step alternately depressed and elastic, his raw scape-grace-looking boys, and Susan, who put no questions and answered none, became the legitimate prey of the inquisitive. Very little was made of them. Anyone could see that though the boys outgrew their trousers and jackets, these were seldom renewed; that Mr. Ford's coat grew whiter at the seams, and his nose rather redder as time passed: and that Susan's temper, as displayed in her conversations at the front door, or from the bottom of the area steps, did not become more mellow as Susan herself ripened. But such general discoveries only heightened curiosity, by suggesting all that remained unknown. That much was left to find out was certain. In the first place, there was Mrs. Ford; what had Mr. Ford done with her? She was not dead. Even Susan admitted that by implication, since, when questioned, she invariably answered in her sharpest tones and angriest key, "that Missus was very well, she was." And it was pretty well ascertained that, well or ill, the missing lady, whom not a soul had seen for the last seven years, was to be found behind those drawing-room blinds, which were never raised in day-time at least. But what did that prove? as the French say. Was she crazy, a prisoner, an invalid, or a hypochondriac? No one knew; and heaven alone knows what extraordinary conjectures were rife in Queen Square on this subject.

Such being the sort of interest Mr. Ford's house excited in the minds of his neighbours, the vigilance of their curiosity may be imagined. As a general rule, there was little or nothing to repay it; but a most interesting exception occurred on a gusty autumn afternoon. A double knock, a genuine double knock, was heard at Mr. Ford's door. Two cautious heads appeared; one at the parlour window of the house on the right-hand side, the other at the attic of that on the left. They were quickly withdrawn as Mr. Ford's visitor looked round and leered at Mrs. Buckly, then nodded waggishly at Mary Anne. He had leisure to do so, for the unusual event of a double knock not having been attended to, he had to repeat it with such an increase of force as secured attention. Susan, the sourest of sour-looking housemaids, came and opened, wiping her hands on a greasy apron as she did so, and looking askance at the visitor.

"Mr. Ford at home?" he said, jauntily swinging his cane.

"I shall see, sir," mistrustfully replied Susan; "what name, please, sir?"

"Captain George. Oh! he's at home for Captain George. Tell him his cousin, Captain George, wishes to speak to him five minutes—that's all."

Susan obeyed slowly, not without first giving Captain George a suspicious look.

He was a tall and handsome man of sixty, or thereabouts. He had brown eyes, dark hair, silvering fast, and mustachios carefully trimmed.

He had, also, very good, straight features, and a pleasant smile, that revealed teeth of pearl; and, conscious of these personal advantages, Captain George displayed them to every female gaze with the most graceful liberality. He now smiled at Susan, spite her evident mistrust, and, following her in, kindly shut the street door, and at once made his way to the parlour; but Susan was first, and, laying her hand on the lock, stared sternly at him. Captain George, by no means daunted, kissed his hand; and as Susan, amazed and indignant, was going to ask him what he meant by it, he added, with a wink, "Good—eh?" in a tone so evidently meant for a third person, that Susan at once looked round.

Peering through the banisters of the kitchen staircase, she saw the face of a boy, eating, with evident relish, into a good-sized tart. At once Susan left the parlour door, and, making a dart at the boy, she shook him soundly.

"So you have been and eaten your poor ma's tart. Eh! have you?—have you?"

Every question was accompanied by a shake. The culprit attempted resistance; a scuffle followed; and the noise attracted a lad of thirteen, fair, and very handsome, who at once put away Susan, and stepped between her and her victim.

"You must not, Sue," he said, sharply; "don't you be afraid, Neddy—I am here."

"Do you know what he has been and done, Master Robert?" asked Susan; "been and eaten missus's tart—and how am I to get her another?"

"He did wrong, but you must not touch him," doggedly said the elder boy; "I don't allow Neddy to be beaten at school, and no one shall lay a finger on him at home."

"She pulled my hair!" whimpered Neddy; "and if I ate the tart, William ate the pigeon."

"Well, then, if I don't settle master William for it!" cried Susan, exasperated, "that's all."

"I tell you—you shall not touch William either," said the elder brother; "no one shall beat my brothers whilst I am by. *I* shall punish them. Send William to me; and you, Neddy, just come this way."

He pushed the boy before him, through what seemed to be a garden door.

Susan stood looking sullenly at them; and Captain George, an amused and observant spectator of this scene, now that it was over, coolly opened the parlour door, and, putting in his head, without waiting to have his name taken in, said in his pleasant way,

"It's only me. Never mind me. It's only Captain George."

The parlour which Captain George thus unceremoniously entered was a peculiar one; and not having seen it for something like seven or eight years, that gentleman allowed his keen brown eyes to examine it curiously, whilst he exchanged a cordial greeting, coolly received, with Mr. Ford.

Captain George's first impression was, that he had never seen so comfortless, so untidy, so dirty a place; his second, that his cousin was even a poorer man than the outward appearance of his house, the behaviour of Susan, and the scene on the staircase, all strengthened by some private information, had led him to suppose. There was everything to justify both impressions. Tobacco smoke hung in clouds in the air; the paper hangings were dark with dirt and stains, where they were not torn away in strips, leaving the white walls bare. The table near the window was a litter of books, papers, dirty tumblers, cigar boxes, and bottles of various sizes. The old horse-hair sofa was broken in many places, and recklessly allowed its stuffing to escape. The chairs looked rickety and insecure. The carpet on the floor was full of holes and rents—a trap to unwary feet. The dusty mantel-shelf, above which hung a dull looking-glass with a long crack, was covered with dreary attempts at ornament. An old picture, a broken china vase, an empty watch-case, stood far apart on that long line of yellow board. The untidy hearth, still strewn with the ashes and cinders of a long-extinct fire, crowned this pictnre of domestic discomfort. Captain George saw it all, whilst he shook his cousin by the hand, paternally patting it with both his, proofs of affection which, as we already said, Mr. Ford received coldly enough.

Mr. Ford was a man of forty-two, who had once been handsome, but who was now too worn and haggard to have any claim to the epithet. He was tall and sharp-featured, with good-natured though obstinate brown eyes, and a weak nether lip, that betrayed temper as well as weakness. His high, broad forehead had intellectual claims, but it was both feeble and haughty. His look, his smile, offered the same contradictions. There was shrewdness in the one, and kindness in the other; but Mr. Ford's look was not always intelligent, and his smile was often sarcastic, when it was not envious. He was, indeed, made up of the contrasts which are found in unsuccessful men, the result of broken aims and ever disappointed hopes, and unsuccessful was written in his whole aspect. His uncertain carriage and half-stoop, his loose gait in spite of great physical strength, his very hands thrust in his pockets, and his feet shuffling in a pair of old slippers, completed the story of the dismal ruin, one of the saddest eyes ever gazed on, that of a man.

Of these unpleasant facts, Captain George chose to remain unconscious. He closed his mental vision, and saw a cheerful parlour, and a happy, prosperous man.

"Went to your chambers, and not finding you, came here," he said, gaily sitting down on a broken chair, and heroically disregarding its warning groan. "A comfortable place you have of it. Poor Mrs. Ford—poor Mrs. Ford—a great trouble." And Captain George meditatively smoothed his moustachios, and, in his compassion for Mr. Ford's troubles, abstractedly poured himself out a glass of rum.

"How is Mrs. George?" rather sulkily asked Mr. Ford, thrusting his hands deeper in his pockets, and leaning back in his chair.

"Not very well—not very well," replied Captain George, speaking softly, as if he were addressing the invalid lady herself; "Mrs. George is very delicate—very much so—like Mrs. Ford—all the ladies are, I am afraid."

"And so you went to my chambers," impatiently said Mr. Ford.

"Oh! to be sure! Fine little fellows those of yours! Gad, sir, I thought we should have had a battle on the kitchen stairs. William had eaten a pigeon, and Ned had tucked in a tart, and Susan was for immediate justice. But what's the big one's name? Robert, ay? Robert held out manfully for his little brothers—shan't touch them; I don't allow my little brothers to be beaten at school, and you shan't touch them; *I'll* punish them; and off he marches with them. Capital—on my word—capital—ha, ha! A regular trump, that boy of yours."

"And so you went to my chambers," said Mr. Ford again.

"That's to say, what brings you here, eh? That big boy is just like you. Just like you."

"So much the worse for himself," morosely replied Mr. Ford.

"Come, old fellow, don't be so sulky," said Captain George, giving him a jovial thrust with the end of his cane; "if I hunted you out to-day, it was to do you a good turn. Why, man, you know as well as any one that Captain George is a good-natured fellow, rather fiery now and then, but a good-natured fellow."

A most knowing wink of the left eye, a wink that recalled to Mr. Ford's memory many a merry night, when Captain George had at least put on wonderfully well the appearance, if he did not possess the reality, of good-nature, compelled a smile, an advantage which Captain George at once followed up.

"I have come to make your fortune," he said, striking his stick on the floor, and giving every word suitable emphasis.

"Have you made yours?" asked Mr. Ford.

"I have come to make your fortune," repeated Captain George, disdaining to answer the question. "A hundred pounds, no more, sir, will make your fortune this very day."

Mr. Ford was just then very much in want of a guinea, and to be asked for a hundred pounds by the least trustworthy of his acquaintance, was not soothing, even though the end in view was so excellent as the making of his fortune. He could not even consider the proposal under its ludicrous aspect. He felt sharp, irritable, and full of his wrongs, and humour and Captain George were equally foreign to his mood. An exclamation which did not convey a benediction rose to his lips, but hospitality checked it, and it subsided into a sort of impatient and half-muttered growl.

"Not a hundred!—well, then, five hundred, say five hundred," facetiously added Captain George.

"You had better not," exclaimed Mr. Ford, looking much excited—"you had better not, Captain George."

"Why, you are just like that boy of yours now," said Captain George—"shan't touch them, no one shall touch my brothers. You are just like him now—a regular trump that boy is!"

"I tell you you had better not," resumed Mr. Ford, with rising anger. "I am not to be fooled out of any more money. And if I had what I lent you, and what I ——"

"Now, what's the use of ripping up old sores," expostulated Captain George, "let bygones be bygones. If you had not been good-natured to me formerly, you know well enough I should not now have this opportunity of doing you a good turn. And, seriously, what is a hundred pounds? Now, what is it?"

Mr. Ford's glass was by him—he took and drained it sullenly.

"A wilful man—a wilful man," said Captain George. "Now, just listen to me; hear me, only hear me, my dear fellow, and I will convince you that the money must be found. Now, just listen; but are you sure we are alone?"

"Ay, alone enough."

"No fear of that pleasant-looking maid of yours," here Captain George winked in the direction of the kitchen stairs, "having her ear at the keyhole."

Mr. Ford impatiently grumbled that there was no fear; upon which Captain George rose, and, cautiously putting his hand to his mouth, whispered something in Mr. Ford's ear.

"Mines," audibly said Mr. Ford.

"Hush—sh! my dear fellow," and Captain George whispered again.

"There was to be a canal once," surlily said Mr. Ford.

"The fortune of war," replied Captain George, with great coolness, "the fortune of war. A hundred pounds will do it this time—not guineas, mind; a hundred pounds!"

Mr. Ford rested his elbow on the table and leaned his cheek on his hand. He had not a hundred pounds indeed, but he had been staggered by Captain George's whispers, and Captain George, who knew his face of old, was quite aware of the fact.

"It is to your strong practical sense I appeal, my dear fellow," he said, insidiously, praising Mr. Ford for the quality he least possessed. "If any one understands these matters you do; and whether you invest or not, I shall be glad of your opinion on my own account."

"Oh! that is it, is it?" sneered Mr. Ford, "I thought you had some object in coming here to-day."

Captain George looked at Mr. Ford with profound admiration, winked, gave him a thrust of his cane, and drawing a packet of papers from the breast-pocket of his coat, he put them on the table with an emphatic thump of his left hand, and a significant "there!"

Mr. Ford took the papers up and glanced hastily over them. Then he began at the beginning, and whilst Captain George leaned back in his chair and surveyed the walls and the ceiling, he read them through with close attention. Mr. Ford was, unfortunately for himself, an excellent judge of business matters, and he soon perceived that the speculation had every appearance of being sound and fortunate. Judgment is of two kinds—critical and practical. Mr. Ford's was critical; no one knew better than he did the weak or the strong point of this world's concerns. In these matters he was keen, clear-sighted and sensible, but even as good critics rarely write good books, so Mr. Ford, who saw so clearly and so well where the elements of success lay, never yet had known how to secure its fruits. The undertakings in which he had embarked were all fair and prosperous, but either he withdrew too soon from them through caprice, or he stayed too long through obstinacy. That practical sense which enables men, ignorant, untaught, and often inexperienced, to do the right thing at the right moment, was that which failed him. He said he was unlucky, and many people said so too; and so he was, but his was the ill luck not of circumstance, but of character, the most fatal of any.

With secret irritation and discontent, he now

read those sheets of foolscap, pregnant with golden promises, none of which could be fulfilled for him. "Even if I had the money, something would come to cross it all," was his bitter thought; "and I have not got it; and that fool, who cannot know this thing will answer—or he would not have come to me—will reap all the benefit."

"Well," anxiously said Captain George, who had been sucking the head of his cane for the last five minutes.

"Well," said Mr. Ford, pushing away the papers with an impatient sigh, "it looks well, but I will have nothing to do with it."

Captain George's face fell.

"Then you don't think well of it," he said, taking up the papers.

"Oh! yes, I do; but just leave me these for a day or so—I had better look at them again."

Captain George obeyed with great alacrity; then, suddenly looking uneasy,

"I say, Ford, fair play; don't invest, and not tell me: fair play—eh?"

"If you talk of fair play, I shall begin and suspect something," said Mr. Ford, sharply; "I have already told you I shall not invest."

Captain George poured himself out a glass of rum, shook his head, rose, and walked out. Mr. Ford saw him to the door. On the last step, Captain George turned round, and nodding with what looked very like drunken solemnity, he said, with much emphasis:

"Deep, Ford, deep—devilishly deep," and walked away.

CHAPTER II.

MR. FORD closed the door on his visitor; then going to the head of the kitchen stairs, he asked, in a subdued tone,

"Susan, are the boys ready to go and see their mother?"

"The boys ha' been and adone all sorts of mischief, sir," shortly answered Susan, appearing on the stairs, and speaking in the same key; "whilst I opened the door to the strange gentleman, one ate the tart, and the other the pigeon, that was for missus's dinner. They're worse than cats, them boys—they are!"

Mr. Ford had a pimple on his forehead, which he always scratched in cases of difficulty. He now recurred to it with a look more perplexed than indignant.

"I am afraid the poor fellows are often hungry,"

sighed Mr. Ford; "you must get something else, Susan."

"I told missus the cat had done it. God forgive me all the stories I do tell in this house. And she said 'never mind.'"

"Well, that is all right; is it not?"

"Why, no, sir, it ain't. The cat made me bring in Mary Ann, and what do you think missus is up to now? Why, she wants Mary Ann up-stairs."

Now Mary Ann was a fiction, the myth of the household, and this was a most inconvenient wish, as Mr. Ford's lengthened face expressed.

"I put it off, saying Mary Ann was ill in bed," pursued Susan; "but that is not all, missus wishes for fruit. Now, sir, Covent-garden is not far off: but I put it to you, sir, can I get cherries at this time of the year?"

"Perhaps hot-house grapes would do," suggested Mr. Ford, looking deeply perplexed.

"Perhaps they will," doubtfully said Susan; "and perhaps they will not; but that ain't all. Missus wants an organ."

"A harmonium, you mean; well—perhaps I can get one on hire."

But when Mr. Ford looked round his wretched home, when he remembered his debts and his downhill name, he wondered who would be so foolhardy as to trust him with an instrument.

"Perhaps an accordion would do," said Susan, looking sagacious; "organs are only fit for churches."

But Mr. Ford shook his head. His wife had been an accomplished musician, and none but a first-rate instrument would answer her.

"God help me!" he exclaimed, distractedly; "it will be all out if she does not get that harmonium, and it will break her heart, Susan, it will break her heart, not for herself, but for the boys and me."

Tears stood in his eyes, and Susan looked sorely troubled, but the accordion had exhausted her short stores of comfort.

"Well," said Mr. Ford, with a deep sigh, "I must put her off for a while; and say I am promised one. Tell the boys to dress, and come to me, Susan, and then I'll see."

Alas! "I'll see," was an old phrase, and Susan knew it but too well. "I'll see" had often paid Susan's wages, and been the final settlement of many a bill; but "I'll see" had never wrought any substantial good. "And if she counts on 'I'll see,' for her organ," thought Susan, as she went up-stairs, "she'll wait long enough."

Poor Mr. Ford remained absorbed in perplexing meditations. From whom could he borrow?—what could he sell to get that harmonium for his wife?

"Decidedly she *is* getting better," he thought; "for once she could bear no noise, and now she wants to make a noise that will fill the house. She is getting better, that is one comfort."

"The boys are ready, sir," whispered Susan, on the staircase.

"Have they got on their good shoes, Susan?"

"They have, sir."

"Mind you stay outside, and make them take their things off at once, Susan."

"No fear of it, sir."

"And, Susan, tell Robert to give them a talking about the tart and the pigeon. They mind him more than they do me."

Susan nodded grimly, and Mr. Ford softly went up the staircase. The three boys were standing on the landing. Their faces were washed; their hair was brushed; their attire was neat and clean. Their father gave them a scrutinizing glance, then opening the drawing-room door, he signed them to enter. They obeyed, in silence. He followed them on tiptoe, and closed the door with so much care, that it made not the least noise.

The drawing-room of Mr. Ford's house offered a very striking contrast to the squalid parlour below. Here time had stood still; the seven years during which the lower regions had lost the rule of the mistress of the house and gone to chaos, had left no trace of their passage upstairs. Mrs. Ford's drawing-room looked as quiet, as decorous as when it had been closed on visitors and guests seven years before. Like its tenant, it was melancholy and faded, a token of better times, when life was young and hope had her day; but the furniture, if not as fresh, was as good as new; a carpet that would still wear many years—for who ever trod on it—spread its faded roses on the floor. The dark velvet curtains seemed to have been just hung by the upholsterer, in their heavy, precise folds on either side of the yellow blinds that were kept rigidly closed; for the invalid could not bear even the mild light of Queen Square. Everything had the same fixed and subdued aspect. The tables were set exactly in their places; the chairs seemed to belong to the walls, where they had grown old-fashioned, unused. The pictures, mere family portraits, were shrouded, in thick coverings, from the weary gaze of the sick lady; the very looking-glass over the cold and dreary fireplace was veiled with a half-transparent tissue, through which it reflected, in dim outlines, the gloomy furniture, but gave back no distinct image to the look of Mrs. Ford. Books, woman's work, graceful trifles were absent from this melancholy apartment, where all spoke of a painful stillness—of a life suddenly and prematurely checked in its flow, and nothing more so than the calm motionless figure of Mrs. Ford herself, as she sat in her chair—with closed eyes and clasped hands, her head bent, her figure, wrapped in a long, loose dark robe, like a monastic garment.

Mrs. Ford was one of those fair women with chiselled features full of repose, who even in the inevitable decay of health and youth, suggest great past beauty. Nature had given her the smooth Grecian forehead, the straight nose, and exquisite lips of the Venus of Milo. She had also bestowed on her the noble neck, the stately figure of that immortal image of woman's majestic loveliness; and though time and disease had done their work, though pain had contracted the brow, though the large blue eyes had grown cold and vacant, though the lips were pale and the cheeks colourless, and the wasted figure had learned to stoop, that subtle part of beauty which survives the bloom and the full outlines of youth still lingered over all.

For the last seven years, ever since the birth of her youngest child, Mrs. Ford had not left the first floor, where we now find her. Visitors—few though they were—were never admitted to her presence. She had no near relatives in England; and her complaint, a nervous one, required absolute rest. Her children saw her rarely, and then in silence. Susan and Mr. Ford alone spoke to her.

Mr. Ford considered his wife's long and mysterious illness one of the many sorrows of his lot, and not without cause. She had been, though he knew it not, the good genius of his life; and it was since her withdrawal from its concerns that it had sunk into the slough of Despond. Since then the furniture had got broken, and Mr. Ford's coat greasy and shabby; since then he had deserted his chambers, and muddled over grog at home; since then the children had grown up, lawless, and bills had accumulated; and nothing had gone well from the day when the firm though gentle mind which had ruled the household and influenced its master, had been conquered by insidious disease.

"My dear!" whispered Mr. Ford; "the children!"

Mrs. Ford looked up. A faded smile passed across her lips. She gazed at the three boys; she embraced the youngest first, then William, then Robert. Then she looked at them again.

"Do they study well?" she asked of her husband.

"Admirably; indeed," coolly continued Mr. Ford, who had kept his children at home for a week through his own inability to pay for their schooling, and the schoolmaster's decided reluctance to trust him any longer—"indeed, I am looking out for a tutor for them, and I think ——." What other invention Mr. Ford was going to indulge in, we cannot say; but it suddenly occurred to him that this school of deceit might not be the best for his children to listen to, and he abruptly added, "Have they not been long enough here, my dear?"

Mrs. Ford nodded assent, and the three boys left the room, to Mr. Ford's infinite relief. He was always on thorns lest they should "let out something," to use his own words. He closed the door upon them, and came back to his wife; he sat down by her side. She shut her eyes. She could look at her children, but the sight of any other face was distasteful to her, especially so was that of her husband.

Theirs had been a love-match. At twenty-three Alicia Norton was what men call "a splendid creature," and women correctively "a very fine girl." She had ten thousand pounds, and suitors for her hand abounded. Some were titled, many prosperous—John Ford, a poor struggling lawyer, was preferred. He was then a handsome man of twenty-seven, but his weak nether lip, his vacillating look, and the irritable cast of his features, would have warned away a wiser woman. Alicia saw the kindness of his glance and smile, and took it for goodness. She heard the confident assertions, the resentful protests of a vain man, and she took them for the aspirations and susceptibility of a man of ambition and strong character. Mr. Ford was neither; he had talent, honesty, and bouyant hopes, but little more. One of his first acts was to invest his wife's ten thousand pounds in a speculation that promised well, but from which wise men soon withdrew. Mr. Ford disregarded, or received with complacent smiles, his wife's hesitating objections. Before six months were over the ten thousand pounds had enriched a few knaves, and were lost for ever to Alicia and her children yet unborn. Spite this mistake, which he would not ackowledge, Mr. Ford did not forfeit at once his wife's confidence. She still hoped in him, and believed in the future; but a few years after this loss, five thousand pounds which Mr. Ford inherited from an uncle, shared the same fate; Mrs. Ford had little or no imagination—love could give her illusions, but once the hard touch of reality had dispelled them, there was in her no power to call them back. She now saw her husband as he was—good-natured, obstinate, foolish, and intellectual, and her pride in him was gone for ever.

Mrs. Ford was a very proud woman. She would not acknowledge that she had been mistaken; no, it was Mr. Ford who had deceived her.

She did not reproach him; but she brooded over her wrongs with the obstinacy of a narrow mind, and the bitterness of a wounded heart.

Of this Mr. Ford remained unconscious. He adored his wife, and was convinced that she adored him. At the same time, he thought himself superior to her, and showed her that he thought so. He concealed none of his weaknesses from her. Nay, he was rather lavish in displaying them to her gaze. She saw that though his kind heart could win him friends, his irritable temper would allow him to keep none. Mr. Ford cast away from him every helping hand, and whilst many derived benefit from him, he derived benefit from none. This result, which he was clear-sighted enough to see, but not frank enough to acknowledge, made him sore. He took scornful views of human nature, and grew sour at home. Yet he still fondly loved his wife. His love increased instead of lessening with years, whilst hers daily grew weaker, and at length died entirely. Something remained: duty, lukewarm liking —but not love.

Alicia Norton could not do without admiring her husband, and it was impossible to live with Mr. Ford and to admire him, spite some sterling qualities. His want of judgment had given her pride a great shock, his folly in alienating men whom a shrewder man could have made subservient to his own ends, irritated and vexed her: his rejection of her advice, his carelessness of her opinion offended her, and the strange blindness with which he still believed in her love, and even boasted of it in her presence, made her despise him. His want of success in his profession, which he neglected for ruinous speculations, the poverty to which it condemned her and her children, made her severe to his weaknesses—and these, alas! were not of the heroic kind.

Mr. Ford was an untidy man at home. He was selfish in little things, pettish, irritable, and despotic by fits. His kind heart, his sincere love, could not soften a woman like Alicia. She had convinced herself that he was to blame for having married her, not she for having married him; and she settled down into a puerile mood of discontent, which she had, however, sufficient strength and dignity not to betray. She allowed her husband to adore her, and even to enjoy the shew of affection which could deceive him. She no longer obtruded the advice he would not always follow, but confined her attention to domestic concerns. Sometimes she hated herself for having ever loved him, and sometimes she hated life for having so ruthlessly lost its prizes: Love, wealth, ambition and its rewards.

"Some lives are one great wreck," thought Alicia, in her despair, "and such is mine."

Her greatest trial was yet to come. Robert grew up like her in person, and like her husband in temper and manner. Mr. Ford spoke in a drawl, interrupted by loud pettish jerks, and Robert showed signs of imitating the paternal propensity. Eagerly Mrs. Ford tried to correct the boy and to make him speak in a clear and distinct tone. Robert's vanity was stirred, and he showed himself remarkably ductile, until that same vanity was more powerfully appealed to by his father's unmerciful ridicule. Inspired by an unlucky spirit of opposition, which always seized him at the wrong moment, he did his best to undo his wife's teaching.

"Why, Robert," he said to him with his derisive laugh, "what priggish pedantry have they put into you?"

Robert, who was not then much more than six years old, had uot the moral fortitude to withstand this taunt. His mother saw him redden.

"Talk like a man," pursued his father, "and not like a methodist preacher. Why, all the other boys will laugh at you when you go to school."

"They shan't," sullenly answered Robert.

This scene, one of many, was the last Mrs. Ford witnessed. She listened to her husband, and never spoke or remonstrated with him. She was not even angry with Mr. Ford. No, the sting went deeper. In Robert's sudden and resentful abandonment of her teaching, she recognized the weak vanity of his father. Was he then to grow up like him? She was near her third confinement, and as she thought of another child her heart seemed to break within her. Was she, Alicia Norton, to be the mother of a race of fools and of social outcasts?

She went upstairs that night in an agony of tumultuous feelings and of wounded pride. The child, a third boy, was born before the morning. Its sex gave her the last pang she could suffer as a mother. Another image of her husband! She never recovered the shock—disease seized her, and made her helpless in her own home. Perhaps the divine chastisement of too much pride.

This was a twofold calamity. Whilst illness held her captive upstairs, the house below was going to the ruin of abandonment, dirt, and squalor; her husband drank and neglected the little business he had, and her children grew up wild, rude, and undisciplined. But the greatest misfortune of all was the complete darkness which settled over Mrs. Ford's mental vision. She became querulous, capricious, and exacting. She brooded over her wrongs until she could think of and see nothing else. She was an ill-used woman, and Mr. Ford was the worst husband a woman had ever had. She was too amiable and too proud to reproach him; she even called in resignation to her aid, and was heroic enough to allow him to see and address her; but his daily presence was an infliction it required all that heroism to bear.

All this would have been ridiculous if it had not been tragic in some of its consequences. It was during this long illness, which would have alienated the love of many a better man, that Mr. Ford's tenderness for his wife burned with purest flame. He proved it in a hundred ways, which, could she but have known the least of them, would have subdued and humbled even Alicia's proud heart.

When the first inroads of pinching poverty began, Mr. Ford resolved that, no matter *who* suffered from this change, Alicia should not. She was not in a state of mind to bear care or to hear of debts, why trouble her with such concerns? Then she could not be denied her fancies, no matter what they might be! No, Alicia must be gratified—he, the boys even, could do without. Thus the miserable condition of the little world below had a double meaning: it was the work of unthriftiness, of loose habits and extravagance, and it was also the work of much love Mrs. Ford's fancies were not very expensive, but they were numerous and wasteful. Often when a savoury and separate meal was brought up to her, she would send it down untasted and ask for a cup of tea. Then she required attendance so exclusive, that for a long time an extra servant was kept; when that became impossible, the work below was neglected and the parlour took care of itself, and the boys tore and mended their clothes if they pleased. The havoc and ruin she caused, Mrs. Ford was never allowed to suspect. The boys had clothes in which they appeared before their mother, and Susan spoke of Margaret and Mary Ann to her deceived mistress. With time she dropped Margaret, finding the fiction troublesome, but Mary Ann she clung to as a convenient scapegoat.

And still Mrs. Ford thought herself ill-used. That there should be comfort she took as a matter of course. That there should be neither wealth nor luxury was Mr. Ford's fault. Another man with his opportunities would have kept his carriage long before this. She did not care about the carriage, nor want it, but it was one of those proofs of success which Mrs. Ford was too matter of fact to overlook. These feelings were always strongest when Mr. Ford paid her his daily visit; she could not and would not show them, and the restraint made his presence doubly distasteful. Poor Mr. Ford ascribed her cold manner to her complaint. And she was so cold, and therefore, as he thought, so ill, on this present day, that it pained him. He thrust his hands in his pockets and looked gloomy. It was hard to have so sickly a wife. Other women were not so—seven years too; but then poor Alicia could not help it—no—and she was so fond of him, too, with it all.

"How is it you are at home at this hour," at length asked Mrs. Ford.

"I had an appointment," replied her husband, not choosing to confess he had not gone out that day.

"With whom?" inquired Mrs. Ford, who seemed in the questioning mood—one rare with her.

"With—with Captain George," was the hesitating reply.

Mrs. Ford opened her eyes, and seemed to search far back into memory for the name. She found it, for her cheek flushed, her look lit, but she did not speak.

"He is the same jaunty fellow as ever," pursued Mr. Ford, "but the very man to dazzle fools."

"He is no fool," said Mrs. Ford.

"I did not say he was, my dear; but he is shallow, which is worse. I have studied that man's character thoroughly, and he is shallow—to the heart's core."

"Take care, Mr. Ford—take care—" said his wife, sitting up in her chair, and leaning her two hands on its leather arms, "that man is not shallow—he is bad—bad."

"Do not excite yourself, my dear," kindly said her husband: "leave Captain George to me. You know it is not easy to deceive me, my love."

"He is dangerous," she gasped—"dangerous!"

"Yes, my love—to some—but not to me. You know my insight into character."

"What did he come for?—what is it?" she persisted.

"My love, you know I do not talk to you on professional matters; but rely upon it, I have not the least faith in Captain George; I know the man," added Mr. Ford, with great emphasis.

Mrs. Ford smiled bitterly. That was how she was treated—that was how her advice was received.

"I am afraid Captain George's loud knock disturbed you," said Mr. Ford; "but it was Susan who opened——"

"And why did Susan open?" interrupted Mrs. Ford: "Susan is to wait upon me. I must insist on Mary Ann attending to the door."

Mr. Ford scratched his pimple, but hit on a bright invention.

"Mary Ann was in the dumps," he said, gravely; "I gave her warning this morning—that girl is getting unmanageable."

And so she was; and Mr. Ford, whom the practice of seven years had not yet made perfect in the art of invention, had resolved to get rid of this troublesome person altogether.

Mrs. Ford shut her eyes again, and sighed; another man would have had a footman by this; but no—thanks to his folly and imprudence, Mr. Ford would live and die with two female servants.

"Mr. Ford," she said, gravely, "do as you please about Mary Ann; keep or dismiss her—what is it to me? but do not take Susan from me. She has enough to do in attending to me."

"Certainly, my love, by all means."

"As to that Mary Ann, I am glad she is going. I am tired of hearing about her misdeeds."

"And she shall go," emphatically replied Mr. Ford.

"Take a first-rate servant instead," pursued his wife; "give her twenty, thirty pounds a year if need be—a little money more or less is not much matter."

"Of course not."

"And, Mr. Ford, get me an harmonium, if you please. I cannot talk, and yet the silence of these rooms is too much for me."

"Certainly, my love. I really do believe you are getting better," cried Mr. Ford, ardently.

Tears of pure delight stood in his eyes at the thought; but he unfortunately smacked his lips in a foolish, exulting, and decidedly vulgar fashion, which was habitual to him.

"And I once loved that man," thought Alicia, turning her head away.

"I daresay you have had enough of me, my dear," submissively said Mr. Ford: "well, I shall leave you," he added, rising, "and I shall see about your harmonium."

She thanked him coldly. Mr. Ford left the room on tiptoe. He did not know, indeed, how to procure the harmonium, but he was confident that his wife was getting better, and his heart felt light and buoyant with the unexpected happiness.

CHAPTER III.

"I MUST get my dear Alicia that instrument," thought Mr. Ford, as he entered the front parlour, "only it is the money!" He sighed; for money was the name of all his cares, and he sank weariedly in his chair. As he did so, he was struck at once with the sight of some dark object in the square, which intercepted itself between the light, and its medium, the window. He looked, and saw a cab standing at the door, with a trunk on the roof. Convinced there was some mistake, he leaned back lazily, and was extending his hand towards his usual companion and friend, the bottle, when a thundering knock shook the house, and, after a brief delay, the parlour door opened abruptly, and Susan broke in on her master. Susan, never very pleasant of aspect, now looked lowering and sullen. Her eyes sparkled with angry fire, and there was an angry spot, not on her brow, where sat a frown, but on either of her sallow cheeks.

"Miss Lavinia Ford," she said, sharply; "an' I had known the lady was coming, it might have been better—but *I* am of no consequence."

"Miss Lavinia Ford," mechanically repeated Mr. Ford, unable to realize the fulness of the new calamity that was coming to him under the shape of his only remaining sister, the last of three; and before he had recollected himself sufficiently to rise and go and meet her, Miss Ford herself, half smiling, half crying, entered the room, holding a bandbox in her left hand. With a flurried look, and an hysterical "How are you, John?" she clasped his neck with her right arm, and cried bitterly on his shoulder.

Then, indeed, Mr. Ford understood it all. His sister was in deep mourning; her godmother was dead, and she had come to his penniless home, a new burden, another care.

A poor man cannot help such thoughts; they are the inevitable curse of his poverty; yet, with all that, Mr. Ford's welcome was cordial, though it could not be cheerful.

"Cheer up, Livy," he said, with a sigh; "there is not much here, but you did well to come. Sit down. Susan, get Miss Ford some tea."

Now was the time for Susan's revenge.

"Please, sir, will you give me the money for some fresh butter?" she said, civilly.

Mr. Ford reddened.

"I have no change," he answered, sharply; "get Miss Ford her tea first."

"I have change," hastily said Miss Lavinia. "Here is my purse; and will you, John, pay the cabman, if you please? I bargained with him for half-a-crown from the station."

"That is a shilling too much; he must not have more than eighteenpence."

Miss Ford looked disconcerted.

"Please, give him the half-crown," she said, plaintively; "it was a bargain, you know."

"Oh, if you like to throw away a shilling, please yourself," said her brother, internally resolving not to be bound to so foolish a bargain. "Well, Livy, so the poor old lady is dead. Don't cry, child, there's a home for you—though a poor one. Susan, show Miss Ford upstairs."

Miss Ford, whom her brother called child, was a maiden lady of forty, at the very least. Her pale blue eyes had an uncertain look; her speech was hesitating and slow; yet her features expressed a sort of firmness, the result of an inert will, and of a watchful conscientiousness. She was of those who pass through life, seeming to yield to all its accidents, yet whose passive obstinacy prevails in the end over many a peril in which the daring and the strong are wrecked. Miss Ford's green bandbox was an instance in point. How it had travelled in the railway carriage, and not in the luggage van, in spite of the guard—Miss Ford had convinced herself there was no moral wrong in violating his peremptory commands—how it had withstood the angry denunciations of other travellers, and hidden under seats at the right time, and emerged again when it was safe to do so, and gently migrated from Miss Lavinia's lap to a convenient place by her side, where it had finally rested—and how Miss Ford's quiet will had guarded it and prevailed throughout, would form a perfect odyssey in the history of bandboxes. This quiet, hesitating, conscientious, and obstinate lady was now surrendered to Susan; and so well aware was Susan that a contest for supremacy was inevitable between her and her master's sister, that, like a good general, she began the battle at once, and chose the first-floor landing for the encounter.

"You must not go in there, marm, if you please," she said, stepping between the drawing-room door and Miss Ford, who was innocently going to open it; "that is Missus's room, marm, and no one ever goes in there but myself and master."

"Is she so very ill?" asked Miss Lavinia.

Susan deigned no reply, but said, shortly, "Go

on, please; I suppose I must put you in the nursery."

Miss Lavinia, who knew that she had nephews and no niece, felt rather alarmed at the prospect of sharing the apartment of three boys; but held her peace, as was her wont, cogitating inwardly on escape.

"In here, please," said Susan, opening the nursery door, and ushering Miss Ford into as dreary an apartment as ever was devoted to boyhood.

And very eloquently did boyhood assert itself in every nook of the vacant room. Tops, marbles, kites, sticks lay strewn about, sharing the floor with the dust. Carpet, there was none, and but little furniture. Three narrow beds, a dilapidated chest of drawers, a broken wash-hand stand, and walls covered with scrawls of writing and attempts at caricature, did not impress Miss Ford with the prospect of an agreeable home. She looked around her dismally enough, and remembered, with a sigh, her pleasant room at her godmother's, with its white dimity curtains, and garden prospect of lawn and flower-beds. Susan watched her countenance with an angry eye, and, conscious of certain domestic sins in the shape of dust and dirt, she resentfully interpreted Miss Ford's dismayed look to her own account.

Susan had many virtues. She was a faithful servant, heroically devoted to the needy family with whom her lot had been cast; she was tenderly attached to her suffering mistress, for there was between them a secret tie which Susan alone knew, a debt which she gratefully remembered and repaid daily; but human nature is weak, and Susan's share of it was very frail in the matter of temper. Hers was of the aggressive and aggravating kind, to use that expressive and popular word in its vulgar sense. Amongst other manifestations of this unamiable quality, was one which most people who had to do with Susan found particularly irritating. To attack was only the common and positive degree of Susan's displeasure; but to ignore plain facts, to become suddenly, blind, ignorant, and foolish, was, to those who knew her, a sure token of her superlative anger. Anxious to let Miss Ford into this little secret of her character, she now said, shortly—she never spoke otherwise—but with every appearance of candour,

"Of course, you've brought your bed, marm?"

"My bed!" exclaimed Miss Ford, taken by surprise. "Oh dear, no!"

"Then perhaps you'll send for it," suggested Susan calmly.

"I have got none," said Miss Ford, beginning to look alarmed.

"Then where do you mean to sleep, marm? We've got no spare beds here."

Miss Ford not answering, Susan pursued in a philosophic tone:

"I always thought that people travelled with their beds; and I am sure it is the best plan, unless when they mean to sleep at hotels. There is an hotel close by, perhaps you would like to go there, marm, until your bed comes. I dare say it will soon be here—things come so fast by rail now-a-days."

Miss Ford looked at Susan, who preserved a stoic countenance—then at the miserable room, which read to her a whole homily of poverty and neglect—and, overcome by fatigue and grief at so great a change from decent comfort to squalid misery, she sat down on the nearest chair and fairly burst into tears. This confession of helplessness conquered Susan.

"Don't take on, marm," she said kindly enough. "I shall bring you a cup of tea presently, and never mind about the bed. You can have mine, and I can manage somehow in the kitchen. Just give me that bandbox; that's what's pulling you down."

But, to Susan's indignation, Miss Ford, who had kept a tight hold of her bandbox whilst she was embracing her brother in the parlour, now, spite her sobs and her tears, grasped it firmly with both hands.

"Please yourself, marm," said Susan, "but there are no thieves here;" and leaving Miss Lavinia to shift as she pleased, Susan left the room. The door had scarcely closed upon her when it opened again, and Susan's head was thrust in.

"Please, marm, to tell the porter when he brings your bed to-night not to make any noise, as Missus is very ill and can't abide it."

Miss Ford was essentially a meek, patient woman, but this persistent insolence was too much for her. She started to her feet with sudden wrath, and, confronting Susan, said in a quivering voice:

"If you say anything more about that bed, I shall slap your face, you hussy!"

Then sinking down once more on the chair, she again burst into tears.

"Oh! very well, marm—thank you, marm!" replied Susan, with a short laugh; "but I don't think you will do it, marm."

And closing the door gently, spite her secret indignation, she walked down-stairs and entered the parlour, where Mr. Ford was just resting after a short but fierce encounter with the cabman, who had gone away angrily, denouncing the bad faith of the lady—no lady—he was sure, who had deluded him with the promise of half-a-crown.

"If you please, sir, I give you notice that I must leave in a week," said Susan, without preamble. "I ain't a-going to stay and have my face slapped for any one; that I ain't."

Now, apart from her fidelity, Susan had just then very high value in her master's eyes. She represented no less a sum than nine pounds five shillings and sixpence, the amount of wages due to her.

"Well, what's up now?" growled Mr. Ford.

"Oh, nothing, sir, only my new missus has promised to slap my face for me, the next time I open my lips; and as of on course I can't do my business without talking, I ain't a-going to stay—that's all, sir."

Mr. Ford looked profoundly perplexed, then annoyed, then angry, and having relieved his feelings with a petulant and irreverent exclamation of—

"The devil take the women—that's all; there's not been a pair in the house more than five minutes, and they are already fighting," he stooped to expostulation with the member of the offending sex who stood before him.

"Nonsense, Susan, we can't part with you—you know," he said impatiently. "Your mistress could not do without you—no one else knows how to wait on her, and you have been like a mother to the boys."

"Susan knew she had, but for all that she must go—she had done her duty, but new faces and new ways and Susan could not get on together; and Mr. Ford had her notice—in a week she must leave."

"You will do no such thing," good-humouredly said her master, who detected lurking softness in her tone. "And, at all events, I am sure you will show Miss Ford that no one can beat you in serving up a good cup of tea."

"Susan knew nothing about that. Of course it was her duty to do her best, and she would do her best for Miss Ford or for any one." And without requesting supplies for fresh butter—a sign of relenting, which her master noticed, Susan left the room and went down to the kitchen.

Some men have a great terror of domestic storms. Mr. Ford fled like a coward before them. Convinced that he should have to face at least Miss Lavinia's tears, and feeling unequal to the infliction, he hastened out of the house, first summoning to his presence Robert, who was in the garden with his brothers, and instructing him to receive his aunt with due honour and affection.

Robert looked disconcerted. They were miserably

poor; what did their aunt, who was poor too, come to them for?

"And mind that Bill and Ned are not rude to her," continued Mr. Ford. "And tell her I am obliged to go out—and so I must: your dear mother wants a harmonium, and I must get her one somehow or other. I wonder," he added, with a sigh, "if that old screw, James George, would let me have the money."

Mr. James George was Captain George's brother—both were related to Mr. Ford; but Captain George was needy and thriftless, and Mr. James George was wealthy and stingy. It did not seem likely that a man of that temper would assist Mr. Ford, yet on that forlorn hope he now went forth. He had scarcely left when his sister came down, her eyes still red with weeping.

"Are you my nephew Robert?" she timidly asked of the lad who stood looking at her shyly.

With tolerable good grace Robert confessed the relationship, and shook hands with his aunt.

"Is this the room in which you take your meals?" she asked, in the same timid, hesitating way.

With a blush of shame Robert answered that it was. He was keenly alive to the proprieties and decencies of life, and he knew well enough what sort of a room this must seem to his Aunt Lavinia. She gave it a very melancholy look; but bad though it was, it could be mended; untidiness was her particular aversion, and she could not help saying,

"My dear, do you suppose if I were to clear that table just a little—do you think, I mean, it would annoy your father?"

Robert stared at the idea that anything should annoy Mr. Ford, the most pacific of men in such matters, and gave Miss Lavinia full authority to act as she pleased. She began by clearing away the empty bottles, then she gathered the books in a heap, then, as carefully as if they were of paramount importance, she put the old envelopes, letters, and bills together. Robert watched her with considerable interest. He began to understand that though poor his aunt was a very valuable person; visions of decently mended clothes and buttons sewed on flitted before his eyes, and, after mature deliberation—Robert was never in a hurry—he kindly offered to assist Miss Ford.

"And Bill and Ned shall help you too," he added; "tell me what you want to be done, aunt, and I'll make them do it."

Miss Lavinia accepted the magnanimous offer. Bill and Ned were summoned, introduced to their aunt, and set to work forthwith. The empty bottles were taken down to the kitchen; the books were put on their neglected shelves; the papers were tied in a neat parcel with red tape, and made to look quite respectable; Master William Ford was despatched for a packing needle and thread with which Miss Lavinia did her best to sew up the rents in the carpet. In short, before an hour had elapsed the room, thanks to the exertions of Miss Lavinia and of her three nephews, who entered heart and soul into the cause, wore quite another look, so that when Susan came up with the tea-tray she had what she scarcely expected to find, an empty table to put it on, whilst Miss Lavinia had the satisfaction of taking her tea in an improved apartment. So remarkable indeed was that improvement that Mr. Ford was struck with it when he came home. Rather a pleasant family picture was that which greeted his eyes. William and Edward were sitting at the table studying their lessons for Robert, for, since they went no longer to school, their elder brother had become their teacher. Robert himself had put by his book in order to hold the skein of silk his aunt was unwinding, and Robert's jacket lying on the table near Miss Lavinia plainly said what the silk was for.

"Why, Livy, you have done wonders with the parlour," said Mr. Ford, missing the usual disorder.

"The room looks beautiful," observed Robert with great complacency.

"I took down the bottles," cried Edward.

"You only took down three," cried William.

"Robert, it was I took them down, was it not?"

"Hush, boys," replied Robert with great dignity, and not condescending to settle the point at issue.

"I hope I shall be able to mend the sofa to-morrow," timidly remarked Miss Lavinia; "I had not time to-day."

"You'll find plenty to do, my dear," sighed Mr. Ford, the momentary satisfaction of Miss Lavinia's improvement being all gone.

He had called on Mr. James George, after ascertaining that the price of a harmonium was far beyond his means. Uncertainty is a painful state of mind, and misfortune itself is not so trying as the apprehension of it; so thought Mr. James George, for, to relieve Mr. Ford at once, he informed him that a shilling of his money he should never see. Mr. Ford, we are sorry to say, was not grateful, he even took this proof of kindness very ill, and his resentment now found vent in words. He addressed his sister, and though he did not think it needful to enter into particulars, he said with some bitterness,

"You remember the Georges, Livy? You know how they used to come to our father's house when we were children, and spend weeks there. They were poor then, Livy, and glad of a comfortable place. Times are changed, Livy. Captain George is a fine gentleman, and lives in a villa at Brompton, and Mr. James George is a City man, who has not time to spare for an old acquaintance. Mind you don't go near Mr. James, Livy, unless it be to borrow money at fifty per cent. He has the credit of lending it freely enough at that rate, on good security, mind."

"I hope I shall never want to borrow money, John," replied Miss Lavinia; "but fifty per cent. is usury, surely."

Mr. Ford laughed boisterously.

"Usury! Business, Livy—business."

His mirth had something so gloomy in it, that Miss Lavinia felt quite depressed. The children seemed very good, and John was kind, but she was afraid, she was, that sewing up the carpet or mending the sofa would not change matters much.

CHAPTER IV.

A FEW days had gone by, and Miss Ford had settled down in her new home, which Susan had condescended not to leave. Spite the unfavourable symptoms which had marked the opening of their acquaintance, Mr. Ford's sister and Mr. Ford's servant had soon tacitly discovered that they were exactly suited to each other. For Miss Ford, who had been treated like a child, and called one all her life, could manage herself and her little concerns; but was by no means fitted for command—and Susan, who, since her mistress's illness, had led and ruled the house, had totally lost the habit of obedience. Miss Ford was precisely, she soon found, the very mistress suited to such a servant; and such a servant, Miss Ford soon discovered, was the only one suited to her. The mutual oblivion, such as the Roman people decreed in their civil wars, was thrown over the unpleasant past; and stimulated by the presence of a censor, Susan condescended to keep the house cleaner, and to make it more tidy. But it was not in her power to mend the broken furniture, to paper the walls, and otherwise restore to decency the external aspect of Mr. Ford's home. Still less had she any power over that important test of domestic comfort, the larder; and Miss Lavinia soon learned, to her dismay, that though her brother lounged at home, and consumed what seemed to her a perilous quantity of spirits, meals were often scanty in his house. At first she said nothing, and quietly gave Susan money for the most pressing wants, but her stock was short; and, foreseeing that, when it was exhausted, matters would return to their primitive state, she thought it best to appeal to Mr. Ford himself. She accordingly managed to find herself alone with him in the front parlour one afternoon, and discreetly opened the matter by encomiums on her three nephews.

"Robert is really a fine lad," she said; "he grows very like you, John."

"I think he is like you, Livy," slily said Mr. Ford.

"Like me!" exclaimed Miss Lavinia, much startled.

"Why, yes. Why should he not be like his

aunt? I say, Livy, I wish you would come and try that harmonium for me. I have found one—a good one I am told, but I do not like to take it without trying it."

"I cannot try a harmonium: I never played on one," said Miss Lavinia, looking frightened; "besides, is it not a pity to have so expensive an instrument, when the poor boys——"

"What about the expense when Alicia wishes for it," petulantly interrupted Mr. Ford.

Miss Ford gave him a timid look, but continued, with her quiet obstinacy:

"The boys want many things, John."

"Let them."

"And they are good boys, John."

"So much the worse for them. They will be poor men, like their father," sighed Mr. Ford, softening, and casting a dreary look over the past. "Lavinia, I might be a rich man now, had I been selfish."

"That you never were, John," said Miss Ford, with tears in her eyes; "I shall never forget when my piece of plum-cake fell into the pond—"

"Ay—ay, child," said Mr. Ford, forcing a laugh; "but it would have been better for me if I had been more careful of my plum-cake through life."

"I cannot ask him for money now," thought

Miss Ford, perceiving she had taken a false step; "but I can tell him of the bills that came in yesterday."

But Mr. Ford was from the north, and, with all his foolish good-nature, he had plenty of northern shrewdness, though, poor fellow, he did not always put it to the best or the wisest uses. He was now quite aware, from certain nervous twitchings about Miss Lavinia's lips, that the discourse about his boys was to end in something very different from them, and he was sufficiently sharpened by daily adversity to guess that this something must be money. Poverty, amongst its other fatal attendants, has one which the great and the heroic alone can escape—meanness. Mr. Ford was mean every day of his life, far less so than many in his position; but enough to feel and deserve to feel the bitter sense of mortification and shame. He owed money, and he could not and would not help it; he was not wilfully dishonest, yet he wronged the hard-working and the poor. His sister Lavinia was heartily welcome to a share of what he had; but he was sure that she had saved money all these years, and the knowledge of that little hoard made him restless. He meant to borrow from her; and to do so, it was urgent that she should not be the first to broach the unwelcome subject of money. Yet Mr. Ford knew in his inner heart of hearts, that though he might borrow, it was more than doubtful that he should ever repay; he kept that ugly fact in those dark depths of conscience where we all have something to conceal; but it would come out in spite of himself—and then a remorseful and relenting "Poor Lavinia, let her keep it," would be internally uttered, soon to be forgotten in the tempting vision of Lavinia's bank-notes and shining sovereigns. Resolved to attempt securing these as soon as possible, he now artfully turned back to the plum-cake of their youthful days.

"What famous plum-cakes those were that your god-mother made, Livy," he said, with a nod; "I have no doubt you are quite a hand at plum-cake, too."

"I shall be very happy to make one for the boys," said Miss Lavinia, gently flattered; "only you know, John, the materials."

"I say, Livy," hastily interrupted her brother, "you couldn't——"

"Lend me fifty pounds," Mr. Ford was going to add, when, to his great vexation, he caught sight of Captain George passing by the window in the square, on his way to the front door.

"Is that a visitor?" asked Miss Lavinia, as a knock was heard at the door.

"It is," shortly answered her brother.

"Then, I think I shall go."

"As you please," answered Mr. Ford, who was very much out of temper.

Miss Lavinia had only time to retire when Captain George walked in, with a "Well, old fellow?" that was comprehensive as well as familiar.

"Well," said Mr. Ford, carelessly tossing him the packet of papers, "it is all right enough—you may invest."

"May I, though?" asked Captain George, with every appearance of anxiety and interest.

"Yes; it is safe."

"Well, and what will you do?"

"How is Mrs. George?" was the irrelevant reply.

"Pretty well, pre—tty well, thank you; but what will you do?"

"I ask you—how is Mrs. George?" sternly said Mr. Ford.

"And I answer, pretty well."

"Well, then, be satisfied."

Captain George whistled, and took up the papers.

"A hundred pounds would do, you know."

"This is a fine day," said Mr. Ford, thrusting his hands in his pockets, and looking out of the window.

"He's in one of his tempers, when nothing will move him," said Captain George, speaking as to a third person; "that man is a rock, sir—a rock."

This speech producing no effect, Captain George, after looking in vain for the rum bottle on the table, exclaimed, seemingly struck with a sudden remembrance,

"By the way—I forgot to show you this—that may change the question, eh?"

He put another paper in Mr. Ford's hands as he spoke. Mr. Ford read it attentively. There was nothing in it but the confirmation of what he already knew; and how bitter was that knowledge! "Ah, if I had but a hundred pounds," thought Mr. Ford, with a heart full of bitterness, "or rather three or four hundred, if I could but avail myself of this opportunity, and get my share of the inevitable prize. It is so clear, so certain a success. Lavinia's money would do for present wants—for the house—for the harmonium which poor Alicia has not got yet ——"

"Well!" here interrupted Captain George; "it is odd, is it not?"

"No," sharply replied Mr. Ford, thrusting back the paper upon him; "I told you it was all right."

"Well, I am sorry you are so obstinate; you always were, you know."

"Of course," said Mr. Ford.

"It is only a hundred pounds," persisted Captain George, with his hand on the lock.

"I am glad to hear it."

"Obstinate," muttered Captain George. "I'll tell you what, old fellow," he added, as they left the parlour together, "you'll die a poor man."

Mr. Ford, who was in one of his silent, surly fits, did not answer, whereat Captain George shook his head, seemingly much affected. Mr. Ford opened the door for him, and started back, surprised. On the last step of the house sat a little girl, of grave yet childish aspect. Heavy yellow curls fell round her little blooming face, lit with a pair of bright grey eyes. She sat with her elbow on her knee, and her cheek in her hand, in an attitude of patient expectation. She was handsomely—nay, richly dressed. Captain George eyed her curiously, then looked at Mr. Ford; but Mr. Ford shook his head, he knew nothing of her.

"Who are you with, child?" kindly asked Captain George, stooping, and patting her cheek.

The question was answered with pert quaintness.

"Never mind," said the little lady, without deigning to look up.

Captain George smiled, uttered an "All right, I dare say," and walked away, gaily humming a tune.

Mr. Ford re-entered the house, bitter and irritated; it seemed to him as if fortune had once more fled away from his home with the papers in

Captain George's pocket. He wondered how much money Captain George would invest—a thousand at least; and he rapidly calculated how much it would bring in.

"Please, sir," said Susan's voice, "is that organ coming?"

Mr. Ford winced at the question. He had deceived his wife; he had deceived even Susan; the harmonium he had found was utterly beyond his reach. He had hoped to lure his sister into purchasing it, by asking her to come and try it; and this hope, a slender one, was the only certainty he had of the instrument he had repeatedly promised Mrs. Ford.

"Missus has been asking me about it again," continued Susan; "I think, sir, you had better tell her it can't be had, than keep her expecting."

"It can be had," sharply said Mr. Ford; "but the instrument is out of order. Tell her she shall have it by next week, at latest."

Susan went away sullen and incredulous, and Miss Lavinia timidly appeared in the hall, where Mr. Ford was still standing. She had evidently been lying in wait for her brother, and, though he guessed with what purpose, he recklessly allowed her to speak.

"John," she said, shyly, "I am sorry to trouble you again."

"Never mind, Livy," replied Mr. Ford, with an ironical sort of kindness; "go on."

"The children are rather shabby," suggested Miss Ford.

"I think you may say very shabby."

"At all events, they want new clothes, John."

"Decidedly they do, Livy."

"And then there are the bills, John. Don't you think you had better pay off a few before they accumulate?"

"A very excellent suggestion," said Mr. Ford, with the same sort of grim kindness and assent.

Considerably encouraged by so ready a hearing, Miss Lavinia proceeded:

"And if you could give me a pound or two for Susan, John, I should like it so. She was quite saucy yesterday, and, at the first wòrd I said, threw her wages in my face."

An execration in which anger, shame, and bitterness blended, rose to Mr. Ford's lips, but did not pass them. He was not used, whatever his trials were, to have them probed so freely, and Miss Ford had not spared him one sting. His dirty and neglected children, his debts, the insolence of his servant, had all been brought up before him, and had separately added their gall to Captain George's last adieu—"Good-bye, old fellow, you'll die a poor man." Who knew it better than

Mr. Ford, with mortgages, debts, and arrest, all hanging over him in gloomy array. But what we know we cannot always bear to hear; and Mr. Ford's short conversation with Captain George had irritated him almost beyond endurance, when his sister unconsciously exasperated him still further. Seeing her startled look, he checked himself and said, sadly:

"Livy, never talk of money to a man downhill; it puts him beside himself—it puts him beside himself, I tell you."

And excitedly snatching up his hat, Mr. Ford rushed out of the house.

CHAPTER V.

He did not go far.

The child was still sitting on the door-step; and Mr. Ford, surprised to find her there, stopped at once. She had not moved or changed her attitude. Still she sat with her cheek resting on her hand, and seeming indifferent to the keen northern wind, that curled the withered and yellow leaves up to her feet. Mr. Ford looked at her attentively, then he laid his hand on her shoulder, and asked:

"What are you doing here, child?"

She looked up wistfully in his face. Her pertness seemed all gone; tears trembled on her long eyelashes; her lips quivered slightly.

"I am waiting for Mary," she said.

Mr. Ford looked around him. There were two gentlemen walking slowly in the enclosure of the square; but neither within it nor without did he see any token of a servant-girl.

"Why did Mary leave you?" he asked.

"She leaves me every day; she goes away, then comes back, and takes me home."

"And where is home?"

But the child seemed unable to answer this question distinctly. She spoke of a great house; but where it was, or what name it bore, or if it had any, she could not tell. It was home—and she knew no more.

"But where does your father live?" urged Mr. Ford.

"I have not got any."

"Is he dead?"

"I tell you I never had any," rather indignantly replied the little girl.

"And no mother?"

"Oh! she's gone," moaned the child; "she's gone."

"Then who takes care of you?"

"The lady."

"What lady?"

But here again the child could not explain. The lady was like home, an image distinct to her own mind—to others, vague and dull. Mr. Ford shook his head. It was plain to him that this richly-dressed delicately-nurtured child had been purposely forsaken. He put but one more question to her; he asked to know her name, half expecting her to inform him that she had not got, and had never had any. Mr. Ford was disappointed.

"My name," she replied, seeming surprised at the question; "don't you know it?"

"No, I really do not. What is it?"

"Mab."

"Mab—Mabel, perhaps?"

"No, it isn't Mabel, it's Mab."

"Little Queen Mab, eh?—and your surname, you have none, of course not."

She shook her head with impatient denial; then clasping her hands around her knees, she querulously exclaimed:

"I wish Mary would come."

But there was no sign of Mary. Mr. Ford remembered his three boys and bad father though many would have thought him; they made his heart yearn towards the forsaken child.

"Let us wait for Mary in the house," he said; and taking her by the hand, he led her in.

She made no resistance. Perhaps she thought this was a thing agreed upon; perhaps she felt cold and tired with waiting in the square, and liked the shelter and protection of a home. They entered together the silent parlour; Miss Lavinia had gone up-stairs to cry in her room—and in that grey day it was not so dingy and so comfortless as in the broad glare of sun-light, yet the child looked startled. Mr. Ford sat down, and took her on his knee. She seemed half frightened at the familiarity of the act; she looked a fastidious little thing, and pushed him away with mingled fright and annoyance. He gently forced her to stay, and, in drawing her towards him, he felt something rustle like paper. He put her down abruptly, and gave her a sharp look; a letter was pinned to her little silk cloak.

Mr. Ford rose and locked the door; then he came back to the child, took the letter which bore no direction, and tore it open. A small bundle of silken papers fell out—notes—bank-notes. The blood tingled in his ears; he picked them up and counted them. There were five notes, and each note was for a hundred pounds.

At first the rush of joy was almost too great. Then came a second thought—the notes were forged; then a third, could he keep them? He hastily put that thought away, and examined the envelope. Within it were faintly traced in pencil, characters reversed, and which could only be read in a looking-glass. Mr. Ford at once went up to the mantel-piece; and, with some difficulty, made out the following words:

"A distressed mother appeals to Mr. Ford's

humanity. If he will keep the child and rear her like his own, the £500 enclosed are his. She will be claimed some day—God alone knows when. Inquiry is useless, and will only cause any future assistance to be withheld."

Mr. Ford hastily thrust this paper in his pocket aud turned to the child. She stood where he had left her, and stared at him amazed and silent.

"Hush!" he said, though she had not spoken; "hush, Mary will come."

He left the room and locked her in, but without taking the key; then he went up to his sister's room and hurriedly tapped at her door.

"Livy," he said, when she opened it, "lend me fifty pounds, will you?"

Words cannot render Miss Lavinia's profound amazement.

"Fifty pounds!" she gasped.

"Yes. I want them for Alicia's harmonium. I have the money, of course, but I cannot spare it, and she has set her heart on that harmonium. I tell you I have money." Mr. Ford hastily produced his bundle of notes and rustled them in Miss Lavinia's face with another hasty, "Now don't shilly-shally, let me have those fifty pounds: you shall have them back next week, and with capital interest, Livy."

Poor Miss Ford was completely subdued by her

brother's manner and bank-notes. Not two minutes before he was bitter, complaining, and poor—now he spoke with the easy insolence of wealth.

"I have not got fifty pounds," she said; "but I have thirty-seven pounds eighteen shillings and sixpence."

"Thirty-five will do, then," said Mr. Ford, rapidly calculating that the two pound odd would do for Susan, "only let me have them quickly."

"I must take off my boot, then," said Miss Lavinia, for in this useful article of her dress she kept her money when she travelled.

"Do what you like, so you be quick," replied her brother, taking a turn on the landing.

Miss Lavinia closed the door, then re-appeared after a while with four notes, much creased. Her brother took them from her with a hasty, "Thank you, Livy, all right," then hurried down-stairs without heeding her prudential recommendation, "to be careful of the money."

An empty cab was passing by when Mr. Ford left the square; he hailed it and drove at once to the dealer in second-hand instruments, where, after much labour, he had succeeded in discovering such an harmonium as would suit his wife, though the obdurate dealer had refused to surrender it without payment. Here Miss Lavinia's thirty-five pounds effected the miracle which Mr. Ford's eloquence had not attained, and he left the house master of the coveted harmonium.

"Number seven Woodbine Terrace, Brompton," said Mr. Ford, re-entering the cab which he had kept waiting. "Poor Alicia, how pleased she will be," was his first thought. His next was, "Are the notes safe?" He felt for them in a tremor. They were safe, and he counted and examined them again. "I wonder what Captain George will think," was his next exulting reflection.

Number seven Woodbine Terrace was one of the pretty little old-fashioned villas, such as were still to be found in Brompton some years ago. The mild air of that locality had been found to agree with Mrs. George, and Woodbine Cottage had agreed with her particularly well. It was one storey high, and stood in its own grounds, as Captain George facetiously observed. It had a grass plot in front, and behind a garden, which, being surrounded by other gardens, allowed flowers to grow, and could even boast a few trees, and a honeysuckle arbour. The door, on being opened by a neat servant, showed a pleasant vision of cool green beyond the hall, and a small back parlour, into which Mr. Ford was ushered, had the same agreeable look of verdure. It was full of choice plants on stands; cages of birds hung in the bow window, a parrot on his perch lifted his drowsy head, and turned his bright eyes on Mr. Ford, and an aged dog, blind and helpless, growled in his basket, but without stirring.

"Mrs. George's pets," said Mr. Ford, with the sneer which he had for every taste, wise or foolish, in which he did not sympathize.

"Master's too," replied the servant. "Hush, Flo! Master took her in a week ago."

"What! that old creature?"

"Yes, sir, more fit to be thrown in the river than anything; but master's so. We have an Italian boy down-stairs that just drives me beside myself—a little lame beggar. Any name, sir?"

"Mr. Ford."

"All right—all right," said Captain George, thrusting his head in through the folding-doors, and nodding pleasantly at Mr. Ford; "what's up, old fellow?"

"I should just like a few words with you."

"Have a cup of tea first."

"No, I must go home."

"We'll see about that. Well, old Flo?" He stretched out a caressing hand to the spaniel, who, leaving her basket, came crawling towards him, whining with pleasure, and finally crept up on his knee.

"No danger of your making such a fool of

yourself, eh?" said Captain George, nudging Mr. Ford's elbow, and still stroking Flo's head.

"A matter of taste," replied Mr. Ford, with a disdainful smile. "I called to tell you that I have changed my mind about that matter; I will have those shares."

Captain George whistled, and stared at his cousin.

"A deep fellow," he said at length; "ain't he, Flo? I suppose you want the shares this evening," he added, in a business-like tone.

Mr. Ford nodded.

Captain George looked at him, and rubbed his chin.

"Business is business," he said; "have you brought the money?"

Mr. Ford thrust his hand in his pocket and threw a bundle of bank-notes on the table. Captain George picked them up, smoothed them open, caressed them, as it were, and smiled; then he put them down carefully, and, opening a bureau, he drew out some pink-coloured papers, which he handed to Mr. Ford. The two men exchanged glances.

"Why had you those shares here?" mistrustfully asked Mr Ford.

Captain George winked, and looked most wickedly knowing.

'Saw it in your eye all the time, old fellow. Captain George looks foolish, but he has been in the wars; Captain George can read an eye."

That Captain George could read an eye was probably very true, but that Captain George had ever been in the wars was one of those matters which sceptical people doubted. The curious had discovered that Captain George had never been in the British service; and Captain George himself so often spoke of Mexico and Peru, that, though he did not say so, Southern America was by the credulous fixed upon as the scene of his exploits.

In his heart of hearts Mr. Ford did not believe that his cousin George had ever held command in any but a militia regiment, and as with the first touch of prosperity the man's whole heart naturally opened, his answer to Captain George's declaration that he had been in the wars was the insolent question,

"And have you really been in the wars, Captain George?"

It was said that Captain George had fought duels on less provocation than this, but he was now pacifically inclined, and, facetiously bidding Mr. Ford take as many shares as he pleased, he watched him doing so with good-humoured patience.

"And now," said he, "that instead of a hundred pounds you are investing five—not fair, old fellow—you will not mind putting your name to these bits of paper. I don't know how you came by them, you know."

"How should I have come by them?" sharply asked Mr. Ford.

"How can *I* tell? But I have been in the wars, and so you will please to write your name on the backs of these little silky gentlemen."

Mr. Ford obeyed with a scornful air; the pink papers sank in his pocket, the silky gentlemen, as Captain George called them, entered the bureau, and the business was over.

"And now you'll take a cup of tea," said Captain George.

"I don't mind if I do," replied Mr. Ford with sudden good-humour; "How is Mrs. George?"

"So, so," replied Captain George—"so, so: walk in."

He pushed the folding-doors open, and Mr. Ford entered a pretty, and especially a comfortable parlour, where Mrs. George sat by a bright fire, presiding over a fairly laid out tea-table. Mrs. George, whom Captain George had married for love many years before, had been pretty, it was said, but time, which often respects plain faces, works sad changes in beauty; and now she was a plain woman enough, with a red nose, small grey eyes, and a long chin, but over all a motherly sort of look, which, joined to a pleasant voice and manner, rendered her a general favourite. Of her virtues as well as of her beauty, Captain George spoke freely. It was hard to say whether he did so through habit, love, or because he was of a boastful temper. One thing was certain, that, though a most faithless husband, he was devotedly attached to his wife. She loved him no less, and, to the few who knew them and their whole history, that strange love afforded room for speculation.

"And how is Mr. Ford?" asked Mrs. George in her kindest tones, and with her most benevolent smile; "quite a stranger of late."

She shook her finger at him, whilst Mr. Ford looked foolish. The world had not softened his northern bluntness, and this forbade either excuse or apology. He took refuge in his cup of tea, and looked at the fire.

"I think we must have that boy up," said Mrs. George to her husband.

"I think we must, my love, Sarah does not like him."

Mrs. George rang the bell; the Italian boy was ordered up, and soon came in limping.

Captain and Mrs. George looked complacently at him; a side-table was laid out by Mrs. George's own hands, and, to Mr. Ford's profound surprise, the Italian boy was told to take his tea, with the addition of some cold meat which Sarah brought up for his use, looking deeply disgusted. Little mattered her looks; Mrs. George poured out the boy's tea, and Captain George carved his meat, and both watched him eating with evident enjoyment. He ate but little, poor child; a pale, sickly boy he was, with a worn and hollow face, and large sunken eyes, that told of much suffering in London streets.

"And where is Flo?" asked Mrs. George; "why is not Flo here?—she would like her tea too—poor old Flo!"

The door was opened, and in came Flo, very slowly, but growling at the boy with unsubdued jealousy and anger.

"Never mind, Flo," said Captain George, laughing; "never mind her, Giachino. She has no teeth—only spite—Eh! you old Flo."

"What on earth do you mean to do with that cross old beast?" Mr. Ford could not help asking.

"Why, feed and keep her until she dies, of course."

Mr. Ford looked his disgust. Captain George struck his fist on the table, till the tea-things rang again, and said, with much emphasis, though without anger,

"You may laugh, Mr. Ford, but Flo's mistress was an old flame of mine, as no one knows better than Mrs. George"—here he gave a wink to his wife, who smiled—"and when she died a week back, I vowed that Flo should have a bit and a sup whilst *I* lived. Eh! old Flo?"

Flo, who, to say the truth, was an old friend of Captain George's, and had known him since her birth, fondly licked his hand by way of reply.

"Every one to his taste," said Mr. Ford rising; "but what will you do with that young vagabond," he added as the door closed on the Italian boy, who, after uttering his pretty *grazie tante*, limped away—"not belonging to an old flame of yours, is he?"

Mr. Ford said this with tolerable insolence, for such was his unfortunate temper. He was one of those men of whom nature has decreed that they shall never know how to joke.

"No—no—no," said Captain George, waving his hand with graceful denial; "nothing of that kind. We'll wait till his foot is well, to think about what we shall do with him; he is no trouble in the meanwhile—poor little Giachino! I picked him up starving, sir—starving! Ugh! what a state of society this is!"

Mr. Ford reddened deeply. He remembered the little stranger at home. Were his motives as pure as those of that scapegrace Captain George, who was known to live by his wits, to cheat, to trick, and whom every man despised, and no man trusted.

"Good night," he said, hurriedly.

"Good night, Mr. Ford," sweetly said Mrs. George.

Her husband saw their guest to the door. Then he gave him one of his favourite thrusts in the ribs, and said, knowingly,

"Had the money all the time, eh?—sly boots!"

Mr. Ford laughed, entered the cab, and drove away. Captain George returned to the parlour. His wife gave him a look.

"All right," he said, laying his finger to his nose; "all right, my dear."

CHAPTER VI.

When Miss Lavinia's first amazement was over, she began to feel alarmed at her facility. She no longer heard her brother's confident tones, nor was she dazzled by the sight of the bank-notes. Besides, since he wanted them for something else, it was just as if he had not got them; and since he had them, why did he require her thirty-five pounds? Surely Mrs. Ford could do without the harmonium for a day or two. At all events, it was very odd why *her* money had to go!

"I dare say he has not gone yet," thought Miss Lavinia. "Perhaps if I were to go down and have a convincing talk with him, he would give me back the notes."

Downstairs Miss Lavinia went; but Mr. Ford was not in the parlour, and in his stead, to the lady's amazement, she found a strange child fast asleep on the rickety sofa. The sight at first took her breath away. Miss Lavinia had always cherished a passive dislike for animals and for children. She, of course, tolerated her three nephews, and did not object to the presence of a cat in the kitchen; but this little creature, come she knew not where from, and sleeping there coiled up like a silky spaniel, alarmed and disturbed her.

She looked at Mab, then she walked away. Then she came back and sat down, and looked at her again, and still the child slept on soundly. At length, unable to bear this extraordinary event in silence, Miss Lavinia precipitately left the room. She went to seek her adviser in cases of domestic difficulty, Susan, and as usual, the conversation took place over the banisters.

"Susan!" she called out, dolefully. "Susan—do you hear me?"

"Yes, marm," answered Susan's sharp voice from below; "on course I do."

"Susan, I am in such distress!"

Susan, not considering that this declaration of trouble required any comment, uttered none.

"Susan, will you come up, please?"

"Indeed, ma'am, I can't—I am too busy."

"But, Susan, I do want you. What child is that in the parlour?"

"What!" screamed Susan.

"What child?—do come and look at it."

Susan, confounded at what she heard, now appeared at the head of the staircase, and, giving a scowl around her, as if she were looking for some noxious reptile, imperiously asked "where it was."

"In the parlour," said Miss Lavinia.

Susan entered the parlour at once, and stared at the little girl, who, awakened out of her sleep by their loud talking, sat up on the sofa, and looked half ready to cry.

"Who are you?—what brought you here?"

The child, offended at Susan's tone and looks, buried her face in the pillow, and would not reply.

"What shall we do with her?" asked Miss Lavinia.

Susan gave her an odd look, pursed up her lips, shut her small eyes, shook her head, and, without answering proceeded to walk downstairs to the kitchen. Miss Ford hastily called her back.

"Susan, take it with you; I cannot stay with it in the parlour."

"Then lock the door, ma'am; I ain't a-going to have it in my kitchen. Besides, those that let it in, can let it out."

"What shall I do?" exclaimed Miss Lavinia, wringing her hands piteously.

Comfort came from a quarter whence Miss Lavinia had not been wont to expect it since her arrival in this house. A sharp double knock at the door announced the return of her three nephews, who had been out for a walk. She opened the door herself, hoping to derive from them either information or support. They rushed in, in their boisterous fashion, and their first breathless exclamation was, "What's there for dinner?"

For, unlike Captain George, Mr. Ford kept genteel hours.

"Roast beef and Yorkshire pudding," replied Miss Lavinia.

The three brothers uttered an exclamation of dismay. Yorkshire pudding was an old and scandalous invasion of the fundamental law, that pudding follows meat. Disgusted though they felt, William and Edward went down to the kitchen, in the hopes of better things. Miss Ford looked at her eldest nephew, and faltered:

"Robert, there is a child in the parlour. Do you know who and what she is?"

"Let's see her," replied Robert, and, putting his aunt aside, he entered the parlour.

The child raised her head from the pillow, against which she had hidden her face. It was covered with tears, yet her fair hair, her blooming complexion had too much beauty, and her attire was too costly, for both not to strike Robert with surprise.

"Who brought her?" he asked, looking at Miss Lavinia.

"I don't know—I don't know anything about her."

"Nor I. Who are you, little girl?" The child turned sulkily away. "I dare say papa knows," said Robert, carelessly; and he first pushed with his foot, then picked up a crumpled paper. Miss Lavinia looked inquiringly at him.

"It is only an old letter," said Robert, hurriedly, and he thrust it into his pocket. "I think I'll go upstairs, aunt."

And, without heeding his aunt's slow remonstrance, upstairs Robert went. He there found his two brothers quarrelling. He soon restored peace between them.

"There's a little girl below."

The information was received with a derisive shout.

"There is," emphatically resumed Robert. "You go and see her, Edward."

Edward would much rather not have gone, but Robert's will was law, and down he went. He soon returned with startled looks, beckoning from the staircase to William, who at once obeyed the summons. Robert heard them go downstairs whispering; he listened for a while, then shut the door, and took out the paper from his pocket. It was the letter his father had received with the banknotes. Robert was puzzled, at first, by the reversed characters, then suddenly their meaning flashed across his mind—he went to the little cracked looking-glass hanging between the two windows, held up the letter, and, though somewhat slowly, he, too, came to a knowledge of its contents.

"Oh, what a beauty!—looking at himself," said the voice of William, who had entered unheard, and now stood behind his brother. Robert turned round, and he was so dreadfully pale that William drew back frightened.

"I'll tell you what," said Robert, in a voice that shook with passion, "if you do that again, I'll —I'll strike you!"

William was a good-humoured, patient lad, but this uncalled for threat roused his ire.

"Will you," he said—"will you?" and he flew at Robert, who had barely time to defend himself, and whose surprise at the attack helped to cool his anger.

"Don't be a fool, Bill!" said he, pushing back his young brother. "I don't want to hurt you—you ninny! Why, I could double you up in no time."

There was, unfortunately, no doubt about that, and Bill's excitement wisely found vent in tears, which Robert allowed to flow, quietly thrusting back the letter into his pocket, whilst William was too much moved to mind him.

"And now do let me be quiet, will you," continued Robert, with the look and tone of a premature man.

The school of adversity has its drawbacks for youth. Robert had found it a hard one. Years had modified the faults which had pierced his mother's proud heart; but though he grew up with her beauty, her reserve, and her pride, he lost none of that vanity which was his father's prevailing error and misfortune. It had been wounded at every turn; the poverty of his home, his shabby clothes, his father's beggared reputation, had given it many a cruel sting, but had failed to conquer it, though they had, indeed, compelled it to silence and a passive existence. The very hardships and sufferings, which that vanity had made it cruel to endure, bore sad fruit. Robert grew up in the conviction that there is nothing like money and a fair name. The wealthy, safe, reputable side of life's high-road attracted him irresistibly. Respectability was Robert's youthful ideal. Poor lad! he could not help prizing that of which he felt the want so keenly. The son of a poor man, unable to acquire more than a very secondary education—unable, as he felt beforehand, to make his way in one of those professions where men win money and repute—what could he ever be? These feelings passed vaguely through Robert's mind; they were feelings and not thoughts, for his character was more formed than his intellectual faculties were developed. He studied hard, but with more application than success; yet work is certain of its rewards, and slow but sure might be applied to him.

But though the blight which had fallen on Robert's childhood, and on his home, since his mother's illness, had forced some fatal defects and dangerous feelings into premature existence, it is but fair to add, that some genuine qualities, some fair blossoms, had sprung up amongst the weeds. Robert had early learned to think little of his father—poor Mr. Ford had found the world in the heart of his own child, yet Robert had had the self-command not to betray his feelings, and even to veil them with a tolerable show of filial respect. There lay his strength—he could forbear—he could suffer in silence, and neither complain nor repine; and that secret and unfortunate contempt which he conceived for the parent he should have revered, helped to foster the tenderness which he felt for his younger brothers. William was but three years his junior and Edward seven, but Robert, seeing how weak and helpless their father was, had learned to treat them with genuine, though imperious fondness, and taught them to rely on his support, and obey his authority. Childhood goes to strength as flowers turn to the sun, and William and Edward knew no law save the will of Robert. As a rule he was just to them. He protected them against insult and attack, fought all their battles, and would have done without his dinner before they should want. There was boyish vanity in this assumption of protection and power, but there was a fine and generous feeling too; the sense in which his father lamentably failed of what we owe to those with whom God has given us the ties of kindred.

But, as we all know, this is a feeling which is often allied with a sort of selfishness. Miss Lavinia's arrival was not seen by Robert with much pleasure, for she came a burden to this overladen home. He softened, however, when he saw the comparative decency she introduced into it. Respectability, under one of its many aspects, appeared before Robert's mind, and he had sense enough to feel his aunt's value. But very different was the vista which opened with the letter he had just read; money, actual money was coming with the little fair-haired girl on the sofa below. Five hundred pounds! the sum seemed incalculable wealth. The poor boy's heart beat with emotion. Five hundred pounds!—comfort, competency, honour, the world's esteem; education and a career for his brothers. He felt dizzy and faint, and William's fierce attack did him infinite good: it cooled and steadied him, and rendered thought an easier task.

"I'll not tell papa I've seen the letter," was Robert's first thought. "I'll keep it," was his second.

But where find a safe hiding place? He looked around the room, and saw none that would be more than temporary. Yet one he was compelled to adopt. William had gone downstairs again—he was alone, and could do as he pleased. He thrust the letter folded small behind the chest of drawers, then whistling carelessly, though alone, he walked downstairs.

Miss Ford had left the parlour, and the two young Fords were in it, amusing themselves with teasing the poor little stranger. William danced around her making faces, to her great rage and vexation; whilst Edward every now and then gave her yellow locks a pull.

"Ain't you ashamed of yourselves to tease a girl so," sternly said Robert. "Don't be afraid, little girl," he added as his brothers slunk away. "I'll settle the first who touches you."

Mab's protection was ensured from that hour; but, unconscious of her debt, and feeling insulted by the familiarity of Robert's address, she said somewhat haughtily,

"I am not a little girl—I am a lady. And if *he* were here," she added, her eyes filling with angry tears, "he would strike you as he did the boy who provoked me."

"Would he!" said Robert with much disdain.

"I should like to see him hit Robert," ironically exclaimed William.

"I tell you he would!" cried the little stranger, stamping her foot; "he is taller and stronger than Robert, as you call him."

"Oh, my!" exclaimed Ned and Bill on hearing this heresy.

"Let her alone," loftily said Robert, with generous forgiveness; "she knows no better. Come here, little girl, and tell me who is he."

"I don't know," sobbed the child, "but he shook the cherry-tree, and the cherries fell—oh! so fast!"

This was not much to the purpose, and Robert's further inquiries failed to elicit clearer information. Not even her name of Mab would the child confess, but, weeping bitterly, asked to go to Mary; and turning from sorrow to wrath, again threatened them with the assurance that "*he* would punish them well, he would. And you are a rude boy," she added for Robert's special benefit.

Robert did not condescend to resent the taunt, and his father's entrance put an end to the scene.

"What's up?" he said carelessly; "well, little one, how are you?"

"Mary!—Mary!" sobbed the little girl on seeing him.

Mr. Ford was affected; he sat down and took the weeping child on his knee.

"You are but a poor forsaken little thing after all," he said with some emotion; "but you have got a home—don't cry—there, don't! We'll take care of you."

"Is the little girl going to stay, pa?" asked Robert, with a look of well-assumed wonder.

"She is."

"And what is her name, pa? She would not tell us."

"Her name is Mab—is it not, dear?"

"Ye—es," sobbed the child.

"That is a short name," said Robert, looking fixedly at his father.

"Her name is Mab—Winter," answered Mr. Ford.

"That was grandmother's name," said Robert.

There was something too pointed in the lad's manner to escape his father. He was a weak and passionate man, and, stamping his foot, he turned on Robert with sudden wrath.

"How dare you stand and con my words, young sir?" he said, stammering with rage.

Mab, frightened at such unexpected violence, ran away, and, in her terror, took refuge between William and Edward, who, amazed at seeing Robert reproved by their ever-yielding parent, remained mute and still. Robert turned red, then pale, and fixing a reproachful look on his flushed and angry father, he said with some firmness and dignity, "I meant no harm."

Nor had he. He had meant no insult, no reproach—it was Mr. Ford's own secret heart that had given his words their sting, and, his first wrath over, Mr. Ford knew it better than Robert. He knew what it was that had exasperated him, how and why he had felt defied, but, raising his voice louder to disguise his secret regret, he said with assumed sternness,

"Hold your tongue, sir; I will not have the child meddled with—remember that."

Thus, twice within a quarter of an hour, Mab's inviolability was proclaimed by both father and son in her new home.

"And now," said Mr. Ford, relaxing into his easy, good-humoured tone, "let us see if there is nothing in my pocket that will make you four good friends."

He produced a good-sized but decidedly flattened parcel as he spoke.

"I must have sat on it," exclaimed Mr. Ford, dismayed, and opening it he displayed fragments of a cake that looked indeed as if it had undergone some such operation. He rubbed his forehead, and looked perplexed, but soon rallying, he philosophically remarked:

"I daresay it is none the worse for it. There, take it—divide fair; and let little Queen Mab's share be the largest," he added, unconscious of the contradiction this double behest implied.

Edward, William, and Mab herself seemed quite of opinion that the cake was none the worse for its misfortune; for they divided it most amicably. Robert remained aloof; his father slapped him on the back.

"I have not forgotten you, Bob," he said, kindly; "you go to school to-morrow, and in the meanwhile take this," and he put in his hand a handsome case of mathematical instruments, long wished, but scarcely hoped for by the ambitious boy.

Robert reddened with joy, and could scarcely falter his thanks; his father sighed with pleasure and relief, as, sinking back in his chair, he watched the happy children, Mab the merriest of all. It was something to know that henceforth he could gratify them without stint, that henceforth they need fear neither the bitterness nor the disgrace of poverty.

CHAPTER VII.

Money is a wonderful thing. Mab's five hundred pounds did Mr. Ford all the good in the world. This sum had found him depressed, gloomy, and worried; it restored him in no time to his genial good-humour and buoyant spirits. Mr. Ford was convinced that his investment was a safe one, and he acted on the belief that time would multiply it tenfold. He had a forgiving, hospitable temper, and the very next morning he went about among his friends and acquaintances, renewing broken ties, and extending invitations. He went about amongst the tradesmen, too, talking loud of his improved circumstances, promising speedy payment; and so convincing was his eloquence, contracting a few more debts. But the greatest change of all was that which Mr. Ford showed in his own home; it was sudden and complete. He took the children on his knee at breakfast; he did not swear; he drank very little spirits. The man's whole nature was thawed in the pleasant warmth of unexpected prosperity. Very kind, too, was he to the forsaken child who had thus become an inmate of his house and a member of his family. He questioned her in private on the evening of her arrival, and his questions were careful and close; but he ascertained nothing save that, for some period of time, she must have been kept in complete ignorance of all that concerned herself. Now and then, when he pressed some point, such as her surname, the home she had been reared in, the names of people she had known, Mab would look deeply perplexed. It was plain that she once had had the usual amount of childish information on these points, and that memory had kept vague traces of the knowledge; but it was plain, too, that she had not been cast forth on the world's broad waters with any of that troublesome information remaining on her mind. Some process, which Mr. Ford conjectured to have been almost complete seclusion, had evidently been adopted to secure her oblivion of what it was wished she should not mention. She had probably been kept in some country house, between a lady and Mary, her servant, until it was ascertained that, with the rapid forgetfulness of her years, she could no longer betray the history of her little past. Perhaps a more acute and persevering examiner than Mr. Ford could have learned more from the child: but his curiosity was not so strong as the sense of his real interest, and prudently remaining content with the sudden piece of good fortune which had visited him under Mab's aspect, he strove no more for knowledge, which, if gained, might have proved inconvenient; and he strictly forbade "the child to be teased with useless inquiries," as he expressed it.

Miss Lavinia was too discreet not to obey her brother's rather severely uttered behest; but people's thoughts are free, and after long and mature deliberation, and many painful and conscientious struggles, she internally came to the conclusion that Mab Winter should have been Mab Ford. Susan, too, though on grounds that would have horrified poor Miss Lavinia, could she have suspected them, concluded "that the little monkey was a Ford every bit of her;" and Robert, convinced that she was not, and could not be a Winter, did his best to ascertain who and what she was the very next morning that followed her first appearance.

His attempt was made in the back parlour after breakfast. Mab was already accustomed to her new home, and though she had flatly refused to sleep with Miss Lavinia, and had insisted on having a bed to herself the preceding evening, she had shown herself tractable and loveable in other respects. With Robert she was at home in half an hour, and indeed in less.

"Mab, you are to call me cousin," he said; "just as you are to call papa uncle, and our aunt Lavinia, aunt." Mab nodded.

"And don't be afraid of William or Edward, Mab, *I* shall take care of you."

"I am not afraid."

"I shall teach you, Mab; papa said so; do you know your letters?"

"No."

"Then look here; this is A, and that is B: do you see?"

Mab's bright eyes opened wide. She went through the whole alphabet in less than a quarter of an hour, and, to her teacher's great amazement, she learned it as fast as she went through it.

"She is a wonderful child," thought Robert, unaware that whilst he imagined Mab was learning, she was only remembering, "and I shall teach her all I know."

It was when they had gone thus far that Robert's questions began.

"There," he said, "*he* never taught you your letters, did he?"

"But he would not let the boy beat me," cried

Mab, firing up, "and he took me in his arms and kissed me—and I love him."

"What is his name?" asked Robert.

"I don't know, but I love him."

"That's nonsense, Mab," coolly said Robert, "you cannot love a person whose name you do not know."

Mab vowed she did, and the conversation which Robert had begun, in the hope of acquiring information, ended in a half-quarrel.

"Mab, do not be naughty, or I shall punish you," authoritatively said Robert.

"He will not let you," derisively replied Mab.

"We shall see that, Miss."

There is no knowing what might have followed if a shuffling noise in the hall, as of men carrying some weighty piece of furniture, had not disturbed the pair. Robert opened the door, and Mab drew to his side and peeped out. Two porters, acting under Mr. Ford's whispered directions, were cautiously moving a strange square mass muffled in green baize.

"Softly, very softly," says Mr. Ford. "Susan, come here," and he whispered lower still. "Lure her into the back room, Susan, lure her into the bed-room, I want to surprise her—and Susan, you know what I told you, no need to trouble her about that."

His look seeks Mab, and Susan nods grimly—of course not, there is no need to trouble missus about that.

"What is it?" asks Mab, struck with secret awe.

"Don't ask questions," replies Robert, looking superior, and reluctant to confess his own ignorance; "besides, it is no business of yours."

"It is," says Mab, indignant.

And it is indeed. Miss Lavinia's thirty-five pounds shall be refunded, but who is to pay for Mrs. Ford's harmonium in the end?—it is you, poor little Mab, it is you.

"Come in and go on with the lesson," said Robert, who, having guessed what burden the porters were carrying up-stairs, no longer felt any interest in the subject. But Mab, though endowed with great facility for learning, was not studious by nature. She now heard William and Edward in the garden at the back of the house, and she longed to be with them. In vain Robert pulled her in, in vain he proceeded from the alphabet to the delightful task of spelling; Mab listened with big envious sighs to the happy shouts and laughter of the boys, and wholly disregarded the efforts of her teacher.

"I wish you would let me go," she said, plaintively.

She stood at his knee, pretty and entreating.

Robert smiled down at her with conscious power, and bade her tell her name forthwith.

"Mab."

"Mab what?"

"I don't know."

"You do, Miss, but you are stubborn."

"Indeed I don't know, Bob."

"Well then, since you don't know; you must learn—you must know how to spell, Mab."

Mab pouted.

"Mab," said Robert, looking shocked, "do you want to remain ignorant all your life?"

"I don't care," petulantly said Mab.

"Mab, I thought you were ambitious."

"No. I want to play."

"Mab, if you do not behave better I shall not marry you."

For a matrimonial scheme had already been privately discussed between these two.

"I don't care—I shall marry William—I promised this morning."

Robert's face darkened, and as jealousy and revenge are natural to disappointed love in its earliest stages, he forthwith ordered Mab to spell the word "examination." Mab had learned her letters without effort, but "examination" was beyond her. She pouted, sulked, and at last cried, but Robert was obdurate; examination she must spell before she left the room. Then Mab resorted to coaxing; she gave Robert a sly pinch, after the fashion of rural lovers; his face softened a little, and he said, "let go," very mildly, but still he persisted in "examination."

"Oh! Bob," whispered Mab, rising on tiptoe to reach her tutor's ear, "I shall love you so if you will let me go."

"I don't want you to love me. I will have nothing to do with an ignorant little thing like you. William is welcome to have you."

"Oh! Bob, I really will have you—I really will!"

In short, the word "examination" was dismissed from their councils. Bob allowed himself to be pacified, and Mab again solemnly promising to marry him and no one else, she was allowed by her lover and liege lord to make her escape into the garden. Robert found more pleasure in remaining alone in the parlour; he had a turn for mechanics, and his leisure moments were devoted to diminutive mills, fortresses, and bridges, all rather straight and angular, but genuine-looking articles for all that.

In the meanwhile, Mab enjoyed herself to her heart's content with Edward and William. She promptly confided to the latter the unfavourable turn their love matters had taken; but William, a rosy good-humoured boy, told her at once not to mind, and that he did not care, a declaration which Mab received with a shrewd nod, and which was immediately followed by what William called "a jolly game."

The garden was rather a wild place, as all such gardens are when they are surrendered to boys. A wooden bench between two poplars adorned one extremity, and a ruined summer-house stood at the other. Flowers there were none, but gloomy ivy covered the walls, and hid at least the smoke-dried brick, so dreary to the eye. Ned was busy in the summer-house digging a grave for a dead sparrow, rescued too late from the cat's cruel jaws; and William, struck with a bright idea, at once imparted it to Mab in a low whisper.

"Suppose you go and hide from Ned."

Mab received the suggestion with transport, and stole away on tiptoe. But where should she hide? Not with Robert in the back parlour, nor with Mr. Ford in the front. Not with sour-looking Susan in the kitchen, nor with shrinking Miss Lavinia up-stairs. She stole up, meditating concealment in the boy's room, but on reaching the first floor her mind changed. That morning, as she came downstairs, she had asked Susan who lived there, and Susan had sternly replied:

"Bogucy."

"And who is Boguey?"

"A dreadful creature with horns."

"I don't believe in him," replied Mab, with much scorn. Nor did she; she was a sceptical child as well as a bold one. Dear to her also was anything that savoured of forbidden fruit; and as Susan had injudiciously crowned her description of Boguey's personal appearance with the most severe prohibitions ever to attempt opening the door on the first floor landing, holding out dark hints of the chastisement that would follow disobedience, Mab no sooner found herself before it, unwatched and unchecked, than irresistible temptation assailed her.

To open the door, look in, see what Boguey was really like, and ascertain if Boguey really existed, and to do that in spite of Susan's warnings and threats, was too great an indulgence for Mab to dream of hesitating. At once her hand was on the lock, and, with scarcely a moment's pause, she boldly walked in.

She saw a handsome though darkened room. It seemed vacant, and she softly stepped across the carpet to the window. On her way she perceived the arm-chair in which Mrs. Ford sat day after day. It was empty; and Mab, who had an indolent as well as an inquisitive temper, and who, moreover, thought this an excellent hiding-place, jumped into it at once. Gathering her feet under her, she sat there for some time, chuckling as she thought of Ned's and even of William's perplexity; and wondering in what part of the house they were carrying on their researches. She was growing impatient, however, and wearying of her own stillness, and of their slowness at finding her out, when sounds rich, though soft, of solemn religious music, suddenly woke in the room. Had Mab been older and capable of reasoning, she might have felt frightened to hear this seemingly solitary apartment alive with strains so sweet; as it was, she only felt amazed and delighted. She listened for a time, remaining quite still; then curiosity prevailing over awe, she cautiously looked round the edge of the chair. Rising above the dark line of the harmonium, she saw a pale face with upraised look and parted lips; Mab was frightened, and jumped to her feet with a scream. At once the music abruptly ceased, and a tall lady, clad in ghostly black, stood before her speechless with amazement.

CHAPTER VIII.

"WHO—what are you?—what brings you here?" at length gasped the lady.

Mab did not answer.

"Speak, child, who are you?—what is your name?"

"Why, Mab, of course," petulantly answered Mab, who was rather tired of hearing that question since the preceding afternoon.

"Mab—what Mab?"

"Mab Winter."

"And where do you live?"

"Why, here, to be sure."

"In this house?—why—then, who are you?"

"I have already told you so," replied Mab, with some temper.

Mrs. Ford rang the bell, and Susan, who was on

her way upstairs on another errand, entered the room almost at the same moment.

"Who is this child?" exclaimed Mrs. Ford, stamping her foot, and speaking with an imperious loudness to which she had long been a stranger.

"You little hussy, you!" said Susan, angrily shaking her fist at the offender, who laughed in her face unabashed.

"Take her away!—take her away!" exclaimed Mrs. Ford, with uncontrollable impatience.

And without more ado Mab was bundled out of the room; Susan, having shut the door, softly and carefully returned to her mistress.

"It was that it might not trouble you, ma'am, that Mr. Ford said you were not to know anything about it," said Susan, standing near the arm-chair, into which her mistress had sunk exhausted.

Mrs. Ford's hands twitched nervously at her long dark robe, before she said again:

"Who is she?"

"La! don't take on so, ma'am. It is not what you think—Mr. Ford be too fond of you for that —and I have no doubt that it was for charity he took her in when he found her yesterday sitting on the door-step."

Still Mrs. Ford's hands were restless.

"La! ma'am, don't you think anything of the kind," persisted Susan; "though, if I must say a bit of my mind, I will say it out—there—it is Miss Ford's child—there."

"Miss Ford's child!" slowly repeated Mrs. Ford. She had not seen her sister-in-law for many years, and now a sudden thought seemed to strike her.

"What sort of a woman is Miss Ford?" she asked; "young—fair?"

"She has been young," prudently answered Susan; "and she is fair and blue-eyed; and I do think, ma'am, that she is the mother of the child."

Mrs. Ford rose to her feet with sudden energy. A terrible suspicion had seized her. What if the person who had entered her husband's house under the name of Miss Ford were not his sister? What if she were that last and deepest insult which can be offered to an outraged woman—a rival in her own home! Worse still, the mother of a child destined to rival her children in their father's heart!

Seven years of solitude had shaken the balance of Mrs. Ford's mind. She could not see the cruel wrong of such a suspicion. It possessed her and roused her to sudden strength and action. Without saying a word to Susan, she walked to the door.

"Ma'am—ma'am!" cried Susan, at her wits end; "you must not go down—indeed, you must not—the place is all upside down to-day; besides—besides ———"

"So, it is true," interrupted her mistress. "I was not mistaken; I have lived to be wronged in my own home."

"For God's sake, ma'am, do not think that!" cried Susan; "do not, ma'am."

She spoke in vain. Mrs. Ford had opened the door, the threshold of which she had not crossed for seven years, and with a steady step she went down the staircase. There was no one to wonder, no one to impede her progress; the street door had just closed on Mr. Ford, and Robert and his brothers were gone to school. Susan still followed her mistress imploringly, saying, "Don't, pray don't, ma'am!" but she was not heeded. Though dazzled by the light she had so long been unused to, Mrs. Ford reached the bottom of the staircase safely, and at once opened the parlour door; but she did not enter.

When she saw that dreary room with its broken and tattered furniture, with its squalid walls and its ragged carpet, she remained one moment mute, then she turned round, and looked at Susan with angry surprise.

"It is no use, ma'am," said Susan, feeling desperate; "the truth must out. I can't keep the place better with one pair of arms. Mary Ann has long been gone, and master said it did not matter, so long as you were comfortable upstairs."

"That is it," thought Mrs. Ford; "that is it. Anything to keep me quiet up there."

"And you don't know, ma'am, what we have gone through downstairs," continued Susan, tears standing in her eyes as she spoke. "Short commons is nothing, I can do with them as well as any one; and the children, though they did not fare daintily, had enough—God bless them! But it was a fight for the dear life, one may say, everything going to rack and ruin, and one pair of arms for it all. When the servants went, I kept up with you about Mary Ann as long as I could; and Mr. Ford, he would make me take a charwoman, and she was a Mary Ann, so that did not go so much against my conscience. But lawk, ma'am, I could not have the heart to keep her; and to know, as I did, that master dined out day after day because there was nothing at home, or not more than enough for the children and me, and that Mary Ann. I soon packed her off, I did; and I feel, ma'am, as if I did well."

Susan ceased her explanation, and looked at her mistress half defiant, half imploring.

"Anything to keep me quiet, upstairs out of the way," muttered Mrs. Ford. "I see—I see."

She turned away, and once more ascended the staircase.

"Ay, do, ma'am," eagerly cried Susan; "it is

enough for one day; do go to your own rooms again."

"Never!" replied her mistress. "Oh! God, help me! What have I been doing for these seven years? But it is not too late! I am strong. I am well now."

It was useless to contend with her; Mrs. Ford was bent on having her own way. Upstairs she went, to the room of her children. Her brows knit and her lips tightened, as she there witnessed new and more dreary tokens of pinching poverty, and long standing neglect.

"I know what you think, ma'am," said Susan, firing up; "but I know, too—I have done what I could, and it is not one pair of arms ——"

"Hush!" interrupted her mistress, raising a warning hand; "whose step is that?"

"It is Miss Ford, ma'am," said Susan, opening the door, and thus giving Mrs. Ford a view of that lady on the landing.

Poor Miss Lavinia turned pale as death, and looked ready to faint on beholding her sister-in-law; but one look convinced Mrs. Ford of her identity, and a second glance, more scrutinizing than the first, also convinced her that Miss Ford was not the mother of the child who now clung shrinkingly to her skirts.

"I am glad you are well again," at length stammered Miss Lavinia.

"Thank you," was Mrs. Ford's short answer. "Who is that child?" she added, pointing to Mab.

"God knows," faltered Miss Lavinia, "looking preciously guilty," as Susan internally phrased it. "John found her sitting on the door-steps, and took her in; but why she was left at his door, he having already three boys of his own, is hard to say. Perhaps, though, that as the Fords are an old Catholic Lancashire family, that may be the reason; for I questioned her last night, and made her say her prayers, and I found she had been reared a Catholic; and I almost thought she had a Lancashire look, too."

Mrs. Ford smiled sternly, first at Miss Lavinia, in whom she saw her husband's accomplice; then at the child, in which she beheld the fruit of his guilt, and saying, with bitter emphasis,

"Ay, she *has* a Lancashire look." She walked downstairs, back to her own room.

"And now, ma'am, do pray rest," entreated Susan.

Mrs. Ford turned almost fiercely upon her.

"Rest!" she said; "rest! I shall sit at the head of the dinner-table this day."

"Very well, ma'am," said Susan, with a desperate sort of resignation; "and what is there to be for dinner to-day?"

Mrs. Ford did not answer her; she was walking up and down the room with restless excitement.

"I suppose the cold beef will do," muttered Susan, and, still amazed at the strange turn events had taken, she went downstairs.

It so chanced that Mr. Ford did not come in early that day, as was his habit; but when he came he was in high spirits. The shares were rising with unexpected rapidity.

"I shall sell out next week," thought Mr. Ford, "and then—" "Then" referred to a new speculation, and one still more promising than the last, of which he had heard that very day. He was full of hope; and, for the hundredth time in his life, sure of success, and, with success, of fortune.

"If dear Alicia would only go on improving," he thought, with a sigh, as he reached his own door, "all would be well."

Susan admitted him, with a countenance overflowing with news. His thoughts at once flew to the child.

"Where is she?—what have you done with her?" he asked, nervously.

"Bless me, sir, I ain't done anything!" rather sourly replied Susan, "and if missus will come down and dine to-day——"

"What!"

"If missus will come down and dine to-day," repeated Susan, "why, surely it is all for the best."

The rush of joy was too great. Mr. Ford turned pale as death, and was obliged to cling to Susan for support.

"Bear up, sir," said Susan, who was ready to cry herself—" bear up—there she is!"

Mr. Ford looked up; his wife was descending the staircase with a slow but steady step. A strange shadow of her former self looked Mrs. Ford. She had put on a dark silk dress, seven years old in fashion and taste. Everything in her attire, from her wide collar to her narrow sleeves, looked antiquated and faded; saddest of all looked her sad eyes and her pale, rigid face; but Mr. Ford was blind—blind with happiness and affection. Alicia was cured—Alicia was well again! He saw nothing else. He went to the foot of the staircase and took her in his arms.

"God bless you, Alicia!" he exclaimed, fervently. "God bless you, my darling!"

He kissed her again and again. Mrs. Ford gave him an icy look—a look that said "enough," but which Mr. Ford knew not how to read.

"Where are the boys?" exclaimed Mr. Ford, excitedly. "Susan, call the boys—tell them to come and see their mother. Where *are* the boys?"

"Better not worry her, sir," put in Susan.

"I shall see my children," coldly said Mrs.

Ford, putting away her husband. With a steady step she entered the front parlour, where the cloth was laid, and the three boys and Mab were gathered in a corner, giggling and laughing.

"Boys," cried Mr. Ford, "here's your mother come back again. Bob, Ned, Bill, here's your mother come to dine with us, my boys!"

Profound silence followed this announcement. The three boys turned round and looked at their mother, but not even Robert seemed inclined to approach her, and Mrs. Ford made no sign, held out no encouragement. Her love had never been one of words, and she was still too much the woman of seven solitary years to care for speech now. She looked at her children with silent tenderness, and shunned, with irresistible aversion, poor little Mab's fair face and golden hair; and that was all.

The hours which Mrs. Ford had spent upstairs since the morning had strengthened her secret resolve, and made it firm and inexorable as fate. She would not reproach her husband: she would not even be unkind to the child: she would not seem conscious of infidelity or wrong; but she would watch—watch and keep guard over *her* children. She would let no usurper step between them and their father. Whatever happened, *they* should be protected. Mrs. Ford's self-denial, however, did not go so far as to ignore Mab's presence in the house, and, turning calmly to her husband, she said, in her clearest tones,

"Why is this child here, Mr. Ford?"

How those five hundred pounds must have clung to Mr. Ford's soul to make him colour up and stammer so!

"The child," he said, feeling, rather than meeting, his wife's keen look; "you mean the little girl, I suppose."

Mrs. Ford bent her stately head, and her husband was going to stammer an awkward "After dinner, my dear," when an unexpected auxiliary came to the rescue. A loud double knock at the front door announced a visitor.

"Please, sir, Captain George wishes to say a few words to you," said Susan, putting in her head at the door.

"Show him in—show him in!" eagerly cried Mr. Ford. "You'll be glad to see Captain George, my dear. Captain George, come in, old fellow. Here's a ghost, Captain George!"

Captain George, who was indeed surprised, started back a little on perceiving Mrs. Ford, but, quickly recovering, he gracefully exclaimed,

"A lovely ghost, old fellow—a lovely ghost!"

"She could not do any longer without me," said Mr. Ford, rubbing his hands with boastful triumph;

"could you, Ally? Sit down, Captain George, and have pot-luck with us."

"In honour of the happy event—I don't mind if I do," replied Captain George, taking a chair at the table with the most amiable alacrity. "But, bless my soul, if that is not little 'Never Mind!'"

"Yes," replied Mr. Ford, relieved, yet embarrassed to have his wife thus indirectly answered, "it is the child we found yesterday on the door-steps. I took her in, and I mean to keep her."

"Oh! I see, I see," nodded Captain George, with an air of sudden reserve; then looking at Mrs. Ford, next whom he sat, and in whose watchful blue eyes he perchance read something, he added, apologetically, "our friend here was always fond of children—always: besides, having no girls of his own, you know."

Mrs. Ford gave him a cold, fixed look; and Mr. Ford, carving the joint which, by some mysterious means, Susan had substituted to the cold beef, was going to help his guest, when his wife icily observed:

"You have not said grace, Mr. Ford."

Mr. Ford, most of whose gracious habits had vanished one after the other during the last seven years, blushed, and muttered an indistinct blessing.

With keen pain his wife saw the grin which stole from Robert to Bill, and from Bill to Ned—

and which Captain George's demure looks nearly converted into an open laugh of derision; but she had nerved herself to bear much, and with as much composure and steadiness as if she had not long been a stranger to the sights of this every-day world, she did the honours of the dinner-table.

It was a strange meal, and a noisy one, thanks to Captain George. He made himself irresistibly amusing to the children, from Robert down to Mab; highly entertaining to Mr. Ford, disagreeable to his sister, and bitterly offensive to his wife. It seemed, indeed, to be his object to draw out all poor Mr. Ford's worst traits and greatest weaknesses. Mr. Ford, elated by the news he had heard in the city, had taken some refreshment on his way home. He reached Queen's Square excited but sober; but his joy at his wife's recovery, and Captain George's presence, rendered him strange and boisterous at dinner. He repeatedly drank the health of Mrs. Ford, and every time he uttered "Your health, my love," across the table, he winked at Captain George, and added, in an audible whisper, "Could not do without me, you see." And Captain George, who drank Mrs. Ford's health fully as often as her husband, and sometimes twice to his once, did his best to lead him on.

"Leave the table," said Mrs. Ford to her children, as she saw that her husband's self-possession was fast deserting him, and go up-stairs," she added.

"Stay," shouted Mr. Ford; "Robert, drink your mother's health; Bill, take a glass, my boy. Ned, where are you?"

Mrs. Ford rose, pale with anger and sorrow. Captain George seemed to take pity on her, for he unexpectedly interfered.

"Nonsense," he said; "let boys be boys, and men be men. Come out with me; we have tired Mrs. Ford long enough: besides, I want to say a word to you on business."

"Oh! you want to do me, do you?" said Mr. Ford, with tipsy slyness; "*I* know you, Captain George—I know you—no go."

"No, no, now; 'pon honour, that's too bad," said Captain George; and whispering familiarly to Mrs. Ford, he added,

"Never mind, my dear lady; it is only for once, and I shall send him home to you in an hour."

And so he did; for they left the house together. Ay, Captain George kept his word. In an hour he sent Mr. Ford home in a cab—dead drunk.

CHAPTER IX.

SOME penitence and some shame Mr. Ford expressed the next morning, But on the whole he made light of the matter; and, half carelessly, half good-humouredly, he laid his transgressions to the joy he had felt at seeing his wife once more down-stairs. He assured her, however, that "Captain George had fished nothing out of him;" and the confusion he could not help betraying, sprang, not from having been brought home intoxicated, but from the recollection which had escaped his mind the preceding day, that Mrs. Ford must have found the house in a strange state of negligence and decay.

"You see, my dear," he said, as they sat down to breakfast, "matters are never quite right when the mistress of the house is ill as you were; but I have already ordered some new furniture—this is too shabby, carpets, sofas, and the rest of it: and I am almost sorry you came down so soon—I really am, my love."

He spoke with a warmth and tenderness that ought to have been convincing, but Mrs. Ford was watching Mab. The child had stolen into the room, where they breakfasted alone, and stood by Mr. Ford's chair, looking shyly in his face, as if expecting a caress. He gave it kindly but mechanically; whilst his hand smoothed her golden curls he still addressed his wife:

"By the way, my dear," he said, "how do you like the harmonium?"

"Thank you, it is a good instrument," she said, aloud—and in heart she thought, "It is his child."

Mr. Ford's face fell. Accustomed as he was to his wife's coldness, he had expected something more. But then poor Alicia could not know how hard a struggle it had been to get that instrument. She suspected nothing of Livy's thirty-five pounds; she did not know that, without Mab's five hundred, gloomy would have been the fate of the whole family. It was no fault of hers, only she did not know.

It was well Mr. Ford did not know what was passing in his wife's mind whilst he was stroking Mab's hair. Terrible is the jealousy that survives love. No tender regret, no fond remembrance, soften its bitterness and wrath. It is the offspring of self-love and pride, and, like them, it is implacable. Relentless dislike sprang up in Mrs. Ford's heart. She thought herself outraged in her dignity—in the sanctuary of woman, home—in her children, ever loved though so long estranged. In that loving tenderness which had kept every care away from her, she read the cold design of a faithless heart. But she said, she showed nothing; neither her husband nor the child could tax her with unkindness, even in those first trying moments; yet it was well for Mr. Ford that he had little tact and blunt perceptions, that he neither saw nor minded his wife's strange coldness, and that he explained away her icy looks and her brief replies. It was well for him that the cruel blow was delayed, and fell not on him then. Poor fellow, he had but one thought, and that was, how he might best please his Idol.

"My love," said he, rising from the breakfast-table, and walking about the parlour, with his hands thrust in his trousers' pockets, "my love, if it does not fatigue your mind too much, will you just tell me what arrangements we had best take about this house, now that you are well and strong again."

Mrs. Ford received this offer with cold acquiescence. It was her due.

"Your circumstances do not seem very flourishing, Mr. Ford," she said, a little reproachfully; "I shall be satisfied if you take another servant and refurnish the house, which is, indeed, in a shameful state."

Mr. Ford always congratulated himself on the extraordinary presence of mind he displayed on this occasion. Instead of letting out the unpleasant truth that he had little or no ready money just then, he brightened up, and said cheerfully, "Certainly, my dear, certainly; but is that all?"

"No, it is not all," replied Mrs. Ford, with some bitterness, "the children want clothes, Mr. Ford."

Mr. Ford brightened up again.

"Certainly, my love; but do you want nothing for yourself?"

"Nothing."

"Don't you think, my dear, that a drive in the country, say Richmond, and a quiet luncheon at a quiet inn, would do you good? Of course we should take Lavinia and the children."

Mrs. Ford shook her head, in token of denial.

"My dear, it is a beautiful day, mild and lovely; we should have a close carriage."

He looked anxiously at his wife. She seemed languid and indifferent; but Mr. Ford, convinced that the excursion would do her infinite good, persisted.

"As you please," she said, at length, and Mr. Ford, delighted to have won her acquiescence, immediately went to secure a close carriage for his wife and himself, and an open one for the children. But when the carriages came round, Mrs. Ford thought that Mr. Ford had better go with his sister and the young children, and let her and Robert go alone; for though the close carriage was a large one, Mrs. Ford could not be crushed.

Mr. Ford did his best to brighten up at this arrangement, and he said, "Certainly, my dear," in his most cheerful tone; but Mrs. Ford's choice depressed him for all that. So she went with her eldest son, and he and Miss Ford and the two younger boys and Mab crowded into the other carriage. The day was fine, and the drive was a pleasant one; but when Richmond Park was reached, Mrs. Ford declined to alight; she sent away Robert and drew down the carriage blinds, refusing to look out, to Mr. Ford's great disappointment.

"Don't you think, my dear, the sight of the verdure would do you good?" asked Mr. Ford.

"My head aches," answered Mrs. Ford, and, leaning back in the carriage, she closed her eyes.

Mr. Ford walked away rather disconsolately—it was a great pity that Alicia's head ached; but perhaps the fresh air and the motion would do her good, so he went and ordered luncheon, leaving the children under the care of Miss Lavinia, whilst Mrs. Ford and her carriage drove slowly on.

"Why, bless me if that is not little 'Never Mind!'" cried a gay voice.

To her great annoyance, Miss Ford recognized Captain George. The gallant Captain was not alone; a stout lady was leaning on his arm, and she was looking at Mab with motherly interest.

"Is that the child?" she whispered, audibly.

"It is the child, my love," replied her husband.

"Sweet little thing!"

She beckoned in friendly wise, but Mab was too busy with Robert to heed her.

"What an extraordinary coincidence!" exclaimed Captain George. "You come to Richmond, and we come to Richmond. Is Ford here?"

Miss Ford stammered that her brother had gone to order luncheon, upon which Captain George discovered that the coincidence was not merely extraordinary, but delightful. Mrs. George had just been wishing to go and take luncheon somewhere, and nothing could be pleasanter to all parties than to take luncheon together. In the meanwhile, what could be more appropriate than to enjoy together, of course, the beauties of Richmond Park? Miss Lavinia timidly suggested that her brother would only order luncheon for six; but Captain George kindly assured her that what would do for six would do for eight, and again suggested that they should enjoy the beauties of Richmond Park. Seeing the hopelessness of her lot, Miss Lavinia submitted.

When Mr. Ford came back rather flushed and warm from his errand, he had some trouble in finding either his wife or his sister. At length he saw the carriage in an avenue, and in the distance he perceived a group, in which, on approaching it, he had the pleasure of recognising his friend, Captain George, who was playing at blind man's buff with the children.

"Didn't expect to find us here, old fellow," cried the Captain, pointing his cane at him; "and what about the luncheon? Soon ready—eh?"

Mr. Ford was the most hospitable of men. Appeal to his hospitality, and he lay bound hand and foot at your mercy. No sooner did Captain George speak of luncheon than the royal desmesne of Richmond Park became Mr. Ford's own. An invisible roof spread above the heads of Captain and Mrs. George; and from intruders, they became sacred guests.

"Luncheon will be ready in an hour," cheerfully replied Mr. Ford; "perhaps I had better go and tell Alicia—she might just walk for a few minutes."

"My dear," said Captain George to his wife, "you will like to see Mrs. Ford."

Mrs. George would be delighted; and though Mr. Ford knew well the meeting would be highly distasteful to his wife, he could not very well prevent Captain and Mrs. George from going up to her carriage. A queen could not have been more stately than was Mrs. Ford to Captain and Mrs. George; she looked at them, and spoke to them with such regal coldness, that the interview did not last more than a few minutes. When they were gone, Mrs. Ford beckoned to her husband, who came up to her, looking foolish.

"Mr. Ford," she said, in a tone of ice, "are these people staying with you?"

"My dear, it is chance brought them here."

"I ask if they are staying with you."

"I believe they mean to do so."

Mrs. Ford shut her eyes, and said no more; but when it was time to go to luncheon, she informed her husband that she could not eat, and would go back to town at once. In vain Mr. Ford entreated and remonstrated; Mrs. Ford was inflexible, and Miss Lavinia, who was present at the debate, preferred a timid request to be allowed to go home with Mrs. Ford. By an extraordinary coincidence, as

Captain George would have said, she, too, had a headache, and no appetite. With a rueful look, Mr. Ford saw the carriage drive away. The children were very happy, and he could hear them shouting with glee, and Captain and Mrs. George were charming company, no doubt; but the trouble and the expense had been taken for Alicia, and Alicia had enjoyed nothing.

Captain George's declaration that a meal sufficient for six persons is also sufficient for eight, was thus falsified, since six persons alone remained to enjoy that which Mr. Ford had ordered. The departure of Mrs. Ford and Miss Lavinia in the close carriage wakened, however, very sincere regret in the bosom of Captain George—for they had come by rail, and Mrs. George would have preferred the close carriage to go home in.

"However, we will make the open one do," kindly added Captain George.

Now, Mr. Ford's carriage was not like the pavilions of Prince Ahmed, in the Arabian story, it could not expand according to the number of the persons it was to accommodate, and Mr. Ford was startled at Captain George's suggestion; but again hospitality interfered, and Mr. Ford looked as cheerful as he could. To do Captain George justice, he made luncheon a merry meal. He told the children wonderful stories of his adventures in early life, and kept them in such glee that Mr. Ford's genial heart warmed towards the man. It did him good to see his boys in such spirits, and to hear little Mab's silvery laugh. And then when the meal was over, who so ingenious as Captain George? He took them all to the park, kindly leaving Mr. Ford to pay the reckoning—and whilst Mrs. George sat on the grass and rested, Captain George invented the most extraordinary and the funniest games for Mr. Ford's boys and Mab. Then, when it was really time to go, Captain George proved that he had been in the wars by the clever way in which he attempted to pack the carriage. Having first enthroned Mrs. George in the most comfortable seat, he did his best to find room for every one else, and would willingly have thrust the children under the seats to accomplish so praiseworthy an object, if the coachman had not put an end to his persevering efforts and his assurances of "there's room for us all," by peremptorily declaring that no earthly consideration should induce him to take more persons home than he had brought to Richmond.

"Never mind, old fellow," kindly said Captain George, "we can go home by rail. My love," he added, bidding his wife a graceful adieu, "mind you are put down at your own door. On no account let it be at the end of the terrace. It is no use letting those fellows off," continued Captain George, addressing Mr. Ford, as they walked away together to the station; "one pays just as much, you know—neither more nor less."

When Mr. Ford reached Queen Square, he found that his wife had gone to bed. She was very unwell, Miss Lavinia said. Wild with alarm, Mr. Ford ran for her medical man, who said it was only excitement, but scolded him roundly for having taken her out—and this was the end of Mr. Ford's day of pleasure.

CHAPTER X.

Mrs. Ford kept her room a fortnight, and, during that time, her temper was so irritable, capricious, and unaccountable, that even Mr. Ford's patience was sorely tried. He knew dear Alicia could not help it, still it was hard. At length Mrs. Ford came down one morning. She found the parlours in all the glow of new furniture; not that it was showy, Mr. Ford's taste in these matters had, at least, the merit of plainness—respectable neatness was his ideal; but the rooms were fresh papered, new carpeted, new curtained, and looked wonderfully improved. She found, too, a new servant, fresh and rosy, Lucy by name, and who had the additional merit of being Susan's young sister, and completely under Susan's dominion. She found, also, her children in neat and comfortable attire, and in excellent health; and to be a contented woman, Mrs. Ford only required to see things as they were. But Mrs. Ford saw things as they were not, and silently brooded over her wrongs.

She had not been up more than a few days, and the house was still under the management of Miss Lavinia—poor thing, she, too, brooded over her thirty-five pounds, not one of which had she seen again—when Susan, tapping at the drawing-room, informed her mistress that a strange lady wished to speak to her.

"Send her to Miss Ford," querulously replied Mrs. Ford; "she is one of Mr. Ford's friends, of course—send her to Miss Ford."

"She will not see Miss Ford, ma'am—she wants you."

"I wish Mr. Ford's friends would stay away," still querulously said Mrs. Ford. "I can see no one—who is she?"

"She would not give her name, ma'am; but she is a very strange lady, with such short petticoats, all tucked up so oddly!—and there is a little girl with her, too."

Mrs. Ford's thoughts flew to Mab. A little girl!—was it anything about the child?

She reddened, and said quickly,

"Show her in."

Susan had not time to obey. In walked a middle-aged lady, in widow's weeds, with iron-grey hair, straight, hard features, not without a sort of good-humour in them, and, as Susan had said, the shortest of short petticoats, accurately tucked up round her ankles.

There is a great deal in petticoats. Whilst they are worn they will have a meaning. This lady's were short, resolute, wilful, and strong-minded. Other women might object to showing their ankles, or take pleasure in sweeping the streets—she evidently would not soil the hem of her garment, and felt she could put forth a foot with anyone.

"Well," said the lady, "don't you know me, Alicia?"

She held out her hand, and a vision of a fresh-coloured, dark-haired girl, who had gone out on her honeymoon to Australia, some twenty years before, with Alicia's brother, rose before Mrs. Ford. It was Thomasina Norton, her sister-in-law and cousin, who, though seven years a widow, still wore her weeds, and would wear them so long as she lived.

"Of course I am altered," said Mrs. Norton, sitting down, "and so are you, 'Licia. I heard you became a beauty, and married—not too well—but don't be afraid, I am not going to breathe a word against him. I know what it is to have had a husband—and I would kill any one who would dare to say a word against mine," impetuously added Mrs. Norton, rising as she spoke. Seven years had passed since Robert Norton had been laid in his grave at Melbourne, but the heart of his widow beat for him still, and tears stood in her eyes, and her lips quivered, as she vindicated him against possible aspersion.

"And where are your children?" she asked, looking round her, as if she expected the young Fords to be in their places like so many pieces of furniture.

"At school," answered Mrs. Ford. "Is this child yours?" she added, glancing down at a little girl of eight, who shyly hid behind Mrs. Norton's skirts; "but no, I remember—you have no children, Tom?"

"No, indeed," briefly answered Tom, for so Mrs. Norton's friends always called her; "No, indeed, I have none." And she uttered the declaration in a tone that implied that it was a doubtful proceeding to have children, and that she, for one, had kept clear of it.

"No, this is Harry's child," she continued. "You remember my brother Harry, 'Sly Harry,' as dear Robert used to call him. Well, Sly Harry he found him, and I never liked him since then; but my dearest husband was the most forgiving of men, and, as almost his last words were, 'Take the baby, Tom,' I took Nelly. Look up, child."

Nelly looked up; a dark, gipsy face, shaded by dark hair, was hers. A face of dreamy sweetness and some beauty, lit up with soft black eyes.

"She is like her father," said Mrs. Ford, slightly moved; for that father, now a widower in Australia, had been one of her rejected suitors.

"Yes, she is like Sly Harry," said Mrs. Norton, with significant emphasis; "but have you got a girl too?" she added, surprised, as Mab softly opening the door, timidly looked in, to deliver a message from Susan. "Come here, little one. Why, she is not a bit like you," continued Mrs. Norton, looking up in her sister-in-law's face.

"She is not mine," was the icy reply. "Mr. Ford has adopted her."

Mrs. Norton whistled; gave Mab another scrutinizing look, and, saying to the two children, who were examining each other with shy, inquiring glances, "Go and play together—go and play," she dismissed them. They left the room hand in hand, and, ere the door had well closed upon them, Mrs. Ford said hurriedly, as if anxious to change the subject,

"Where are you?—why did you not come to stay with us?"

"I am in comfortable lodgings, my dear, where I am sure not to be in the way."

"Say we were too poor to receive you," rather bitterly said Mrs. Ford.

"Well, what about it?" stoutly rejoined Mrs. Norton; "it is no sin to be poor, that I know of; and if your husband is not a successful man, he is your husband, and you love him none the less. Oh! Alicia, don't talk of poverty to me—you have your husband still; and I, the rich woman—for I am rich—I envy you."

"You envy me!"

"Not your children, mind you! That little, sly, deceitful Nelly is the plague of my life. She looks soft and sweet; wait a bit; there will soon be a battle between her and that little grey-eyed thing. It is only with boys that Miss Nelly Norton agrees. Oh! she and her cousins will get on wonderfully, depend upon it!"

"They will be back for dinner," said Mrs. Ford. "Take off your bonnet, Tom, and stay with us."

But Tom thought she would like to keep on her bonnet, England was but a chill place. And what had Alicia been doing with herself all these years? for Tom's talk was more varied and fluent than connected.

"Nothing—nothing," drearily replied Alicia. "Imagine a long blank, and you have my whole history."

"A blank with three boys! But I heard you

had become such a beauty. Your good looks are gone, then, Alicia—all gone."

"I dare say they are."

"I dare say there is no doubt about it. You know me of old; I contend it is no scandal to talk of a friend's face. My sister-in-law, Mary, never would tolerate my saying that her son was plain, He is plain—can I help it? But she says it may prevent him from getting married. 'Now, Mary, you know *that* is nonsense,' said I, 'James's face is not a thing that either you or he can put in your pockets, and not bring out till the wedding day is over. It must be seen, do what you like, and so where's the harm of saying the plain truth about it?' Not but that there's much in a face," continued Mrs. Norton, after a short pause, "and in one's whole person, too! Now, my dear husband could never endure tall women. He had not seen me since we were children, and he took it in his head that *I* was tall. Not a bit, said his aunt, Tom is neither tall nor short. She is of a nice middle height, just the wife *you* want. She is like her father, but hers is a refined and feminine resemblance, of course. In short——"

A piercing childish scream here interrupted Mrs. Norton. She seemed at no loss to understand from whom it proceeded, for she said, very calmly, in answer to Mrs. Ford's startled look,

"I told you so; Nelly has pinched or bitten that little fair thing; bless you, it is her way. Well, grey-eyes, what has she done to you?" she added, opening the door, and questioning Mab, who sat on the staircase, flushed and crying, whilst Nelly stood, silent and cool, in a corner of the landing.

"She bit me," sobbed Mab.

"Of course she did. *I* know her. Nelly, come in here, and sit down on that chair."

"We will go downstairs, if you please," said Mrs. Ford, rising; "I hear Mr. Ford's voice below."

And, without heeding Mab, who remained crying on the staircase, Mrs. Ford and Mrs. Norton went down, followed by the demure-looking Nelly.

Mr. Ford was below, and as he and his wife's sister-in-law had never met, this, their first interview, was awkward, though cordial. Mr Ford was excited, and Mrs Norton observant; there was that about him that did not please her—indeed it required his quality of a husband to soften her severe appreciation of some of his evident deficiencies. Very restless was Mr. Ford, talking at random, and rolling some money that lay loose in his pockets, and seemed to trouble him.

"Just come from Australia, ma'am—a fine country—a fine country; where is the child? Livy, where is she?"

Miss Lavinia, who was sewing unheeded in a corner of the parlour, rose and said, "I shall go and look for her."

"My sister, Miss Ford—Mrs. Norton—I am anxious about the child, Alicia—she always comes to welcome me—where can she be?"

"She is sitting on the staircase crying," coldly said Mrs. Ford; "she and Nelly quarrelled, I believe."

"Oh! ah! bad as boys, eh!—a fine place Sydney is, ma'am."

"I come from Melbourne," said Mrs. Norton.

"True—a fine place Melbourne— a rising country—gold diggings and all."

"The diggings are not the best part of the country," shortly said Mrs. Norton, still eyeing Mr. Ford with an observant air."

"What is the matter, Alicia?" he exclaimed, seeing his wife, who stood by the window, give a sudden start. Before she could answer, he looked out; a handsome carriage had rattled to the door, a footman had given a loud double knock, and Captain George had stepped out and entered the house, to be almost immediately ushered into the parlour by Susan.

Captain George was very much altered. His jaunty air had given place to a grave and demure aspect, even as his gay apparel had been replaced by the deepest mourning. Mr. Ford stared at him in mute amazement, and Captain George stared at Mrs. Norton, who looked at him with cool defiance; but this was soon over, and, turning to Mr. Ford, Captain George said, with much gravity:

"I see you are shocked—I have indeed lost a valued relative, a maiden cousin on my mother's side."

"Did she leave you that handsome set-out?" ironically asked Mr. Ford, nodding towards the carriage.

A sly gleam of satisfaction twinkled in Captain George's brown eyes, but it was quickly repressed.

"She did," he demurely replied; "that is to say, the bulk of her property was divided between my brother and myself, for she made no will. She was taken off with a suddenness which ought to be a warning to us all to be duly prepared."

Captain George drew on his gloves, thoughtfully and sadly as he spoke; then, trying to smile,

"I am getting old and moralizing, I think," he said; "but life is a riddle—a riddle."

Captain George shook his head slowly, then relapsed into the good-humoured mood on seeing Mab led in by Miss Ford, and greeted her with a "How do you do, little 'Never Mind?'"

"My name is not 'Never Mind.'"

"And so you are a rich man now," said Mr. Ford, with ill-disguised envy.

"Not exactly—not exactly," correctively replied Captain George; "my share was but small—say something between ten and twenty," he added, knowingly, laying his finger to his nose; "but bless me, I was forgettiug that doll I promised the other day! What do you say to it, little 'Never Mind'—bless me, I forget again, that is not the name. What is the name?"

"Oh! let me have the doll, let me have it!" cried Mab, forgetting her resentment.

"Certainly, I always gratify a lady's wishes," graciously replied Captain George—"always."

He tapped at the window; the footman at once answered the signal, and in a few seconds appeared, carrying a square deal box, which was respectfully placed before Mab, and whence she drew forth a very handsome doll, that nearly sent her wild with joy. Captain George, after looking at her benevolently, once more directed his discourse to the grown-up persons present.

"I think, madam," said he, addressing Mrs. Norton, "that I have already had the pleasure of meeting you."

Mrs. Norton put her hands behind her back, and replied that perhaps he had.

"I believe," continued Captain George, "that

I had even the happiness of being of some trifling service to you."

Mrs. Norton smiled sternly, and doubted it.

"Excuse me," resumed Captain George, "I was a witness in your favour—but I should not have mentioned it; a sad case—a sad case, but men will be wretches, and not value their own happiness."

Mrs. Norton glared at him, and requested to know his meaning.

"Nay—nay," said Captain George, "not for worlds, since the subject is distasteful. Besides, he is dead and gone—it is amiable and feminine to forgive."

"Do you mean to say, sir—" cried Mrs. Norton, at the pitch of her voice.

"I mean nothing, my dear madam, nothing," hastily replied Captain George. "Ford, old fellow, a few words with you, eh!"

And before Mrs. Norton could recover her amazement, Captain George had stepped into the back parlour with Mr. Ford, and the door had closed upon them.

"I never knew anything like it, never!" said Mrs. Norton; "that mean upstart, to dare and breathe a word against my dearest husband! But he shall not get out of it, Alicia, he shall not. As if he did not know me all along! Why, the moment he entered the room he knew me, as I knew him. You shall have a bit of my mind, Captain George—a bit of my mind."

And Mrs. Norton once more, quite cool, put her back to the front parlour door, and stood there, pleasantly waiting for Captain George.

She waited some time. His conference with Mr. Ford related to sundry money matters, which Captain .George, now grown grand, requested Mr. Ford to transact for him. When this was over and settled, Captain George suddenly exclaimed:

"By the way, Mrs. George is very anxious to see little Never Mind before we leave; we are going to Italy for her health; can you spare me the child for an hour?"

Mr. Ford hesitated, but said, "Yes."

"Don't be afraid, sly-boots," facetiously said Captain George; "I don't want to find out anything."

"But will she go?" hurriedly asked Mr. Ford.

"To the world's end, if I hold out vistas of other dolls; but call her in and try her."

Mr. Ford opened the door that led into the front parlour, and called Mab. Captain George's request was preferred to the child, and his hint of more dolls produced the readiest acquiescence.

"Then we shall go at once," said Captain George; "and I think I shall slip out here," he added, opening the door that led to the hall—"that lady in the weeds and grey hair looked rather savage. Tell her, my dear fellow, it is a case of mistaken identity—mistaken identity," continued Captain George, with his old impudent wink.

And leading Mab by the hand, he coolly walked out past the front parlour door, and stepped into his carriage. Mr. Ford handed Mab in to him; and Captain George, wrapping her up in a loose warm shawl, clapped the door to, and uttered the magic "all right." The coachman at once drove away, and thus was Mrs. Norton defrauded of her vengeance. She had, however, the satisfaction—a great one, no doubt—of seeing Captain George kiss his hand to her from the carriage window, ere it drove away.

"Wait awhile, wait awhile," said the exasperated lady; "I shall be up to you yet, Captain George."

But we do not wish to raise false expectations; let us declare it plainly: Mrs. Norton never was up to Captain George.

"Well, my dear," said Captain George, to Mab: "how do you like going to see the lady?"

"Is she pretty?"

"She has been pretty; but has and is are different, eh, little Never Mind? Besides, you saw her at Richmond. Give me a kiss."

A decided refusal was returned to this presumptuous request. Very good-humouredly did Captain George bear with his repulse, and with equal good humour did he go on bantering his young friend, as he called her, until the carriage reached number seven, Woodbine Terrace, Brompton. Mab, still wrapped in the shawl, was carried into the villa; it was a furnished one, and bore but few tokens of the next day's jour ney. She was conveyed at once to the presence of Mrs. George, just taking her tea in the parlour.

"I had given you up, my love," she said, pleasantly; "how do you do, my little dear?"

"Come, little Never Mind, go to the lady. I was detained, my dear—otherwise you know I would not keep you waiting."

"No, my dear, I am sure you would not. Sit by me, my love; what is your name? I have forgotten it."

"Mab, Mab Winter, now."

Mrs. and Captain George exchanged a look.

"His mother's name," said the Captain, pouring himself out some tea; "a clear case."

Mrs. George nodded, and helped Mab to some cake. But Mab did not care to eat. She was sorry she had come, and said so.

"I want Robert," she said, tearfully.

"Hush!" replied Mrs. George, "I have got something for you—look."

She put her hand in her pocket, and drew forth a coral necklace. Mab blushed with pleasure, and allowed the Captain to fasten it round her neck; then stealing a sly look at the looking-glass, she nodded at herself, and went on very pleasantly with her tea. But when it was over, the longing for home returned, and was once more expressed.

"Nonsense," said Captain George, "we have not done with you yet. Wait till the tea-things are cleared away—that is all, I say."

Mab waited, and magical indeed was the sight that rewarded her patience. The tea-tray was replaced by Noah's Ark, and a wonderful collection of strange looking animals, who strayed to the further ends of the table. Exclamations of wonder and delight burst from her every time a new one appeared, and Mrs. George smiled, and Captain George rubbed his hands with glee.

"Capital! eh?" he exclaimed every now and then—"capital!"

They were all very much absorbed. A gentleman entered the room, and by Mab, at least, he was not heeded. Captain George saw him, indeed, gave him a nod, and said, "Take a chair, James," and there ended his welcome; and Mrs. George never moved, and smiled, but rather coldly.

This gentleman—a tall, grey man—was Captain George's younger brother, Mr. James George, a city man, and a rich man, too, if report spoke truly, and certainly a very different man from the gay Captain, in external appearance. Respectability and decorum were stamped on his whole person, and his deep mourning added to the solemnity of his aspect. He took his chair in profound silence, played for a while with his watch-guard, and looked at Mab.

"Some tea?" suggested Captain George.

"None, thank you. Who is that child?"

Here Mab looked up, and fixed her large grey eyes full upon him.

"Miss Mab Winter is her name," said the Captain, looking very much inclined to laugh.

"Winter!" musingly repeated Mr. George. "Anything to the Fords?"

Captain George threw himself back in his chair, and laughed outright.

"Oh! James—James!" he exclaimed, as soon as he recovered his breath. James looked at his brother with austere surprise.

"I am at a loss to divine the cause of your merriment," he said, in solemn displeasure. "I said, 'Anything to the Fords,' a natural question, and I repeat it, 'Anything to the Fords?'"

Captain George looked amazingly tickled, but

did not laugh—his younger brother had always ruled him; he now said, gravely enough,

"Poor little Mab was left at Ford's door—Heaven knows by whom—and he took her in, and gave her his mother's name."

"Bless me, what an extraordinary story!" exclaimed Mr. George, arching his eye-brows; "and he gave her his mother's name, too—quite peculiar!"

"Very," drily said Captain George.

"And where were you before you were taken to Queen Square?" said Mr. George, addressing Mab, rather suddenly.

The child had never ceased looking at him, like one fascinated or perplexed.

Mr. James George was a peculiar, and not a pleasant-looking man, when you examined him closely. His small grey eyes, veiled by heavy drooping lids, had a sly and eager meaning. There was will in the lines of the thin mouth, and fearfulness in the long retreating chin, and, over all, a smoothness, tempered by dignity, which did well enough for superficial observers, but could avail nothing against the instinct of childhood. Instead of answering his question, Mab continued looking at him with all her might. He seemed annoyed, and, raising his voice, said again,

"Child, where were you before you were taken to Mr. Ford's house? With whom were you?"

"I don't know," said Mab, a little crossly.

"You must have been somewhere—where was it?"

"I don't know—there!"

"With whom were you?—with your father or your mother?"

Mab shook her head.

"I was with Mary and the lady—I wish I were at home with Robert," she querulously added.

"In what sort of a house did Mary live?" persisted Mr. George—"was there a door to it?"

"No."

"No!"

"No, it was a gate."

Mr. George looked slightly disconcerted, but resumed his cross-examination.

"A house with a gate—and—a garden?"

"Oh! yes—a large garden—a park!"

"A park—hem!—and in what county?"

Mab was silent.

Mr. George suggested Derbyshire, then Buckinghamshire, then every English, Scotch, and Irish county, patiently enumerating the name of each, but all fell idly on Mab's ear, no token of recognition crossed her face as she heard him. Not much more successful was he when he required a personal description of Mary or of the lady. Mary had red hair, and the lady wore glasses, and that was all Mab knew or could tell.

"A hopeless case," said Mr. George, with every appearance of disgust; "and a very low-born child, I suspect. I am surprised," he added, turning to his brother, "you have her here. I have a strong impression that she was taken from a workhouse, and dropped at Queen Square. Observe, she speaks of a gate—workhouses have gates; then of a large garden, which she is pleased to call a park—the very thing; the lady probably is the matron; and Mary—Mary, most likely her mother. That," added Mr. George, rising, and putting on his gloves, "is my opinion of the case—my dispassionate opinion. But it is not much use in giving it," he added, glancing at the table covered with the tenants of Noah's Ark. "You have, as usual, been making a fool of yourself, and my clear-sightedness and advice are both disregarded. Let it be—let it be. Good evening, Mrs. George."

Captain George threw himself back in his chair and stared at his brother like one amazed.

"Now, James,——" he began.

"I think you had better not," rather pompously interrupted his brother—"I think you had better not, Captain George."

"Hang it!—I had forgotten all about you, James—I had, upon my word," exclaimed Captain

George, striking his fist on the table; then suddenly changing his mood, he shook his forefinger roguishly at his relative, and winked most knowingly. "Didn't know you, old fellow—didn't know you—know you now, though. It was a deep one—it was."

Mr. James George looked unable to speak. He had known his brother for some years, as he would have said himself; but never had the Captain taken the liberty of calling him old fellow before—never.

"Mrs. George," he cried, more amazed than offended, "can you explain—*can* you explain this most extraordinary behaviour?"

Mrs. George glanced reproachfully at her husband, who compelled himself to look grave, and declaring there was nothing to explain, rose to let his brother out; but no sooner were they in the hall together, than he broke again into a chuckling "Didn't know you, 'pon my word, didn't know you, James."

"I protest I cannot understand," said Mr. James, looking very indignant.

"Of course not," replied Captain George, with infinite amusement in his tone; "it cannot understand. Ah! it was a sly old fox—it was. Ta-ta—no use looking daggers at me."

It was no use, and so Mr. James George probably felt, for though he did look daggers, he said not one word, and walked out of number seven, Woodbine Terrace, a dignified and sullen-looking man.

Captain George was still chuckling when he returned to the parlour. Mrs. George looked very ready to drop into a doze, and Mab, wearied and offended at Mr. George's questions and remarks, was looking dispiritedly at Noah's Ark.

"I want to go home," she said.

"I think you had better take her home," suggested Mrs. George, rousing herself up.

"Wilson can drive her home," replied Captain George, stretching himself lazily on a sofa, "she will be quite safe in the carriage."

Mrs. George seemed to think so too. Accordingly Mab was once more wrapped up in the shawl, placed in the carriage with the box that held Noah's Ark under her feet, an arrangement which Captain George roused himself to superintend; and after having consented to give that gentleman a parting kiss, she was driven back to Queen Square. She was fast asleep when the carriage stopped at Mr. Ford's door. That gentleman came out himself for her, and expressed his dissatisfaction at the unceremonious manner in which Mab had been returned to him. It was as well that his wife did not hear him, nor see his knitted brows, but she was in her room. Mrs. Norton and Nelly had been gone some time, and Miss Lavinia, who sat sewing, and the three boys, who were deep in their books in the parlour, alone witnessed Mab's return.

"Why, the child might have got her death of cold," grumbled Mr. Ford, as he brought her into the warm room; "sit down by the fire, Mab; she is quite numb, I declare. Well, what do you want now?"

"Noah's Ark, please; it is in the carriage."

Susan was bringing it in, and Noah's Ark on being set on the table, elicited exclamations of wonder and delight, in which even the grave Robert joined.

"That must be an expensive toy," said Miss Lavinia, putting down her work.

"I dare say it is; why, what red thing is that round your neck?"

"A coral necklace," promptly replied Mab; "Mrs. George says I am to keep it."

The coral necklace disturbed some conjectures Miss Lavinia had already been forming concerning Mab's parentage, and in which Captain George figured. No, it could not be that; Captain George would not take her to show her to his wife.

"Nelly has got a coral necklace," said Robert.

"Oh! Mab, what a pity you did not see Nelly—she is so pretty."

"And so good-natured," said Edward.

"She kissed me," put in William.

"No, she didn't."

"She did."

"Hush!" said Robert, checking a quarrel which this new Helen was going to cause between the two brothers; "Mab will see Nell to-morrow—she told me she would come."

"I have seen her," cried Mab, with flushed cheeks, "and I don't like her—she is spiteful, and she bit me."

"And I am sure Nelly is too amiable to bite," decisively said Robert, "I cannot believe it of her."

Mab's eyes filled with jealous and resentful tears, but she said nothing.

"She will bring Frederick, her brother," said William; "I like Frederick."

"You have never seen him," sharply said Robert.

"No matter—I like him."

"So do I," quickly put in Mab, "I like Frederick, and I shall shew him my Noah's Ark, and my doll," she added, looking round for it.

Alas! for the sight that met her view. The doll lay with her face to the floor, a shattered and disfigured image of her former self. Mab uttered a cry, then burst into tears.

"It was you did that," said Robert, reproachfully, to William. But both William and Ned denied the charge—no, it was Nell—Nell who had deliberately taken the doll, and smashed it.

"Never mind, Mab—it is only a doll," loftily said Robert.

But Mab did mind, and, for the first time since her arrival in Queen Square, she went weeping to bed.

CHAPTER XI.

WELL it is for childhood that its griefs are short-lived, but better it would be if its dislikes were as brief. Mab was by no means of a resentful nature, yet the injured doll rankled on her mind, and she disliked Nelly from that evening. With Nell's brother Frederick, a fine good-humoured lad of ten, Mab, on the contrary, formed a close friendship, so close, indeed, as to excite some jealousy in Robert. Yet he had no cause. For Robert, her teacher, friend, and future husband, Mab had from the first day of their acquaintance contracted a reverential affection, and the rest of her favours she distributed pretty equally between his younger brothers and Frederick Norton.

No one meddled with the children. Miss Lavinia avoided them by temperament, Mr. Ford was always out, Mrs. Ford thought but of her own boys, and heeded neither the likes nor the dislikes of Mab ; and Mrs. Norton sarcastically called Nell a flirt and Frederick a simpleton, and when she watched the ways of these six children, did so purely and simply for her own entertainment, and by no means for their improvement.

Quarrels were frequent in that little world, and as a rule, these dissensions, however they might begin, ended with Robert and Nell on one side, and Mab and Frederick on the other. Ned and William either remained neutral or they sided, partly through affection, more through fear, with their elder brother. But Frederick was sent to a school in the north, and Mab remained undefended. These were hard days for the child, for Robert, always so kind when they were alone, grew severe, despotic, and harsh when Nell was present. Nell knew how to flatter him, and, better still, how to work on his weakness. With a smile and a "I know you are afraid of Mab," or again, "You dare not hurt Mab's feelings," she could make Robert as unkind and as unjust as she pleased, or, what came to the same thing in Mab's opinion, she could secure impunity for her own insults or her ill-nature, both of which Mab had to bear, although Robert was present. These attacks were more persevering than varied. Childhood is not generous, and Nell's taunts had Mab's unknown birth for their chief object. She had found that this was the surest sting, for Mab was pretty and clever; she cared little about her clothes, but she did care when she was told that she was a foundling, and that she lived upon charity. Sometimes she tried to retaliate, but Nell was cool and never lost her temper, and Mab could not keep hers long enough to vex the enemy—besides, what could she taunt Nell with? Nell had relatives and friends; Nell wore fine garments, and was rich; Nell was pretty, too, and if she was not so intelligent as Mab, she knew more than Mab did.

On a bright afternoon, the long contest between her and Nelly came to an end. The final scene was not very different from those that had preceded it, but it was rather more bitter. Robert was, as usual, the real motive, though neither Mab nor Nelly mentioned his name. Mab wanted him to play with her, and Nelly did her best to prevent him; and while he suspended his decision, the war of words went on.

"You are only a foundling," said Nelly, curling her pretty lip at Mab.

Mab shook with emotion, but did not answer.

"I heard aunt saying that she supposed your birth was a disgrace—and aunt would not say it if it were not true."

Shame, pride, and passion contended in Mab's heart. She looked at Robert—she thought, she hoped he would defend her from an insult so flagrant and uncalled for; but Nelly looked very pretty in her bright blue silk dress, and she always stood high in Robert's good graces. He looked a little superciliously at the two young beauties who were contending for his favour, and he forbore to interfere. Mab's heart felt as if it would break. She was alone, insulted and unprotected.

"*He* would have taken my part," she cried, pale with anger, and scarcely refraining from tears; "and I hate you, Robert, and I will leave the house, I will."

"Do," said Robert, austerely—"we do not want haters here."

"And never come back," added Nelly. "Come here, Robert, I want to show you something," and she drew Robert into a corner with an affectation of mystery.

That corner irritated Mab more than anything else. Who and what was Nelly that she should take Robert aside, and laugh and talk with him, to Mab's exclusion?

"I will run away," she thought—"I will!"

She looked out of the front parlour window. The sun shone on the green of the trees in the square; the world looked bright and inviting;

Robert and Nelly, after discussing in their corner, had gone to the garden without minding her. There was nothing and no one to oppose her project. Mab stole out of the room, and opened the front door. The square was silent and lonely, yet the child stood irresolute on the threshold of that home, which, though it was turning so unkind, was still home. She paused like a young bird on the edge of its nest—then remembering that she had said she would do it, she went down the steps, and entered the square. At first she walked irresolutely around the iron railings, then coming to the gate and finding it ajar, she pushed it open and entered. There was no one within the enclosure; she was alone with the trees and the golden sunshine, and the discoloured statue of queen Anne. She sat down on the earth at the foot of the pedestal, and looked before her with sadness and discontent. She felt very forlorn. No one had minded her flight, and, as time passed, no one, it seemed, had missed her. Why was it so? Why was she not like Nelly, and Robert, and his brothers—precious and beloved?

Her poor little childish mind struggled in vain to find a ray of light in that strange mist. There came flashes of memory to her, of a kind lady, and a wild seashore, of a dark youth; but even to herself she could give those images no definite form.

They were gone, all gone, and had long been so. The memory of the latter days only showed her another lady, a large house, and Mary. Then came Queen Square and the present.

Her head ached with all these thoughts. She felt unhappy too, and cried silently and bitterly. She no longer cared to wander, but neither did she care to return to the house. She was satisfied to stay where she was, weeping and feeling chill and miserable.

The red light of the setting sun was fading away from the old brick houses of the square, the hands on the church dial marked five, the leaves no longer looked golden—they hung withered and thin on every bough, the blue sky had turned grey, and a cold breeze shook the quivering branches above the child's head.

"I wish I were dead!" sobbed Mab, "I wish I were dead!"

She took her little skirt and gathered it over her head, she hid her face in her lap; for she began to feel afraid, twilight was creeping around her, and there were strange whisperings in the air. She did not see grey clouds gathering in the autumn sky, she did not feel at once the chill and penetrating rain, and when she felt it, she did not stir. The passive despair of childhood had entered her heart. She stayed there wet and shivering.

It showed of how little account Mab was in the house that she was not missed though so long absent. Neither Robert nor Nell troubled themselves about her, and when Miss Lavinia, perceiving that she was not below, as usual, inquired where she was, Susan, with whom Mab was no favourite, replied sharply—

"Oh! the little monkey is sulking somewhere," and no more was thought or said on the subject.

Mr. Ford came home early, and he missed Mab at once.

"Where's the child?" he asked, looking round.

But no one could tell him where Mab was. The house was searched for her and searched in vain. Robert and even Nelly got frightened. Mr. Ford detected the conscious looks they exchanged.

"What is it?" he asked; "what do you know about her?"

"She said she would run away," reluctantly answered Robert.

"Run away! What for?"

This time Mr. Ford got no answer.

At length the truth, or part of the truth was wrung from the two children, and it became evident that Mab had kept her word, and had run away.

But where could the child, a stranger to London, have gone?

Sorely troubled, Mr. Ford went forth into the square and called out aloud. He got no reply. It struck him that Mab might be within the enclosure. He looked and caught sight of some black object at the foot of the statue.

"Mab," he said, "Mab, are you there?"

A sob was Mab's only answer.

"She got shut in," was Mr. Ford's first thought, but the open gate proved it erroneous. He entered, went up to the child, and picked her up from the damp earth; with concern he saw that she was wet through, and he felt that she trembled violently.

Mr. Ford carried her to the house, and at once called Susan with imperative tones.

"Undress her and put her to bed," he said, "whilst I go for Doctor Smithson."

Susan obeyed. Mab was carried upstairs, undressed, and put into her little cot.

"I am afraid the child is really ill," said Miss Lavinia, with concern; "do look at her, Susan. She is quite flushed, and her hands are burning."

"The mischievous little monkey to go and get wet," crossly answered Susan.

"I will run away!—I will not be called a foundling!" moaned little Mab, in her delirium.

"Had we not better go and tell Mrs. Ford?" timidly suggested Miss Lavinia, looking at Susan.

Susan returned the gaze.

"I think, ma'am," she said, emphatically, "we both know and can see Mrs. Ford don't dote on her; besides, she could come if she pleased, and if she do not please, whose business is it save her own?"

"Very true," murmured Miss Lavinia.

By this Mr. Ford returned, not with Doctor Smithson, whom he had not found, but with a strange medical man, whom, in his anxiety for Mab, he had gone for. The Doctor looked at the child, felt her pulse, said it was a doubtful case, and withdrew with the intimation that he would call again next morning.

"I must go to my work," stoutly said Susan, walking downstairs.

"I think I had better keep Robert and the boys away, for fear it should be a contagious fever," suggested Miss Lavinia.

"Very well," answered her brother; "I shall mind the child—only tell Alicia I am with her, and not to sit up for me."

He sat down by her little bed. He nursed her through that long night of fever. It was not love, it was not kindness, it was the secret though unacknowledged sting of conscience. She who had brought prosperity to his home, had been driven from it with insult. They had taxed her with being a foundling, with living on his charity, and he knew, in his heart of hearts, what would have become of him and of them, but for her!

As dawn broke in the sky, Mab ceased to moan, and fell asleep.

It was then the door opened, and that Mr. Ford, looking round, saw his wife standing on the threshold. She, too, had come, but it was not out of kindness to the child, it was because she felt that she should find him there. She felt sure, only she wanted to see it.

"Mr. Ford," she said, "had you not better go to bed."

"Thank you, my love, but I do not like to leave the child."

"Why not?—she is asleep."

"She might waken."

Mrs. Ford smiled bitterly. What more could he have done—she would not say for his own child, Mab was his—but for her children? She looked at the little face, now pale and weary, lying on its white pillow, then she raised her eyes to Mr. Ford's, wearied with watching, and, with another bitter smile, she withdrew. He felt vaguely uneasy at her manner. Alicia looked odd, but it was very kind of her to come in and look at him. "She always was so fond of me," he internally exclaimed. "The dear creature, to get up, and come and look at me—just like her!"

Mab's fever had left her the next morning. The medical man pronounced her safe, but recommended rest and seclusion. On the fourth day, however, Robert was admitted to her presence.

She would not look at him.

"Mab, don't you know me?" he asked.

Mab buried her face in her pillow, and Robert tried to kiss her, but she pushed him away.

"Go and kiss Nelly," she said.

"Nelly is gone, simpleton. Gone to such a grand boarding school."

The intelligence softened Mab, she turned her face to Robert, received his kiss, but, as she returned it, she said, impetuously,

"Robert, if ever you let me be called a foundling again——"

"Hush, ninny," he interrupted, "don't you know I am to marry you."

Thus was made up this quarrel, which had given Mab five days' illness, Mr. Ford some fatigue, expense, and anxiety, and which, besides hastening Mrs. Norton's resolve of sending Nelly to school, had given a keener pang to Mrs. Ford's aching heart.

CHAPTER XII.

Mrs. Ford now bent her mind on one object—Mab must leave the house, and go to school. She did not delay in mentioning this plan to her husband, though she felt convinced he would oppose it. She was deceived, his acquiescence was ready and cheerful.

"Of course," he said. "Of course, Alicia, you are quite right. Boys are not fit society for a girl. She will be much better at school."

But Mrs. Ford's scheme received unexpected opposition from Mab herself.

"I will not go to school," she said; "I will not."

Mr. Ford argued, menaced, and entreated. Mab heard him with silent tears—a school for her was a collection of Nellies, all taunting, all insulting her, all calling her foundling—and all she said, when he ceased speaking, was,

"Do not turn me out—do not."

Mr. Ford was much affected, and, as to all he said, this was Mab's invariable reply, he gave up the point in despair.

"I cannot, my dear," he said, "Providence sent the child to my door—I cannot turn her out, as she says. We must wait till she is older."

Mrs. Ford was extremely indignant at Providence being thus brought in, but with the inward reflection, "I must be insulted to the last, and to the last I must bear it," she submitted. Now there was a person who visited at Queen Square, and who thought that the "last" was not far off. This was Mrs. Norton, and, as she was a zealous advocate for putting people on their guard, she managed to get Mr. Ford alone, and plainly told him than his wife was going wrong.

"Going wrong!" exclaimed Mr. Ford, pausing with his hand on the door as he was in the act of leaving the room; "not a bit of it. Alicia was never better in her life."

"I tell you Alicia is going wrong," persisted Mrs. Norton.

"How do you know?" was the sharp rejoinder.

"Why, she has such a colour for one thing."

Mr. Ford smiled derisively.

"And then she stoops so, that it is quite frightful.'

"Pooh! she has left off stays, I suppose."

"Stays!" exclaimed Mrs. Norton very indignantly; "what have stays to do with stooping? Look at me," she added, throwing open her shawl and grasping her waist in both hands, she turned round to display its straightness to Mr. Ford's view, "do *I* wear stays? And look at me! Why, stays ruin the figures of women. Nelly shall never wear stays while she is with *me*. Of all fatal and pernicious inventions stays and boots are the worst. Oh! you may look at my feet. I wear shoes, sir, and only wish I had the moral courage to wear soles, the only sensible plan that ever was adopted; but boots you shall never see on *my* feet, unless they put them on me when I am dead."

Atoning for her want of moral courage by the firmness of this declaration, Mrs. Norton sat down and no more was said about Alicia's health; but the warning had not been thrown away on Mr. Ford. The very next day he called in Dr. Smithson, his wife's medical attendant, and waylaid him as he was leaving the Square, after seeing Mrs. Ford.

"Well," he said anxiously

"Well," dubiously replied Dr. Smithson, "I do not like this change. I fear Mrs. Ford is worse."

"Worse! Why, Doctor, she does now what she has not done for years. Goes about, bears the light, does not mind talking, and sees to the house concerns."

"I know it—but that is just what alarms me—for it is only the result of some strong shock to the nervous system."

"Not at all," confidently replied Mr. Ford; "*I* am in perfect health, and nothing but uneasiness on my account could give Mrs. Ford a shock sufficiently strong to account for your suggestion. Mrs. Ford idolizes me, sir, rejected splendid offers for my sake, and even her children, though her love for them is assuredly great, only occupy the second place in her affections."

Dr. Smithson smiled gravely, but said again,

"Allow me to assure you that Mrs. Ford is by no means cured."

With this he took his leave.

Mr. Ford was staggered, but only for a moment.

"I dare say I know as much about her case as any medical man," he thought, with that secret complacency which never forsook him, "of course I do. What is medicine? Observation, and I am essentially an observant man. I have no particular merit in being so, it is my nature, my bent—I cannot help it. Now, I have observed Mrs. Ford very closely all these years that she has been ill, and I have never seen her as she is now. If she had received a shock, should *I* not have detected it at once? Of course I should."

Although Mr. Ford came to this satisfactory conclusion, and went off to the city in high spirits—for, to use his own words, "matters were going on splendidly"—Mrs. Norton still felt convinced that Alicia was going wrong, and kindly attempted to lecture her into going right.

Now it so happened that Mrs. Ford had very little liking for her brother's widow. She had been honoured and indulged and obeyed for seven years, and could not tolerate the abrupt manners of Mrs. Norton, who was indeed the last person to humour, indulge, and obey any one, having probably bestowed all she had to spare in these matters on her deceased husband.

When she called, therefore, on Mrs. Ford a quarter of an hour after Dr. Smithson's departure, and found that lady alone in the drawing-room, sitting languidly in her chair and the blinds down, Mrs. Norton took her to task, and, before uttering a word, deliberately walked to the windows and drew up the blinds.

"Now, Licia," she said, putting her hands behind her back, and looking austerely at her sister-in-law, "what do you mean by going on so?"

Mrs. Ford coloured angrily. The light annoyed her, and it was impertinent of Tom to draw up the blinds.

"I ask you what you mean by going on so," again said Mrs. Norton.

As she spoke the drawing-room door opened, Mab, sent by Miss Lavinia, put in her blooming little face, and began softly:

"Please, ma'am—"

The sight of the child exasperated Mrs. Ford.

"Begone!" she exclaimed, turning almost fiercely upon her, "begone, and never come near me!"

The frightened child shut the door and vanished.

"Bad—very bad—," muttered Mrs. Norton shaking her head. "Licia," she stoutly added, speaking aloud, "what makes you hate that little grey eyes so?"

Mrs. Ford looked moody, and did not answer.

"Now," pursued Mrs. Norton, "I am a bitter enemy, for I *never* forgive," she emphatically added, "and so that Captain George will find when I can get hold of him; but Licia, I can't hate a child, I would scorn it, Licia," she added, warming with her subject. "I keep my resentment for grown-up men and women; I know we are told to forgive them, but I answer to that, Fiddle-de-dee!"

Mrs. Ford closed her eyes, leaned back in her chair, and made up her mind to listen.

"Nature," continued Mrs. Norton, without seeming aware that Mrs. Ford had not yet addressed or answered her, "Nature says 'don't forgive,' and I obey Nature. Besides, I have got a drop of Irish blood, and I am resentful and vindictive. It is very wrong and unchristian, of course; but I am so. Nelly's mother affronted me once, and I never forgave her. I would not bow to her, and when I meet that Captain George, I will not bow to him," added Mrs. Norton, summing up her resentment in this vindictive declaration.

But as Mrs. Ford gave her no reply, and as she had only spoken once since Mrs. Norton's entrance, and then not to that lady, Tom became aware of her silence, and asked, rathed shortly,

"Do I bore you, Alicia?"

We are sorry to record Mrs. Ford's answer. It was at variance with all the laws of politeness.

"Yes," she said, briefly.

Poor thing—she could not help it; she was relapsing fast into her old state, when sight of faces and sound of voices were alike distasteful to her. Mrs. Norton was not at all offended, and assured her sister-in-law that she was even pleased with the frankness of her answer.

"I like sincerity," she said, emphatically; "for I practise it. Now I met Mrs. Deacon yesterday, and what do you think she told me? Why, that Anna, little Anna Grey, was dead. What! I said —Anna Grey, who ran away with Captain Johnson? Now, I put it to you, Alicia—was there any harm in saying what everybody knows to be the case? Anna Grey did run away with Captain Johnson. But Mrs. Deacon was mightily offended. 'If she did run away with Captain Johnson,' she replied, very shortly, 'she came back, Mrs. Norton.' 'Well, Mrs. Deacon,' I replied, 'I do not think that was the best part of it; I think she had much better have stayed.' Off flounced Mrs. Deacon, saying, 'If she did run away with Captain Johnson, she was a good little thing, at all events: and there are some people who are always picking holes in other people, to make themselves out better than their neighbours, Mrs. Norton.' I let her go," continued Mrs. Norton, magnanimously, as if, by not detaining the offending Mrs. Deacon, she had shown her infinite mercy, "I let her go, but I am not sure that I shall bow to her again. However, I dare say I shall—for I like sincerity; and perhaps Mrs. Deacon was only sincere."

Mrs. Ford could endure no more. Impatience conquered every other feeling.

"Excuse me, Tom," she said, querulously; "but my head aches."

"Then why did you not tell me to go at once?" asked Mrs. Norton, in her sharpest tones; for perhaps Mrs. Ford's sincerity was becoming too strong. "Why did you not tell me to go, Alicia?"

Alicia twitched her nervous hands, and said, in the same querulous tones,

"If you would go down to Lavinia—she is below."

"Go down to that silly Miss Ford, who never found a man to marry her," cried Mrs. Norton, indignantly, tying her bonnet strings; "thank you, Alicia! However," she added, more calmly, "as your head aches, I shall leave you—only take care of yourself—and don't hate the child," she continued, with some pathos in her voice, "don't hate the poor little forsaken creature that was left at your door, Alicia. I have often seen her little scared face; and I tell you that though I never had a child of my own, Alicia, it has made my heart ache."

Mrs. Ford drew herself up haughtily.

"But she did not frighten me," as Mrs. Norton said afterwards, and thus they parted.

Little did Mrs. Norton suspect how bitter were the thoughts of the poor sick woman, diseased in body as in mind, whom she had been lecturing.

"I am dying," thought Mrs. Ford, "I know I am; and he will marry Mab's mother when I am gone."

Thus she thought, and it was very bitter. But Mrs. Ford had a refuge, a mother's refuge, when such feelings oppressed her; she went to her children's room, not that they were there—but it held their clothes, their little beds, their toys, their books, the nearest and dearest tokens of their being and presence. There, whenever cankering sorrow proved too strong, she went and worked for them. She could not work on this day; Mab's face haunted her. She sat down on the nearest chair, and, with jealous envy, she thought again of the little golden-haired child who had stepped between her children and their father.

"And what will become of them when I am gone!" was the secret cry of her aching heart; "I cannot live, I know I cannot. And must a strange woman, the mother of that child, fill my place, and be set over my boys? God help me! God help me, indeed!"

She wrung her hands, wild fancies entered her troubled brain as she looked around that room which she had restored to pleasantness and comfort. She remembered a legend she had heard in her childhood, how the wronged orphan girl had called on her dead mother, and how that mother, breaking the bonds and cerements of the grave, had risen to protect her child.

"Oh! if it were but true," thought Alicia; "if the dead could but return, how I would come and watch over them! But it is not true," she thought again, after a dreary pause; "the dead are locked fast in their graves—fast as in a prison house. There is no rising again, no coming forth to watch and avenge—not till the last sad judgment-day. Once gone, I am powerless and helpless, and—God help me!—what can I do when I am here!"

Alas! it was true enough. She could do little or nothing. She had no property to bequeath, no will to make, no trustees, no executors to appoint, and her love would soon be as useless to her children as a treasure cast into the deep sea, fathoms away from mortal ken. Oh! for ten years of life! for ten years more!

Mrs. Ford rose and walked feverishly about the room, then, mechanically, she stopped before the little chest of drawers that held the clothes of her children. "Will *she* trouble herself about them when I am dead?" she thought, referring to Mab's unknown mother; "it is not likely—then, let me do what I can whilst life is mine."

She opened the chest of drawers, and took out its contents one by one. Mrs. Ford had been a careful housekeeper in her day, and she had kept a housekeeper's fondness for order and neatness. Tenderly, almost fondly, she took out the little shirts and socks of her younger boys; gently she unfolded them one by one and set aside those that required mending.

"Perhaps they will allow Susan to do that," thought Mrs. Ford, persistently returning to the same subject; "but, no, they will not keep Susan —Susan was too fond of me. Lavinia, perhaps; no, she will not be here either. My children will be surrendered to the stranger. God grant she may not prove too unkind! Oh! God help me—I *cannot*, I cannot bear it!"

She sat down again, helpless, forlorn, and downcast. She leaned her head against the chest of drawers, and her tears flowed slowly and unconsciously. She felt that her case was beyond human aid, and, for the moment at least, she had no trust in divine assistance. On her lap and on the floor around her lay strewn the things she had taken from the drawers. She looked at them apathetically, with a cold and careless eye. Suddenly she started, she had caught sight of a slip of paper lying in the white folds of Robert's linen. What brought it there? She stooped and picked it up. It was inscribed with characters strangely reversed. Tumultuous suspicions crowded her mind. The paper shook in her hand; but yet it could not be what she thought. That would not be hidden in her children's clothes. She did what Robert, what her husband had done before her—she held it up to the looking-glass, read its contents, then sat down again, crushed with the blow.

CHAPTER XIII.

Some minds have been framed by nature so as to shrink more than others of equal integrity from the breath of dishonour.

Alicia was not merely an upright woman, incapable of wrong doing, she also held the least dereliction from the severest laws of right in inexorable abhorrence; and Mr. Ford's want of delicacy in many little things which he could not conceal from her, his shortcomings of the heroic standard in this as in all else, had contributed to alienate his wife's proud heart. Still she thought him honest, incapable of abetting fraud and wrong, incapable of injuring the innocent and the weak, and now she knew how the case stood.

Not for a moment did she doubt the genuineness of the letter that betrayed his secret. That, then, was the meaning of every contradiction that had irritated and stung her insane jealousy. They were living, she, her husband, her children were living on the wages of sin. The child whom she had secretly hated as the wronger of her children, was in reality the wronged one. The comfort, the creeping luxury of their home, were the fruits of iniquity—of the plunder of a child.

She rushed downstairs in a transport of grief, and the first object that met her sight as she entered her own room was the harmonium. She remembered at what time it had been bought—she knew now with what money! She crushed the paper she still held. No doubt, no thought of possible innocence softened the bitterness of her feelings. She did not believe that letter had been written by Mab's mother. What mother would thrust her child on Mr. Ford? She believed that Mab had been put out of the way, not of shame and disgrace, but of wealth and of an inheritance, and she thought that her husband had been chosen because he was poor, needy, and weak of principle; because it was known he would keep the money and tell no tales.

And she was his wife!

"Oh! the other thing was nothing," thought Mrs. Ford, clasping her hands in despair, "*this* is the crowning misery."

"Did you ring, ma'am?" asked Susan, who, after tapping at the door, now looked in.

"No, but come in—I want you, Susan."

Susan looked at her mistress and shook her head.

"You are doing for yourself, ma'am, you are."

"Susan, I am struck," said Mrs. Ford, "I am struck."

"Struck, ma'am, where?"

"Here!" and she laid her hand on her heart.

"Now, ma'am, it *is* not what you think. Indeed and indeed, ma'am, it is not."

"Hush!" said her mistress, "you are thinking of one thing, and I of another; but I can tell you nothing, nothing, Susan—only this: I am struck—struck to the heart, and for ever!"

Susan looked at her mistress in doubtful amazement, and stood before her silent and perplexed.

"Susan, help me to go to bed," said Mrs Ford; "it is all over—oll over."

"What is, ma'am?"

"Life, Susan. It is all over; help me to go to bed."

Susan, much alarmed, yet unwilling to betray her fears, assisted her mistress, who seemed scarcely able to stand, into the next room, undressed her, and helped her to get into bed.

Mrs. Ford sighed deeply, and closed her eyes as her head sank on the pillow.

"Susan," she said, "this bed is my grave. I shall never rise again—never."

"Shall I go for Miss Lavinia, ma'am?" asked Susan, getting more and more frightened.

"No—send Mab up to me. Do as I bid you, Susan—send up the child."

Susan shook her head doubtfully, but she obeyed, and in a few minutes little Mab came in, shrinkingly. With evident reluctance she approached Mrs. Ford's bed, and with some alarm she felt that lady's feverish hand laid on her shoulder.

"Do not be frightened, child—I will not hurt you," said Mrs. Ford, "I only want you to answer a few questions. Where were you before you came here—to this house?"

Mab's face expressed decided annoyance. She had been questioned more than she liked. Mr. Ford, Robert, Miss Lavinia, Susan, Captain George and his brother, and Mrs. Thomasina Norton, had each in turn endeavoured to worry the truth out of her.

"I don't know," she said, crossly enough, "not a bit. I was there, you know."

"Go and fetch that picture book," said Mrs. Ford, pointing to a thin quarto on a table.

Mab ran nimbly enough for it, and came back beaming.

"And now," said Mrs. Ford, "open it and show me *there*."

The book was one of views of mansions in various parts of England. Mrs. Ford, who knew already that Mab described her home as one of some extent, thought that some resemblance might strike the child's eye and give a clue, howsoever faint. But Mab, though not an untruthful, was an imaginative child, and Mrs. Ford sighed to see how many *theres* Mab found in the book, every one unlike the other. One had castellated walls, one was pure Elizabethan, another, again, had turrets, and a fourth was an Italian-roofed mansion, with cool porticoes and marble colonnades. It was the same, when, in the course of her questions, Mrs. Ford came on that *he* who had provoked and perplexed Robert.

"Was *he* there?" asked Mrs. Ford, with injudicious eagerness.

Mab looked puzzled, and put her finger on her lips.

"I don't know," she said, at length, "it is so long ago, but *there* was a fine place, with beautiful trees and a great deal of water, and he used to walk with me, and help me to pick up shells."

"Then it was by the sea?"

"Oh yes! and he gathered the acorns."

"It was in autumn!" ejaculated Mrs. Ford.

"I don't know, but he was very fond of me—we used to play at hide-and-seek in the square."

"What square?"

"Why, this of course. Don't you know?—round the statue of queen Anne."

Mrs. Ford's countenance fell. It was plain that dreamy invention and present realities mingled unconsciously in the mind of the child, and that *he* had become a myth round which all sorts of strange fancies blended in little Mab's brain. It was useless to set her right, useless to reprove her. Mrs. Ford only sighed drearily.

Mab laughed to herself.

"I could tell you something," she said, saucily, "I could—but I won't."

"I shall bribe you—what will you have?"

"Play for me."

She nodded towards the harmonium. Mrs. Ford tried to lead her away from this inconvenient whim, but opposition only made Mab obstinate. She would have music or nothing. Mrs. Ford yielded. She rose, trembling with fever, and seated herself before the instrument. She played—and played very sweetly, though very sadly, a movement from an old master.

"And now tell me," she said, faintly.

Mab rose on tiptoe, and said, mysteriously,

"You know that grey old gentleman I saw that evening, when I got Noah's ark?"

"At Captain George's?"

Mab nodded.

"Well."

"Well! he put so many questions to me—but I did not tell him."

"Tell him what?"

"That I had seen him there, you know."

"You saw him!" exclaimed Mrs. Ford.

"Yes," confidently replied Mab, "I did; he kept his hat over his face, but I knew him quite well, he is so ugly."

Mrs. Ford rose with a low cry. She knew now whence the blow had come, and knowing it, she saw the evil was hopeless.

"My dear! what is the matter?" exclaimed Mr. Ford, entering the room. "Why, you will get your death of cold in your night-clothes; you surely are not unwell?"

Mrs. Ford never answered him. She tottered back to her bed with chattering teeth, and moaned aloud as her head sank once more on her pillow.

"What is the matter?" said Mr. Ford, sitting down in a deep arm-chair by her.

"A spasm," gasped his wife, "do not mind it; it is nothing."

"Of course not," cheerfully said Mr. Ford. "Come here, little Mab," he gaily added, drawing her up on his knee, "Oh! you like that, you little puss, eh?" and he gave her a kiss.

"He can, he dare kiss her," thought Mrs. Ford; "oh! what a man!"

In that buoyant tone which in him indicated the height of good humour, Mr. Ford now said to his wife:

"My dear Alicia, I wish you would leave off that old-fashioned dress you had on this morning. It is horrid. You must leave it off, my love."

"Must I?" said Mrs. Ford, bitterly: "yes, I think I shall."

"Of course. Ten pounds will surely buy you something better, and it would be a hard case if I had not ten pounds to spare my wife. What paper are you crushing so, my dear?"

Mrs. Ford gasped that it was nothing.

"Then there's the drawing-room," pursued Mr. Ford; "it will not do. You were ill so long I did not like to disturb you, but now we must renovate the place, we must. Besides, our position is altering daily. You see," he added, thrusting his hand into his pocket, and playing with some loose gold there, "you see, Alicia, a man of talent *cannot* be kept down. A few months ago, we were—well, no matter, but now I am in a rapid way of making a really handsome fortune. You would be amazed if I were to tell you how a miserable sum of five hundred pounds which I had by me has swollen into—well, no matter. It was all the opening;

there was no opening formerly—but now the opening has come, and of course it is all right. I knew it would be in the end. I always told you so; 'only give me time, Alicia,' I said, 'and I will make a rich woman of you yet.'"

He kept rolling the sovereigns in his pocket with one hand, whilst the other played with Mab's hair. Mrs. Ford pressed her two hands to her beating heart, but she said nothing; she had resolved not to speak yet, even though that heart should break.

"And it is surprising when once luck sets in, how it will pour in," continued Mr. Ford, in the same cool and easy tone; "those sly Georges! they had an inkling of it; I could not keep it from them, owing to various causes, and that deep old dodger, James, has this very morning asked me for Robert."

"What?" cried Mrs. Ford.

"My dear, how you excite yourself! Why, it is a capital thing for the boy. James George is one of the great men of the city, and these men are up to everything, of course. Well, he stopped me this morning, near the Bank, and wanted to know if I had no sons. I told him I had only boys, but he said, very handsome though true, boys reared in business habits as mine must be, were invaluable, and could I spare him one. I put him off with Bob's age, but he would not be frightened; however, I played and played with him until he became as fidgetty as a bee, and actually offered me sixty pounds a year for the lad's services in his counting-house."

"Sixty pounds a year for Robert!"

"My love, do not look so amazed, but I forget you know nothing of business. Robert is just what I was at his age—invaluable. Why, his name alone, Robert Ford, is a guarantee."

"But you did not accept, you cannot have accepted?" cried Mrs. Ford. "You must see that this is a trap, a bribe, a dreadful snare for that boy and you."

Mr. Ford looked amazed.

"My love," he said, "your mind is wandering. And as to accepting, why, of course I did. Robert's duties begin next Monday."

"You must break your word!" exclaimed Mrs. Ford, in despair; "I will not have my child's soul bartered. I tell you, Mr. Ford, you must break your word."

Mr. Ford looked bewildered and perplexed.

"Break my word, my love," he said. "I really would if I could to gratify you, but it is out of the question; Mr. George made me sign——"

He said no more. His wife, who had sat up in the energy of her remonstrances, now sank back with a low moan.

She had fainted. It was hours ere she returned to consciousness; and when she did, she was passive, inert, and cold; once more the woman of former days.

There seemed little in such an event to please anyone, yet when Mrs. Norton called in a few days, she had the satisfaction of finding her prophecy fulfilled.

Of course she was very sorry for it, but, as she belonged to the class of the "I knew it," and "I told you so,"—a countless tribe in every generation,—her eye brightened as she informed Mrs. Ford that she had accurately foretold her present condition. Mrs. Ford, who now kept her bed, heard her without heeding her. She was listening to Robert talking to Mab in the drawing-room, for she would now scarcely let the child out of her sight, and her heart ached to hear Robert, who had already entered on his duties at Mr. George's, say to his little companion,

"This is all very well for the beginning, Mab; but *I* cannot stop at sixty pounds a year, can I? I must push on William and Edward, as I get on myself."

"Of course," answered Mab.

"God help me!" thought Mrs. Ford; "the boy is his father's echo. Good fortune, success, inspire him with no mistrust, with no surprise. God help me!"

"And now," continued Mrs. Norton's voice, which had been going on for some time, "I shall tell you what you must do, Alicia. You must take á piece of flannel and fold it four times—so —you see—but do you see?"

"Yes, I do."

"I thought your eyes were shut. Well, as I said, you must fold a piece of flannel— Bless me, who is that talking below?"

Mrs. Ford knew her husband's voice, and, from its tones, she knew, too, that he had been drinking. He came up the stairs talking loudly to Susan.

"Missus is but poorly, sir," austerely said the servant.

"Over-excitement," replied Mr. Ford. "Well, I have got something for her. Go downstairs, Susan, and bring me up the parcel on the dining-room table; and hark ye, Susan, take this—you are a good girl, Susan; I have a regard for you, Susan."

Opening his wife's room door as he spoke, he slipped a sovereign into the astonished girl's hand, and gave her a Lancashire slap on the shoulder that helped her a step down the staircase; then, without seeming to perceive Mrs. Norton's presence, he walked up to his wife's bed, with his hat still on, and his flushed face telling plainly of gin and water.

"Good evening, Mr. Ford," drily said Mrs. Norton.

"Good evening, ma'am. I heard from your friend—Captain George, you know. He sends his love."

Mrs. Norton did not look angered in the least, but she bent her keen eye on Mr. Ford, and read his face.

"Something has happened to that man," she thought, as she surveyed the haggard lines of his countenance. "I never saw him look so before, never."

Never, indeed, had Mr. Ford worn that wild look, half fearful, half defiant. Never had his voice been so boisterous, and yet so sullen. He seemed unable to keep silent.

"I have been with Mr. George," he said; "a thorough good fellow is Mr. George. You know the Georges, my love?"

His wife shuddered, and answered that she knew them.

"Robert is getting on capitally, it seems; astonished the oldest clerks in the office. That boy is just like me; I told them so."

"And I once loved that man," thought Alicia.

"Capital luck to-day," hiccupped Mr. Ford. "Now," he added, turning to his wife, and not heeding Mrs. Norton's presence, "how much do you think I cleared to-day, Alicia?"

Mrs. Ford opened her eyes wide, her pale lips parted, and she gasped forth,

"I do not know."

Mr. Ford stooped, and whispered hoarsely,

"A thousand pounds, Alicia, a thousand pounds," and, thrusting his hands into his pockets, he began rolling the gold there with a sort of wild exultation.

"Here's the parcel, sir," said Susan, opening the door; "shall I open it?"

"Do, Susan, do. I like you, Susan. On my word I do."

Susan simpered; at another time she would have snapped at this declaration of affection; but the sovereign had softened her much, and she quickly undid the parcel.

A black silk dress of the finest quality was its contents.

"Oh, my!" exclaimed Susan. "Well, I never?"

"Hold it up, Susan—hold it up. There's silk for you! Well, Alicia, what do you say to that?"

Mrs. Ford did not answer; her features remained rigid, and her clasped fingers worked strangely.

"Missus's head aches, sir," quickly put in Susan. "It was a pity to show her the handsome dress to-night. She will see it better to-morrow, sir."

"True enough," said Mr. Ford, with a nod; "put it away—there, that will do. You may go, Susan."

"I think I shall go too," rather drily said Mrs. Norton, rising; "I fancy Mr. Ford has something to say to you, Alicia."

Mr. Ford started, and stared at Mrs. Norton, and even Alicia roused herself; for there was something in this speech that struck both as a home-thrust; but, without appearing to notice the impression she had produced, Mrs. Norton took her leave. Robert and Mab went downstairs at the same time, and Mr. Ford remained alone with his wife; he seemed in an unusually communicative mood.

"And you never ask me how I cleared those thousand pounds," said he, throwing himself into the chair Mrs. Norton had just vacated. "No curiosity. Eh, Alicia!"

"Ay, ay, do tell me," she whispered, eagerly, "do tell me, John."

"Well, there it is; don't look at me so, my dear; are you really ill?"

"No," she answered, faintly, and she closed her eyes; "go on."

"I told you, the other day, about those five hundred pounds."

"What five hundered pounds?"

"An old debt. Well, I invested them in what every one thought the worst speculation in England; but *I* saw—bless you, *I* saw. I bought cheap, sold dear, bought again, sold out, and in short that is how I am a thousand pounds richer to-night than I was this morning."

"Then that money comes from the five hundred pounds?" said Alicia.

"It does; but why do you ask?" replied her husband, a little sobered by her look and tone.

"And where did those five hundred pounds come from?" she persisted—"from the Georges?"

"Ye-es," stammered Mr. Ford, "from the Georges. They have come into thirty or forty thousand pounds lately."

"But Captain George made you lose more than five hundred pounds formerly."

"My dear, you know the man; besides, Robert has got into that capital situation."

"And who was she that died and left them all that money?" cried Mrs. Ford, sitting upright in her bed; "who was she, Mr. Ford?"

He turned very pale.

"I—don't know," he gasped: "a maiden cousin, I believe."

"And is she dead?—is she really dead?" asked his wife.

"Of course she is dead," began Mr. Ford, laughing aloud, rather hoarsely; but he stopped short, and turned ghastly pale.

Mab had stolen upstairs again, and now stood by his side, expecting the caress he always gave her. He stared at her; he took out his handkerchief and wiped his forehead, and looked at his wife, whose blue eyes read him through and through; then, stammering something about the heat, he left the room and walked downstairs.

Little Mab sat down abashed in a corner of the room.

"He knows it," moaned his wife, "he knows it, and he has sold his soul for five hundred pounds."

It was late when Mrs. Ford fell asleep that night; but at length her eyes closed, and slumbers sound and deep overtook her. In the middle of the night she was awakened, however, by a low moaning near her. A night-lamp always burned in her room, and by its light she saw her husband sitting on a chair wiping the cold dews from his forehead, and gasping for breath.

She sat up, first thinking he was ill, then, because she felt eager and watchful; he seemed struggling with nightmare, and still between sleep and waking.

"You need not look at me so, Alicia," he said, staring at her; "I shall deny it all—I shall deny it, Alicia. Where is the child?"

"Hush?" she said, stretching out her trembling

hand to him, "hush—it was a bad dream—a nightmare."

"I tell you I do not know who she is," he said, half angrily. "I would not ask. What business of mine was it, I know nothing."

"Awake," whispered his wife, bending towards him, "awake, John, you are dreaming."

He did awake with a start and a deep sigh, then he looked suspiciously at his wife.

"I daresay I have been talking a precious deal of nonsense?" he said, after a pause; "people always do when they are dreaming."

Mrs. Ford looked unmoved.

"You took something that disagreed with you," she said, coldly; "only I wish you had not come in here to disturb my sleep."

"I am going, my dear," said Mr. Ford, recovering. "I took something that disagreed with me, as you say, I have no doubt."

He walked to the door, then came back.

"I remember I had cutlets, depend upon it that was it."

"Pray leave me," was his wife's cold reply.

And slowly and submissively Mr. Ford went back to his room.

CHAPTER XIV.

FROM that evening forward, Mr. Ford was an altered man. Until he had known how and why Mab had been left at his door, his guilt had sat lightly upon him. He had smothered the secret voice that bade him search and inquire, he had been satisfied to believe in the letter, and to close his eyes to all further knowledge; but Mr. Ford had to do with men who wanted no unconscious accomplice, for such they held to be dangerous. Perhaps, too, they did not believe in his blindness; however that might be, they would not indulge him in it. Mr. Ford could never know the whole truth, and he could not prove one tittle of it; but he could talk, and suspicion is unpleasant and inconvenient. No better plan offered itself to them than to bind him by advantages—great to him, small to them.

Such were Mab's five hundred pounds, and

Robert's situation. If Mr. Ford should prove ungrateful, or too exacting, and human nature is liable to both, dangers which he little suspected were kept in store for him, ready to doom him to irretrievable destruction.

Thus, unwilling though he was, Mr. Ford was compelled to suspect, and once suspicion was awakened, conscience forced him to interpret every token, every sign, until the bitter and perfect knowledge came.

Then began the fearful battle of conscience and remorse in John Ford's soul. He knew beyond a doubt Mab's name, station, and wealth. She was of an ancient race. A fair home, a noble inheritance were hers. Of these he had unconsciously at first, willingly in the end, and always guiltily, helped to rob her—and for what? For five hundred pounds! He had sold the rights of the forlorn orphan child, and his own honour, for that miserable pittance. True, he had thriven on the wages of sin; his own honest though imprudent ventures had never prospered, this the bribe of iniquity to faltering principle had been the fruitful seed of an abundant harvest.

There were moments when the thought maddened him, when he cursed the gold that came so readily at the call of evil, and that had been so tardy to appear in his days of struggling integrity.

At other times, his own success rendered him callous. Then he doubted Providence, and scorned retribution; then honesty was folly in his eyes, and successful wrong the only wisdom. In those fearful moments, Mr. Ford went about the house with a buoyant step and a bright eye; his joke was ever ready for Susan, he would throw the boys sixpences, and buy his sister a shawl or a new dress.

"Master is quite pleasant to-day," Susan would say, whilst the boys exulted over "Pa's jolly good-humour," and Miss Lavinia would think how kind John was.

But these were only flashes that rendered the succeeding darkness more apparent. There were days when instead of rejoicing in the triumph of his iniquity, instead of reckoning up his gains, and laughing at the honest fool he had been so long, Mr. Ford felt his heart fail, and his spirit tremble; when he woke at night, with cold perspiration on his forehead, a detected and disgraced man in the eyes of the world, a condemned man before the awful tribunal of God's justice. Then he was sullen, gloomy, and when spoken to, or irritated, savage. Then Susan would wisely remain in her kitchen, and Miss Ford in her room; then the boys would keep out of their father's way, and Mab alone could venture to address him. It was not love, it was not tenderness, it was shame that subdued him in the presence of the child. Whatever his mood might be, she was safe from his anger, safe from his sharpest speech. He could not add a deeper wrong to a wrong already so great.

There was another mood into which Mr. Ford often fell, and this, the saddest of all, was the inert and the hopeless. He then saw the past in its true aspect, himself a sorely tempted and needy man, his tempters strong and secure against him. Even though he had turned the child from his door, he could neither have served nor have saved her. And, if he was helpless then, how much more so was he now! He had no proof: his word was nothing: that the guilty ones were armed against every assertion he could utter, was morally certain. He must bear his fate, he must live in his sin; he was bound to it as Ixion to his wheel. He must go on wronging the child, and thriving on that wrong, rearing himself a prosperous home, a fair name, the world's regard, his children's fortunes out of it. Sometimes Mr. Ford had thoughts of a dark escape out of the snare. He would walk on the bridges, and look down at the black Thames with wild longing. What kept him back? That which had made him weak? That infirm purpose that had found him so ready to fall into temptation, saved him at least from a great sin. He who had not known how to live well did not know how to die desperately. To linger through life a prey to useless remorse, to unproductive shame, to contrition that could not atone—such was his lot.

And whilst he sullenly submitted to, or fiercely struggled against that lot, his wife, unable to bear the new misery his guilt had entailed upon her, was journeying fast to the grave. Everyone knew it save Mr. Ford and the children. He had so long seen her ailing that he could not believe in her danger. Alicia was very poorly, but she would, she must get over it. He acted on that belief, and Mrs. Ford, though she constantly spoke of her approaching end, acted on it, too. Her mind was full of plans in which Mab took a prominent part. She could scarcely bear to let the child out of her sight, and fatigued her by that incessant watchfulness. Mab wanted to be below with the boys, with Susan even, and not in the dull sick-room; but Mrs. Ford grew restless when she was not by, and querulously complained, "They were always taking the child away."

Mrs. Norton, who proved a very constant and assiduous nurse, was struck with this inexplicable change. Why had Alicia grown so fond of the child all of a sudden? Many other things struck her. She felt convinced that some dreary secret weighed on Alicia's mind, and that in this secret her wild, haggard-looking husband had a part. That it related to Mab, she did not suspect; she thought of money matters, and she had not sufficient respect for Mr. Ford to feel very confident of his integrity. "I dare say he has done nothing to be transported for," she coolly thought; "only Alicia is such a methodist in her notions."

Indeed, it only seemed to Mrs. Norton common charity to set Alicia right, and she proceeded to do so on a cold December afternoon.

Mrs. Ford was excitable that day. She sat up in bed, her cheeks flushed, her eyes very bright, far too bright.

"Mab, where is Mab?" she asked.

"Mab is gone down," replied Mrs. Norton, "the child wants to stir, Alicia."

"But I want her, Tom, I want her."

"What for?"

"I want to see that she is safe."

"Safe! Oh! she is safe enough. What should make her unsafe?"

"But I want to have my way," querulously exclaimed Mrs. Ford; "I am dying, I know I am, and yet I am not allowed to have my way."

"Dying! nonsense."

Mrs. Ford probably concluded it was nonsense, for she resumed,

"Besides, I want Mab. The child is dreadfully neglected. I want to teach her. I have no doubt she will have a high position some day, and she must be suited to it."

Her mind was evidently wandering; Mrs. Norton always made it a point to set people right when she could do so.

"Now, 'Licia," she said, "how can you talk of Mab's having a high position? A child left at your door, and taken in by your husband's charity! Nonsense!"

Mrs. Ford looked wildly at her.

"Oh, Tom!" she said; "Oh, Tom!" She clasped her hands, and could say no more.

"Now, Alicia, what does ail you?" asked her sister-in-law. "What is it?"

"Don't ask, Tom, don't."

"Well, then, what is it? I know it is about your husband."

Mrs. Ford shuddered.

"Oh! the weight of sin!" she moaned. "The weight of the sin you know, and cannot prevent! Of the sin that will condemn you on the terrible Day of Judgmemt!"

"Now, Alicia, don't go on so," half-indignantly exclaimed Mrs. Norton; "your husband is neither a thief nor a murderer. And even if he were," she excitedly added, "would you not rather be lost with him, than saved without him? Of course you would," continued Mrs. Norton, warming with her subject.

Mrs. Ford looked gloomy, but did not answer.

"For my part," continued Mrs. Norton, coolly, "this is a subject on which my mind has long been made up. My dear husband was what you good people call a heathen; well, then, I am a heathen too. I am firmly resolved to be wherever he is in the next world, as I was in this. I shall live and die as he did."

"You prefer the creature to the Creator!" exclaimed Alicia, amazed.

"I suppose my feelings are free," replied Mrs. Norton, with some asperity; "and, if I were you, Alicia," she added, more gently, "I would stick to my husband through this world and the next. And I should prefer being lost with him, to being saved without him."

Alicia's mind was naturally too religious to like so extraordinary and indecorous a profession of faith.

"This is a subject on which you may talk as you please, Tom," she said, with some irony, "for who is to put you to the proof?"

"Thank you!" replied Mrs. Norton, colouring up, and rising; "I am much obliged to you, Alicia; but I will say this, it would be better if you loved your husband more, a little more, and then his sins would trouble you less."

With this Mrs. Norton took her leave.

This conversation effectually checked a passing wish, which Mrs. Ford had for a moment entertained, of taking Mrs. Norton into her confidence, and of abiding by her advice. It was plain by this singular declaration of theological belief, that Mrs. Norton's judgment was not to be trusted whenever a husband was at stake.

Then Alicia thought of her sister-in-law, Lavinia. She was conscientious, pure-minded, and honourable. "Perhaps she will give me comfort," thought Mrs. Ford, yearning, as we all do, for human aid and sympathy; and, as soon as Mrs. Norton was gone, she made the attempt.

"Lavinia," she said, addressing her sister-in-law, who had come up with the night-lamp, and had settled herself down to read in an arm-chair, "Lavinia, what would you do if you found yourself unwillingly abetting a wrong. For instance, enjoying property that had been unjustly taken from another?"

Miss Ford looked up from her prayer-book. The night-lamp, whilst it left the rest of the room in darkness, lit Mrs. Ford's white sheet and curtains, and fell full on on her wasted face.

"But that could not be," exclaimed Miss Lavinia, much startled. "I would die of hunger first. I would beg my bread!"

"But if, for instance, you were married; if your husband were guilty, and you were obliged to share his guilt, though abhorring it?"

"I would not!" cried Miss Lavinia; "I would fly from him to the world's end——"

"And break one duty to fulfil another. Oh, Lavinia! that is not it yet—that is not it!"

"Well, then, I would pray to him to repent and atone," said Miss Lavinia, excitedly.

"And if he would not?"

"If he would not, I would throw myself on God's mercy, and leave him to his fate."

As she spoke, the door opened, and Mr. Ford entered the room.

"Lavinia," cried Mrs. Ford, sitting up in her bed, "leave us—leave us. I have something to say to my husband."

Miss Ford and her brother exchanged startled glances. She looked wild, very wild, and it was rare to hear her say those words, "My husband."

"Very well," said Miss Ford, feeling vaguely agitated; "very well, Alicia. I shall go."

She left the room as she spoke.

CHAPTER XV.

"WELL, my dear, how do you feel?" asked Mr. Ford, sitting down in the chair his sister had just left.

She opened wide her large blue eyes, unnaturally bright, and gave him a look that startled him.

"Mr. Ford," she said, "how do *you* feel?"

"Oh! very well, my love—if you ——"

"I do not speak of your body, but of your soul. How does it feel, Mr. Ford?"

"My love!" he exclaimed.

"Call me Alicia—Alicia Norton," she said, sharply.

Mr. Ford looked doubtfully at his wife. Could she know. It seemed impossible, and yet what did she mean?

"Be true to yourself—be true to the child," exclaimed his wife, clasping her hands imploringly, "be true to the poor child, who was left at your door."

"I took her in, what more can I do?" said Mr. Ford.

"Right her—she is wronged; she was found in the way and sent to you for that—do her justice."

"My dear," he soothingly replied, "what do I know about the poor child? I do all I can for her—perhaps, as you say, she was found in the way, but how can I help it?"

"He will not understand—he will not understand," moaned his wife. "Mr. Ford, do you know this?" she cried, drawing from beneath her pillow a slip of crumpled paper, which she thrust into his hand; "do you know this?"

"Ye-es," stammered her husband, turning red and pale; "it was pinned to the child's dress."

"And there was money in it, money which you took."

"Five hundred pounds—no more."

"And you took that money?"

"Why not?" he replied, rallying, "the interest of it will barely pay for her maintenance."

"You confess it—you sold your honour for five hundred pounds—for five hundred pounds!"

Mr. Ford's countenance was no longer pale, but grey and leaden.

"Have you anything more to say?" he asked.

"Yes, John, I have. Do not say I have not spared you; I have kept your secret till it has killed me, and now, on my death-bed, I can keep it no longer. I must separate my cause from yours. I must not let the sin of the guilty father be visited on my innocent children."

Mr. Ford groaned aloud. The keenest pang he could know—shame before his wife—had overtaken him. Cold perspiration stood on his forehead; he wiped it away, and said, apathetically,

"Go on, Alicia."

"Go on," she repeated, "and what more can I say? You know that my threats are vain. That I cannot, if I would, ruin the father of my boys. You know that I am helpless and powerless, and that I can only ask you to have mercy upon them, to have mercy upon your own soul. Do you know who that child is?"

Mr. Ford remained mute, and stared at his wife in silent anguish.

"He does, he does know it," she moaned, wringing her hands, "and he will not atone, and the sins of guilty parents are visited on the offspring—it is Bible truth, it is Gospel truth, and my children will be reared on the fruits of iniquity."

"Have mercy on me, Alicia!"

"Have mercy on yourself. Think not of the money—let us perish, starve, beg our bread, but let us repair the wrong. Have mercy on your own soul, Mr. Ford; think of your salvation, of the next world. Saints have trembled to think of it; have mercy on your own soul."

"Alicia, do not be hard upon me."

"Do you know who she is?"

He did not answer.

"Because, if you do not, I will tell you. She is the rightful owner of the money the Georges are now enjoying. Right her, and all will be well yet."

"I cannot—I have no proof."

"Have the matter searched, take her to a magistrate, wash your hands of that guilty money, tell all—be an honest man once more."

"Alicia, you ask me for my own ruin and dishonour—I cannot—I will not."

"Right the child—right the child, and make your peace with God."

"I cannot, you ask me for death—for worse than death a hundredfold. Besides, it would be useless; it is too late."

"Too late!" she moaned; "then it might have been done—too late!"

"Oh! Alicia, don't be hard upon me! You do not know how I was tempted. Not a farthing in the house, and that devil came and lured me with as fair a chance of making a fortune as man ever had, and we were deep in debt, and Lavinia had come, and you wanted that harmonium, and I had not a shilling to pay for the boys' schooling, and you knew nothing of how matters were going on down-stairs, and, as I said, you wanted ——"

"You did it for me," exclaimed his wife, wildly, "you did it for me!"

"Alicia, you say I have sold my soul, well, then, I would have sold my soul for you—I have always loved you beyond everything else in this world,—and hard as you are on me now, I love you dearly still."

His wife shuddered, and, sinking back on her pillow, turned her face to the wall.

"There, go—that will do," she said, motioning him away—"it is useless to say more, leave me."

But he did not go.

"Alicia," he said, "if restitution were in my power I would restore, I would, Alicia. As it is, believe me when I tell you I will be true to her—I will toil like a slave for the boys, and, since it is your fancy, Alicia—they shall have none of that money."

"Leave me," said his wife, "my heart is sick—sick even unto death. Oh! God, I thank thee that I am dying!"

Mr. Ford rose, trembling.

"Alicia," he said, "I cannot leave you thus—you must say something to me."

She did not reply.

"Alicia, have you nothing to say to me?"

"Leave me."

"Alicia Norton, have you nothing—not one word for me?"

"Leave me," she said again, "do not make me speak."

"Alicia, you are hard. I thought you loved me."

He said it thinking to draw forth assurances of affection, but the truth which had been smothering her for years, broke forth.

"He thought I loved him!" she exclaimed, clasping her hands in strange amazement—"he thought I loved him!"

"I am sure of it, Alicia," he said, trying to smile.

"I do not—" she cried, "I will not die with a lie on my lips—I do not love you—I have not loved you for years!"

Death itself seemed to enter Mr. Ford's heart. His long blindness vanished in a moment—the faith of years perished without recall. He smiled vacantly at his wife. She did not love him, the object of such fond worship, of so many sacrifices, had been alienated for years. He had fed himself with foolish illusions, gloried in that affection, made a boast of it, and it was all over; she had not loved, and now he felt and saw it—she despised him.

"I suppose you could not help it, Alicia," he sighed, "but it's a blow—it's a blow!" And reeling like a drunken man, he left the presence of his contemner. It was a blow, one of the blows which men like Mr. Ford never recover.

He still reeled when he got into the square. Where was he going? Where instinct led him, to the presence of the man that had begun all his woe.

Captain George had left Mrs. George in Italy, and had come back to England on some important business, as he was pleased to call it. He had taken up his abode in some chambers, as he styled them, in the vicinity of Piccadilly, and to these Mr. Ford now made his way, It so chanced that Captain George was within and alone. Mr. Ford found him attired in a magnificent dressing-gown, lying on a couch, and dividing his attentions between a novel on one hand—Captain George was fond of light literature—and a rum bottle on the other.

"How do you do, old fellow?" said he, nodding kindly to Mr. Ford; "sit down; here you find me a lonely bachelor, reading one of the prettiest stories I have read for a long time—I must take it to Mrs. George—she will like it of all things.

Now, Ford, do you know what I like in a story?—It is when it is kept up—it must be kept up, you know—only, how is it done? I protest, sir, it is a mystery to me. However, I like this one amazingly, and, not feeling over-well this evening, I thought I might as well stay at home and go on with my third volume."

"Captain George," said Mr. Ford, who was extremely pale, "I have something of importance to say to you. I know who the child is—the child that was left at my door."

"Do you?" replied Captain George, looking much interested; "and who is little 'Never Mind?'"

"She is the one whom you called your cousin, Captain George, that maiden lady, as you said, who left your brother and you a handsome fortune."

Captain George burst out laughing.

"Look at him," said he, pointing his finger at his guest; "he says it with a grave face too—look at him! Oh! he is a rare one, old Ford is—a rare one for a joke!"

"I tell you I will not be your dupe!" cried Mr. Ford, almost fiercely; "you have made me desperate, and I do not care who hears me—so mind and drop those ways."

The loudness of his voice sobered Captain George.

"Well," he said, coolly, "what about the little impostor?"

"Here is your money," replied Mr. Ford, throwing some notes on the table, "and I wash my hands of your proceedings and you."

"More easily said than done," quietly said Captain George, turning down the page he had been reading. "Why did you take that money?"

"Why! because you came to me in my desperate necessity! But I knew nothing ——"

"Oh! oh!" interrupted Captain George, with a significant nod, "that will not do—never do. You knew well enough who the child was all the time, and very handsomely too you were paid. James said a hundred would do, but I said no. The man is poor, James, and he has a family, let it be five hundred—a terrible battle I had with James; but I won the day, and now there is your gratitude; I declare I am sick of human nature. Ugh!"

"When you say I knew who the child was, you say that which is not true," exclaimed Mr. Ford, pale with passion; "I knew—I suspected nothing."

"And took and invested the money without inquiry—without referring to a magistrate, and you a legal man too! Pooh! pooh! my dear fellow, *that* will never do—say something else—*that* will never do."

Mr. Ford said nothing else.

"I tell you we are invulnerable," complacently

resumed Captain George; "we have legal death on our side. But nothing is impossible—you may find out a weak point in our case, and show us up at the Old Bailey if you like! What about it?—If we fall, you fall first. *I* can prove your guilt, and you cannot prove your innocence."

"My guilt!" said Mr. Ford, scornfully.

"Your guilt," said Captain George, smoothing his moustache. "Now, just listen to me—it was beautifully managed! You remember the day you called on James; I think you wanted him to stand security—something of that kind—for a harmonium. Well, that day James was robbed of a hundred pound note. He knew the number, and stopped it at the bank. Exactly three days after this, that note, bearing your name and address, came into our hands. We have it still. We were merciful, however; but mercy has its bounds, and if you will trump up stories of children left at your door with bank-notes pinned to their cloaks, we must in self-defence ask you to explain how this stolen note came into your possession. Perhaps you will say it came with the child! My dear fellow, who will believe you?—just tell me that—who will believe you?"

Mr. Ford had not expected this. Out of this snare he could see no issue. It was true enough that he had called on Mr. James, and he remembered now that he had remained alone for a few minutes in the same room with that gentleman's desk. He certainly could have stolen the note, and if the stolen property bearing his signature was in their hands, what proof of innocence could he give?

"Oh! James is a deep one," said Captain George; "and do not think that is all!—he has more in store for you—only he has not trusted even me with his plans. But this I can tell you: stay quiet, and you are safe. We have no sort of interest in ruining you. We have put you in a very fair way of making money, and you are making money, I know. James has taken one of your boys off your hands—in short, we have been most liberal, and your connection with us is the only piece of good luck you ever had in your life. Do not quarrel with Fortune when she comes to you, my boy—take the advice of an old soldier who knows something about the lady's ways. She comes rarely, and once rudely received returns no more. Take it easy, keep quiet, and you will be the better for it. With regard to the little impostor at your house, James and I, with the unconcern of innocence, had her for an evening, and we ascertained, sir, that she was quite safe—quite safe. I do not object, however, to showing any kindness to her. There, sir," he added, taking a few gold pieces from his pocket, and rolling them up in one of the notes Mr. Ford had put on the table, "you may give her that, with Captain George's love."

"He laid both the gold and note in which it was wrapped, on the table before Mr. Ford. Perhaps Mr. Ford ought to have pocketed the money, and remembered that both gold and notes were Mab's, but he did not; the insolent tone, the sneer, put him beside himself; he tore the note open, and, taking out the gold, he deliberately flung it in Captain George's face.

"Take that, and the curse of an honest man, whom you have made a rogue, along with it!" he said, with foaming lips.

Captain George was no coward, but he could keep his temper under control, and his resentment now took no active shape. He darted a bitter look at Mr. Ford, and he shook his trembling forefinger at him, but he said not one word. In silence, too, Mr. Ford turned away, left the room, walked downstairs, and let himself out into the quiet street lit by a calm moon and shining stars.

CHAPTER XVI.

SUSAN saw Mr. Ford leaving his wife's room. She was struck with his wild and haggard looks, and entered her mistress's apartment unsummoned. She found Mrs. Ford sitting up in her bed, and looking strangely excited.

"Send me Robert," she said; "send me Mab—be quick, lose no time, Susan."

Susan obeyed, and in a few minutes Mab and Robert stood by the sick lady's bed.

She took their cool young hands within her own hot and burning ones, and looked pitifully at them both.

"Robert," she said, "you know poor little Mab's story—she is alone, friendless, and forsaken—be true to her, be very kind to her, Robert."

"I will," sturdily answered Robert. "I am kind to her, and I teach her all I know."

"You like Nelly best," said Mab, pouting.

"No, I don't, you ninny, I like you best. But Nelly is like a stranger here, and that is why I am attentive to her."

"But you will be kind, very kind to little Mab," said his mother again. "Oh! do, Robert, for your sake, for the sake of your brothers."

"I will be kind to her," sententiously said Robert.

Mrs. Ford sighed deeply. She had done all she could do. She had committed a child to the care and kindness of a child, and there ended her power.

"Leave the room," she said to Robert; "but first put Mab upon my bed, and now leave the room."

Robert did as he was bid, not without some wonder. Still more amazed was Mab, to find herself hoisted up on the high white bed, and seated there face to face with that cold, haughty Mrs. Ford, of whom she had always stood in awe, and whose tardy kindness could not conciliate her childish heart. The door closed on Robert, and these two remained alone, the child and Mr. Ford's wife.

"Mab, Mab!" she said, in a voice full of pathos; "poor little Mab! how unkind I have been to you; but forgive me—I am going to die. Forgive me, Mab."

"Do not! do not!" cried Mab, frightened.

"Forgive me, and forgive my dear children," still pleaded Mrs. Ford.

Mab stared, without answering.

"Say it softly after me," whispered Mrs. Ford. "Say this: 'Dear Lord Jesus, forgive me, as I forgive them, for they are innocent.'"

"Let me go!" cried Mab; "let me go!"

"Hush, darling, hush!" said Mrs. Ford, detaining her. "Only say it after me, it is so easy; say it after me."

But terror had entered Mab's heart. Mrs. Ford's pale face and burning eyes, her broken, impressive accents, had undone the object she wished to attain. With a wild scream, Mab attempted to break from her, and, being unable to do so, she sank back on the bed in a fit. Mrs. Ford had no need to summon assistance—Susan and Miss Ford entered the room at one moment.

"Take her away," said Mrs. Ford, sinking back on her pillow, with a sigh of despair. "I only frightened her; she would not forgive them."

No one understood her meaning. Mab herself, when she was removed out of the room, and soothed out of her strange terror, could give no distinct account of what had passed, nor of what had caused it. There was not much time to mind or question her. Susan and Miss Ford exchanged looks as they watched Mrs. Ford's pale face. The emotions of that day had been too much; death was stealing over that troubled countenance, and, with death, peace, repose, resignation. Meekly folded were the clasped hands, serenely parted were the pale lips, soft was the look of the dying blue eyes.

"To Thy keeping, dear Lord—to Thy keeping," she whispered. "Thou wilt watch, Thou wilt care for them—to Thy keeping I leave them."

There came still a greater change.

"It is all over," said Susan, awestruck. She bent over her mistress, and started, to hear her saying, "Be kind to the child."

These were the last words that bore a meaning; some other disconnected sentences she uttered. Then came the great struggle; the battle which life ever loses. And now it is all over. Close the eyes, compose the limbs, it is all over—never again, in this world, shall Mr. Ford and his wife meet.

Where did he spend that night, which brought an event long expected, yet sudden in its coming? No one ever knew. It was grey morning when he let himself in, stole upstairs, and entered the room where his dead wife lay. Was he shocked, amazed, or merely grieved? No one could tell.

The day was well worn, and he had not come

out; and not a sound had given a token of life from the room of death. No one ventured to go near him.

"I can't, miss—I can't," sobbed Susan, in answer to Miss Lavinia's request—"I know he has made away with himself, I know he has, and I can't go in."

"I shall go and tap at the door," faltered Miss Lavinia, trembling violently. She went and knocked gently, but got no answer.

"John!" she called, "John, speak to me, for God's sake!"

But the adjuration, though repeated, was fruitless. Miss Lavinia came back to the parlour, pale as a ghost, and shaking in every limb.

"I cannot imagine what has happened," she stammered; "I knocked, I called, and could get no answer. We must send one of the children."

But the three boys, who were crying together in a corner of the parlour, would not go. To entreaties and arguments Robert returned a sullen "no," and William and Ned, more honestly confessed "they were afraid." Mab, who sat dressing her doll, seemingly the only unconcerned one midst the general grief, here looked up, and said, promptly, "I'll go, aunty."

She rose as she spoke. Miss Lavinia was a little surprised.

"And why will you go?" she asked.

"I know uncle has had no breakfast," said Mab, her face working with emotion; "and I shall tell him to come down and eat."

No one opposed her project, and up Mab went. She knocked at the door, and got no reply; but either Mab did not know the nature of death, or it had no terror for her, for, opening the door, she walked in. At first she did not see Mr. Ford. A second look showed him to her.

He was lying on the bed near his wife. His arm was thrown over her; his face was laid on her pillow, and he was moaning—drearily moaning.

"Alicia! Alicia!—I loved you!—I loved you!"

Sad lament of a wrecked heart, poured forth to the dull ear of the dead. He did not hear little footsteps falling on the floor, he scarcely felt the childish hands that clasped his, but he heard the soft, tearful voice that said imploringly,

"Don't, uncle, don't!"

Perhaps the paroxysm of his grief was out, perhaps there was something in her young, innocent touch, in her fond, little voice that moved him. He rose, and looked at her—the light eyes, the fair hair, seemed Alicia's, but Alicia's when she was fond and loving. His heart swelled within him.

"I have wronged her," he thought, "perhaps *she* will love me." He clasped the child in his arm—he wept freely, abundantly; she cried, child-like, out of sympathy, and from that hour there was a bond of love between the wronger and the wronged one.

"It will atone," he murmured, glancing at the marble face on the pillow; "it will atone, Alicia."

END OF PART THE FIRST.

PART THE SECOND.

MR. FORD'S SON.

CHAPTER I.

TEN years had gone by.

They had told on Miss Lavinia. She was fifty, grey and wrinkled. These ten years had not been years of pleasure to her. She had had a house to keep on very little money—an irritable brother to please—a wayward girl to rear—and boys' clothes to mend. But Miss Lavinia was of a meek, contented disposition. It had not been all sunshine, she was obliged to confess, but then Providence had willed it so, and what Providence had willed must needs be right. Dear Robert had been very kind, and little Mab was very good at heart, and John meant well, and the boys were good boys, and she had had a home where she could almost do as she pleased, and all was as it should be.

But this satisfied spirit all at once forsook Miss

Lavinia, on a bright summer afternoon. Many things had annoyed her. Robert had gone out without bidding her a good morning. Mab had been pettish—the boys had laughed at her—and she and Mr. Ford had fallen out over the accounts.

This was a frequent source of contest between them. Mr. Ford was much altered, and not improved in temper. The once reckless and prodigal man had become sober, stingy, and mean. He fretted over what he considered Miss Lavinia's reckless expenditure, he teased her night and morning about economy, he denied the boys the simplest things, though he raised no objection to their being provided by Robert; to Mab alone he was liberal, not extravagantly, but sufficiently; but with his sister he carried on a perpetual warfare, of which that source of all evil, money was the root.

Miss Lavinia could have borne better with it, had she not felt some doubt of what her brother daily asserted—that he was a poor man. The world said the very reverse; the world declared that Mr. Ford was more than well-off—that he was rich, very rich—that everything he touched turned into gold; and Miss Lavinia, who had a natural leaning towards the opinion of the majority, thought the world must be right. True, her brother wore his garments threadbare, and denied himself every comfort—luxury was out of the question. "But that is the way of misers," reasoned Miss Lavinia, "and I am afraid, I really am, that John, who used to be extravagant, and, at least, generous, has turned miserly. I dare say it is grief for the death of his wife, poor fellow! I wonder, though, he never mentions her."

For never, since the day when Alicia Norton had been laid in her grave, had the widower uttered her name. It had been pronounced in his presence by Susan, by his sister, and his children, but he had heard them with a rigid countenance, and had betrayed no sign of emotion. Little by little, and as time passed, Mrs. Ford had ceased to be remembered, or, at least, mentioned, and her husband had not sought to renew the subject. She had slept neglected, and, seemingly, forgotten in her grave. A plain stone, with initials, marking the spot, weeds and rank grass taking the place of memorial flowers.

"I cannot make out master, I cannot," was Susan's indignant comment, when she came home from her first visit to the cemetery; "that master, who used to dote on missus so, should allow her poor grave to go wild in that fashion—it is a shame, there, and I shall tell him so."

But Susan did not. She felt certain that Mr. Ford never once visited his wife's last resting-place; she even noticed that he had her portrait, a crayon sketch, removed from the drawing-room, and that he caused to be put away many little tokens that might have reminded him of her being—but Susan did not speak. She vaguely acknowledged a grief different from, and, probably, far deeper, than her own. She guessed a wound hopelessly hidden in his very heart; a sorrow nothing could soothe, and much could waken into bitter life. Only one thing she knew and could vouch for, Mr. Ford had tenderly loved his wife, and she supposed that, after his own fashion, he mourned for her.

This Miss Lavinia never doubted; all that surprised her was his fondness and extraordinary partiality for Mab. He had his own children, and Robert was a pattern young man, but none of them seemed so near him as the little foundling. "Now, that is not just," argued Miss Lavinia; "Mab is a good girl, but she is not equal to Robert—besides, she is not his own child; but since he is not just to me, his own sister, how can I expect him to be just to his own son? I wish, though, he would let me have more money, I really cannot do it on thirty shillings a week. I must tell him so."

Miss Lavinia had already told him so that morning, and in vain, but she had a patient obstinacy, which repulses could not weary, and as her brother, at that precise moment, entered the front parlour, where she was sitting, she took the opportunity to speak.

Ten years had told on Mr. Ford too, and that in more ways than one. His hair was white as snow, and fell in waves around his face. The expression of his countenance was completely altered; his look was keen and shy, his lips were rigidly compressed, he stooped more than ever; but his step was firmer than of yore; purpose was written in his whole aspect, purpose, and, to a close observer, sorrow, corroding and sure: one of those griefs which the strong only master after fierce struggles, and against which the weak contend in vain.

"Livy, are you alone?" he asked, looking keenly around him.

"Yes, John, I am alone. I wanted——"

"Yes, Livy, I have no doubt you wanted," was the sharp reply, "when are you not wanting? And I, too, want, Livy. I want to speak to you, and about Robert, too. You will ruin the boy if you go on so. I have just seen fine doings in the kitchen. A steak for Robert, and for Robert only. What is the meaning of it?"

Miss Lavinia was habitually truthful, but escape, save by partial untruth, was impossible, so she said firmly, internally resolving to do what she declared as done:

"*I* paid for that steak, John. And, John," she added, rousing herself the more readily to attack that defence was difficult, "I have thought about it again, and I really cannot keep house for eight on thirty shillings a week."

"There is a way to do everything," sharply replied Mr. Ford, "and I am afraid, I really am, Livy, you are not a good manager. That steak does not look like good management, and I cannot help thinking you could make the thirty shillings do if you would lay in a stock."

"Out of thirty shillings a week, John!"

"Why do you not do as I do?" he persisted. "I buy coals cheap——"

"It does not make much difference, for we are half starved," interrupted Miss Lavinia.

"I buy coals cheap, and other things can be managed in the same way."

"But I cannot buy meat beforehand."

"Indeed, Livy, you can, and you ought to cure your own beef; and, since you will be such a prodigal as to drink beer, why do you not brew your own beer?"

"Brew my own beer!"

"Well, no," said Mr. Ford, hesitatingly, "you would be extravagant, I fear; but, at all events, I really think you might grow a few vegetables in that garden of ours."

"My goodness!" exclaimed Miss Lavinia, whose mind at once pictured plots of cabbages and ridges of potatoes.

"Now, scarlet runners are both useful and ornamental," persisted Mr. Ford; "they are gay to look at when in blossom, and really nice to eat; but you have no economy, that is the truth of it. You really have none, Livy. Now, what did you do with those thirty-five pounds I returned to you ten years ago—spent them foolishly, I have no doubt, in steaks for Robert and so on, and if you had left them to me they would have brought in capital interest."

"John, I cannot keep house on thirty shillings a week," despondently persisted Miss Lavinia.

"Not if you give Robert steaks, and the boys tea, and rashers of bacon, and hot suppers, of course not. No, Miss Lavinia, good housekeeping and economy cannot go on so. Milk and water and plenty of bread will do for the boys, and tea for Mab and you. You may also have some slight luncheon; you are not young, and Mab is growing. Then a good plain joint for dinner, hot one day, cold the next, a dish of greens or potatoes and suet dumplings, but no fal-lals, or kickshaws and dainties; tea and a slice of bread and butter will do afterwards, and what more is wanted?"

"But how am I to provide that out of thirty shillings a week?" said Miss Ford.

"How!"

"Yes, John, how?"

"What is the price of bread?"

"Sevenpence the quartern loaf."

"And what do you give for meat?"

"I pay ninepence, but of course——"

"Ninepence; well, then, Livy, here it is: twelve loaves a week, seven shillings, and twenty pounds of meat, fifteen; seven and fifteen are twenty-two, the extra eight shillings will do amply for beer, vegetables, &c."

Miss Lavinia looked bewildered at this mathematical division of the thirty shillings, and despondently replied, "It would not do."

"It must do," doggedly said her brother—"I am a poor man, Livy, and I can afford no more."

He left the room as he spoke.

The word "must" always calmed Miss Lavinia. Since the thirty shillings must do, why, there was no more to be said or thought about it. She dived down to the bottom of her work basket for a pair of socks, and, after unfolding them, began meditating on a problem which many mothers and aunts have found perplexing: "Why, and how it is, young people will wear out so fast."

"I wonder they will," thought Miss Lavinia;

"I suppose it is the depravity of human nature."

"They," in this case, meant her two younger nephews, William and Edward; for Robert, who really was more careful, as he was older than his brothers, was never included in any of Miss Lavinia's "theys."

Robert was kind and respectful to his aunt, and the quiet regard of her nephew was the treasure of Miss Ford's life. John was odd, Mab was a good girl, but there was a daring strength in her character, of which Miss Lavinia stood in awe; William and Edward liked her, but in a boyish way, and shrewd, though timid and nervous, Miss Lavinia knew that in a boyish way, too, they quizzed her. But dear Robert was ever attentive and kind. He handed her her chair at dinner; helped her to choice bits when he carved, and paid her every one of those little attentions, which, as women find in the decline of life, drop away with youth as roses from the tree with summer time. No wonder, then, that Miss Livinia's eyes sparkled as they rested on Robert with fondness and pride. He was so handsome, so good, so superior. He was Robert her darling; his faults were virtues, his good qualities matchless perfections. The love of a whole life was bestowed on Robert; a love tempered with humility—for what, save that love, had the giver to bestow? It was all his goodness to care about her. This condescension made him all the loftier a being in her eyes. Robert, his fine person, his talents, his manner of expressing himself, ay, even his hundred a year, in Mr. George's office, were endless themes with Miss Lavinia. "And he earns a hundred a year," was one of her conclusions, when she had been descanting on the perfections of her favourite. No wonder, therefore, that, from the sinning "they" of Edward and William, she now wandered to the irreproachable "him" of Robert, and, again looking at the socks, internally exclaimed, "How unlike him!"

"Is uncle here?" said a pleasant voice.

Miss Lavinia looked up, and saw Mab's head in at the door.

Mab, too, was altered since we saw her last. The child of six had become the girl of sixteen, and wonderful was the change. Mab was neither beautiful nor pretty, she was that something beyond both, for which there is no name. She had golden hair and a radiant face. Brightness was her prevailing aspect. Life, light, and joy played and moved around her. Few could see her and not smile with pleasurable emotion. She had fine grey eyes, and a pure complexion, but her features, though not unpleasing, were irregular; her charm was the charm of the morning, the charm ever fresh and new of light and gladness.

"Come in," said Miss Ford, smiling at the young girl's bright face, "I want to speak to you."

"And I want uncle," said Mab, without entering.

"And I wish you would speak to your uncle," despondingly said Miss Lavinia; "he is upstairs. He is really not reasonable. He wants me to keep house on thirty shillings a week, and I can't. Do calculate it with him, Mab, and prove to him that his twelve loaves a week, and his twenty pounds of meat, will never do for eight people."

"I can't let you have more than two pounds a a week, aunt," decisively said Mab.

"I should be very glad of two pounds."

"Then you shall have them, aunt."

The door closed, and the bright face vanished.

CHAPTER II.

"We do not want a drawing-room now," had said Mr. Ford, a few days after his wife's funeral.

Accordingly, part of the drawing-room furniture was removed to the parlours and bedrooms; and Mr. Ford kept for his own use, as more retired and secluded, the rooms which had been his wife's. They were almost bare, but they pleased him so. The whole man was altered, as his family soon found.

They saw something, but not all. Mr. Ford had been weak, dogmatic, self-confident. Something of all that he was still; but with a wide difference; he had learned to doubt his own integrity, and the change that doubt wrought was fearful. The very foundations of his moral world were irremediably shaken. Right and wrong were still clear to him, but he knew that his power to do one and to resist the other was weak. Repentance had come indeed, but not the power of atonement. It is hard to retrace the path of duty when we once have swerved from it. Turn which way he might, that fair and open path of truth and justice receded from before John Ford. His life was one of daily lies, acted or spoken. He could confess the truth about Mab to none; it might have been dangerous, and was assuredly useless. His children, Mab herself, grew up in the belief that she was living upon their substance and his charity; it galled him, yet he could not help it. Especially bitter was the deception when he had to receive Mab's gratitude and affection. Her caresses felt like fire, her fondness was a torment.

"Oh, if she knew!" he thought; "if she knew!"

From thoughts so bitter he found but one refuge, the acquisition of money. He could not restore Mab to her name and wealth, but he could earn and save money for her. Money had caused her misfortune and his error—money should be the atonement. With feverish ardour he set about his task; twice within ten years he had reached affluence and twice ruin had overtaken him; and now, nothing discouraged, he was bent on a third venture: hence the economy against which poor Miss Lavinia contended in vain.

On leaving that lady, Mab lightly ran upstairs, tapped at the back drawing-room door—Mr. Ford's sitting room—and, without waiting for an answer, entered with the familiarity of one who was always welcome. Mr. Ford was sitting before a table in the window; on hearing her he turned round hastily, and at the same time spread his hands in evident alarm over a heap on the table, and Mab saw with amazement that it was a heap of gold and banknotes.

"You should not come in so," he said agitatedly, "you should not, Mab. It is not right."

Mab did not reply.

"Now you will go and tell Lavinia I am a rich man," he continued, speaking with much irritation, "and I am not; and I have been refusing her money, and I will not give her more than thirty shillings a week—it must do."

"It cannot do," replied Mab, decisively.

"Well, then, I cannot help it."

"Oh! uncle! and all that money."

"It is not mine, child, it is not mine. It is left in trust with me, and I cannot spend a farthing of it."

"Well, then, I suppose we must starve," coolly said Mab. "It is no use, uncle, thirty shillings cannot do."

Mr. Ford looked helpless and piteous.

"You do not know what you are doing," he

groaned, "you do not, Mab—you are robbing Peter to pay Paul."

"Uncle, we cannot live on less than two pounds a-week."

"Two pounds!"

"Yes, uncle; the boys are hearty, and——"

"And I am going to be eaten out of house and home by the boys!" almost screamed Mr. Ford. "Does not Robert earn? Do they not earn?——"

"Oh! uncle! how can you be so unjust! Why, dear Robert almost keeps the boys—it is I, uncle, who am the burden of the family."

Mr. Ford looked at her rather wildly.

"Mab, I cannot do it," he said imploringly, "I cannot, Mab."

But Mab was pitiless. She went up to Mr. Ford, and whilst she twined one arm around his neck, she menacingly stretched out the other towards the heap on the table. But instead of a displeased frown, Mr. Ford gave her an approving smile.

"Do," he said, "do—take the notes and feel how crisp they are. Eh! Mab! And the gold! There is nothing like it, is there, Mab?—and it will be all yours one day, my little Queen Mab. Why, you will be quite a rich woman yet, only, do not tell them so."

"Then the money is yours, uncle," promptly said Mab.

"No, child, it is not, but you see it is in trust, and I manage it, and, of course, I have a sort of right over it, and you shall have it—only do not take it now, Mab—do not."

"Why so?" she said, taking a sovereign and gaily tossing it up and catching it again in the palm of her little hand.

"Oh! Mab!" he said pitifully, "be careful of the money—you do not know the toil, the anxiety, the care, every one of these jingling pieces has cost me. And then when it went all—as it did twice—Mab, I thought I should go mad—I thought I should."

Mab dropped the gold she held, and untwining her arm from Mr. Ford's neck, she said,

"Oh! uncle! how can you be so fond of money?"

"Fond of money!" he groaned; "I hate, I abhor, I detest it—it has been the curse of my life—but you see this money is not mine," he added, calming down and gathering it up to put away: "so I must be careful of it."

"Uncle, you must give me ten shillings."

"Must I?"

"Indeed you must."

"Well, then, here is a sovereign, and let it do two weeks—you understand, Mab."

Mab nodded.

"And will you have any money for yourself?"

asked Mr. Ford, lingering over a five-pound note.

"For myself alone!" said Mab.

"To be sure."

"No, uncle. I do not care about money—I have no use for it—and since you are so fond of it," she compassionately added, "you had better keep it."

"And so, Mab, you wish for nothing."

"Oh! yes I do—but where is the use—I cannot have my wish."

Mr. Ford saw with concern that her face was clouded, and that her bright eyes were dim.

"What is it?—tell me—you shall have your wish."

Mab shook her head.

"It is no use, uncle—money cannot give it me—not even all the heap you had there a while ago," she added, casting a look of philosophic pity at the drawer of his bureau; "no, I want things beyond the reach of money."

"I cannot guess riddles, child," a little impatiently said Mr. Ford; "and I wish you would not talk so loud about heaps of money—you know if you tell Lavinia what you saw——"

"Don't be afraid," said Mab, with the same lofty compassion. "I know better; but, uncle, you have said it—you cannot guess riddles, and it is just a riddle troubles me—I wish," she continued, looking at him sadly, "I wish, uncle, I knew how old I am."

Mr. Ford gave a start. Mab pursued:

"You cannot imagine how it annoys me. I really think I am older than I look. Some guess me at seventeen; perhaps I am, uncle, what do you think?"

"You have been ten years with us," stammered Mr. Ford.

"And that is all you know," continued Mab; "I suppose I cannot have been ten when I was left at your door—eh! uncle? Then I am afraid I am only sixteen or so; and yet, uncle, I feel so old—sometimes, so dreadfully old!"

Mr. Ford looked very uneasy. He always looked so when Mab touched on this matter; and Mab, who had concluded in her own mind that it was because the time of her coming to his house reminded him of his wife's death, rarely alluded to the unwelcome subject. She saw how painful an impression she had produced, and, with a forgetfulness of self which was her redeeming trait, and her prevailing virtue, she left him, went to the harmonium in the next room, opened it, and began playing one of Mozart's most divine pieces.

Mab had early shown great musical taste, and Mr. Ford, so careless about his own children, had cultivated it at some expense and with much zeal.

Mab had received lessons from the best masters, and had made great progress. She excelled in religious music, and Mrs. Ford's harmonium was her favourite instrument. Mr. Ford's saddest or most irritable moods yielded to the charm of her playing; and now, though still moved with the reminiscences Mab had unconsciously called up, he paused in the act of closing his bureau to listen to her.

"It is amazing what an ear I have for music," said Mr. Ford. "I know nothing about it; but I have a wonderful ear. Poor William puts me out horribly with his fiddle—my ear is too correct, you see, Mab. What are you playing?"

"An Agnus Dei, uncle."

The instrument was a fine one, and Mab had both power and skill to waken it into life. The "Agnus Dei" was one of Mozart's most tender and plaintive laments, an appeal of sinning and suffering humanity to the God of all mercy; and Mab gave it infinite pathos.

Mr. Ford listened, and gazed intently at Mab's face as it rose above the instrument. That bright girlish countenance, which in everyday life expressed archness and good-humour, became grave and almost sublime under the power of music. To Mr. Ford's diseased and excited mind, Mab looked like the avenging angel who closed the gates of paradise on our first parents.

"Hush!" he said, with an abrupt motion of his hand, "don't tell me God forgives sinners—I tell you, Mab, some sins are never forgiven."

"Poor uncle," softly said Mab, looking at him with deep pity, for religious doubt and melancholy were amongst the sorrows of Mr. Ford's new life. Since his wife's death he had surrendered to his sister the religious education of his children. He did not believe in repentance, he had no faith in forgiveness; the gates of mercy were closed upon him—he said it, he felt it. No one could argue him out of it—Mab could produce a momentary impression, but even she could do no more.

"Poor uncle," she said again, "I am so sorry for you!"

But Mr. Ford's despair had already given way to other feelings.

"You will not tell them about the money," he said, nervously.

"No, uncle, I shall not," answered Mab, without showing any surprise.

She was accustomed to these abrupt changes. She knew, too, that he no longer wanted her, and, closing the instrument, she softly left the room. Once she was on the staircase, however, she gaily ran down with her prize to Miss Lavinia, who, on seeing the money, breathed a sigh of relief.

"But shall we always get it?" she asked, doubtingly.

"I shall see to that," replied Mab.

As she spoke three young faces passed by the parlour window, nodding at her.

"There they are!" she cried, and she ran and opened the door for them.

Edward, a fresh-coloured lad of seventeen, entered first; then came William, languid and delicate; then Robert, now twenty-three, fair, tall, and handsome, and grave enough for thirty. Mab allowed the two younger brothers to enter the parlour, and looked up demurely in Robert's face. He smiled sedately, softly stroked her hair, and said, "What news?"

"None—only ——"

"Only what?"

"I don't know my lesson."

"Mab!"

"Yes, I knew it was very wrong, but don't scold, Robert, don't."

Robert hung up his hat, and seemed to think about it.

"And don't look sulky," persisted Mab.

"Mab," he said again.

"Well, Robert, it is no use to be cross. I hate ethics—they upset me."

"Because your mind is not well balanced," replied Robert, coolly. "We will talk it over after dinner."

Mab looked provoked, but her displeasures were always short-lived, and this faded as rapidly from her sunny face as it had appeared there. Besides, the hall was not the spot for a discussion on the merits of ethics; so, letting Robert enter the parlour, Mab followed him in. At once William and Edward took hold of her. They had brought home a comic album, and wanted to test its efficacy on Mab. "Do look!" and "Just see this one!" "No, look at this, Mab!" were the exclamations which rose from the corner of the sofa, where their two brown heads, and Mab's fair hair, were bending together over the volume. Mab's clear, girlish laughter answered them with a sound which many would have found pleasant. But it made Miss Lavinia look nervous, and Robert, who had taken a chair near her, annoyed.

"Don't be foolish, Mab," he said, a little impatiently.

"I am not," she replied, with a saucy toss of her head; "I am very wise; I am practising the philosophy of Democritus."

Robert leaned back in his chair, and looked superior to such trifling. Miss Lavinia seemed hurt that her favourite should be answered so lightly.

"My dear, I wish you would be steadier," she said, "you are seventeen; it is quite time to give up nonsense."

Youth has an extraordinary gift for mirth. The word "nonsense" upset the gravity of William and Edward, and they both burst out laughing. They laughed until they were tired, but Mab did not join in their merriment. She saw that Robert looked gloomy, and that tears stood in Miss Lavinia's eyes. She put the offending album away, rose, and, going to her aunt, said softly,

"Aunt, is it time for dinner? Shall I go and tell Susan to do Robert's steak?"

The homely question, put in Mab's sweetest tones, and with her most winning look, was probably meant and felt as an attempt at conciliation, for Miss Lavinia brightened, and Robert's brow relaxed.

"No, my dear, stay with Robert," replied kind Miss Ford, who knew that Mab's society was more acceptable than her own to her elder nephew and she rose, and left the room with unselfish alacrity.

Mab sat down in the chair her aunt had vacated, and took up a sock from the work-basket.

"Oh! do come and look, Mab," said Edward.

"Stay here, Mab," authoritatively observed Robert; and Mab, who had half risen, sat down again, not without a little sigh of regret. "You know, Mab," he added, in a more gracious tone, "that you are my property."

"So I perceive," answered Mab, half pleased and half provoked.

But the exercise of power, sweet to us all, was particularly sweet to Robert. He knew, however, how to clothe the iron hand in the silken glove, and, by a few kind words, rather tenderly whispered in Mab's ear, he restored her to a seeming of good humour. But seeming it was, for Mab was meditating either escape or revolt, when Susan's sister, Lucy, opening the parlour door, gave her the means for the former.

"Please, miss," she said, addressing Mab, "the old captain has been and come down the area steps, and he is in the kitchen frightening Miss Ford to death, and he will not go away without seeing master."

"I shall go and tell uncle," readily said Mab; for since Mr. Ford had grown so irritable and strange, Mab alone was privileged to disturb him, and intrude on his privacy.

Upstairs she went again. William, who had followed her out, overtook her on the first floor landing. William had bad health, and he had been nursed by Mab through several illnesses, since which he had remained her pet. He it was who asked of her what both he and Edward wanted; for Mab was a sort of prime minister in the house. She stood between Mr. Ford's displeasure and his younger sons, and through her flowed his scanty good graces. Thus she was invariably applied to by William and Edward, and even by Miss Lavinia. Robert alone asked and received nothing through her means. There existed between him and his father a line of separation, which Mab vainly endeavoured to break, and for which he was too proud to seek her influence. But his brothers were not troubled with such superfluous pride, and it was to get something through Mab's means that William now followed her.

"Well, what is it now?" asked Mab, turning round, with a half smile; "I warn you I have got money out of uncle to-day, and can ask for no more."

"We don't want money," answered William; "but I wish you would ask papa to let us have Fred here. You remember Frederick Norton. He arrived to-day—we saw him—such a good fellow he is! We want to have him here."

Mab looked startled. It seemed a stretch of her influence to trouble Mr. Ford with a guest.

"I cannot," she said. "No, William, I really cannot."

"Yes—you can if you please—you will like Fred so—do, Mab, now there is a good girl."

Still Mab hesitated; but William, who, spite his languid, careless looks, knew how to press a point, urged this until Mab promised.

"And now let me go," she added, breaking from him, "aunt wants to get rid of Captain George, I am sure."

This time Mab tapped at the back drawing-room door; a ready "come in" at once gave her a right to enter. She found Mr. Ford deep in accounts, but he looked up from his books with a smile on seeing her.

"Well, my dear, what is it now?" he asked; "is dinner ready?"

"No—not quite, and yet you are wanted below, uncle."

Mab looked like one who has unpleasant news to give, and who knows not in what words to give them. Mr. Ford's countenance became troubled.

"Is Captain George below?" he asked nervously.

"He is in the kitchen with Aunt Lavinia. He went down the area steps. Uncle, what does that man always come here for?"

"God knows," groaned Mr. Ford—"for my sins, I believe. Go down, Mab, and tell him I cannot see him—bid him leave the house."

"I am afraid of him," said Mab, with a frightened look, "he is so dirty and so tipsy, uncle. I would not mind giving him money, if I had it, for he is poor, I believe, but he disgusts me."

"Give him money!" wrathfully cried Mr. Ford, "the thief, the robber, the swindler—not a farthing to save him from starvation—not one, Mab!"

Mab, who had a very moderate liking for Captain George, raised no demur to this harsh sentence, but she asked what was to be done.

"Why does he not go to his brother?" indignantly exclaimed Mr. Ford; "his brother is rich, is he not? Why does he not go to him?"

"Do not trouble about him, uncle," said Mab, "I shall dismiss Captain George, but I have something else to say to you. Frederick Norton has arrived from Australia."

"I know it; I saw him to-day."

"And when is he coming?" asked Mab coolly.

"When?"

"Yes, when is he coming to stay here, I mean?"

"I will not have him!" cried Mr. Ford; "I will not, Mab—do not try that."

"But, uncle, if William were to go to Australia, as he talks of doing, where would you expect him to go, unless to Mr. Norton's. Then, of course, Frederick must come here."

"And why should William go to Australia?" angrily asked Mr. Ford; "it is his brother Robert has put that into his head. Just as he told you to ask me to have Frederick here."

"No, uncle, he did not—but I am sorry I mentioned it, I see you do not like it; and now I must dismiss Captain George, must I?"

She turned to the door, but Mr. Ford recalled her with a sigh.

"Stay, child," he said; "why should that man so much as look at you?—I shall go—I shall go."

He went, and Mab followed him slowly.

As they reached the hall they both heard Captain George's whining voice below, holding argument with Miss Lavinia.

"I made his fortune," said the Captain, "and look at my reward!—I made John Ford's fortune, let him deny it if he can—and look at him, and look at me, Miss Ford."

Mr. Ford ground his teeth and shook his fist in the air, and muttered something Mab could not hear; but he went down the kitchen stairs, and if he dismissed Captain George, he did so quietly, though briefly, for Mab's hand was still on the parlour door, when the Captain's step, rendered shuffling by a pair of old slippers, was heard coming up. She entered hastily, but the Captain had heard her, for almost as soon as the door had closed upon her, it opened again, and his head and shoulders appeared in the opening. Time had not improved the Captain. His eyes were watery, his nose was swollen and red, his moustache shabby, and his once brilliant teeth were almost all gone. He leered round the room and gave a longing look at the table now laid for dinner; but with something of the graceful courtesy of old times, he waved his hand to Mab, and, without noticing the haughty looks of Robert, who stood with his back to the fireplace, or the defiant glances of Edward and William, he said:

"Mrs. George sends her love, my dear. You remember Mrs. George."

Before Mab could reply, Captain George suddenly vanished, and his half-angry exclamation: "Now, Ford, that's too bad!" followed by his rapid exit at the front door, showed that this sudden disappearance was not entirely effected by Captain George's own free will.

CHAPTER III.

Mr. Ford entered the parlour with a flushed and angry face. The first person he saw was Robert, still standing with his back to the fireplace, and to him his wrath was at once directed.

"Who has been talking to Captain George in the kitchen?" he asked, staring angrily at his eldest son.

"I have," composedly replied Robert.

"And what business have you to be talking to that vagabond. He did not ask for you, I suppose?"

"He did not," still very calmly answered Robert, "and I certainly had no business with him, but he frightened my aunt, who appealed to me for protection—I went down and gave it, that is all. Captain George having promised to be quiet, I left him."

Mr. Ford growled something between his teeth,

thrust his hands into his pockets, and walked up and down the room in a fit of smothered passion. Robert took up a newspaper, and neither looked nor spoke. William and Edward pulled long faces at each other, and exchanged winks; and Mab, watching Mr. Ford, patiently waited her opportunity to interpose a gentle, conciliating word, a task of love and peace which she unweariedly renewed day after day, though ever in vain. She did not know, she could not suspect, that she was the cause of the ever-widening breach between father and son. Ever since his wife's death Mr. Ford had felt morally certain that Robert was in possession of his secret. He could not tax him with a word, not even with a look of disrespect, yet he was certain he had not his esteem, and the thought rankled in his heart. For whom had he sinned? For Alicia, who had died reproaching and contemning him; for his children, for Robert, who neither loved nor respected him; for William and Edward, whom Robert had estranged from him, over whom he assumed, as he exercised, the power and the care of a father.

An embittered heart is rarely just. Mr. Ford forgot that if Robert took much on himself, it was because his own neglect had been great. He forgot that if he had loved his children, he had not always shown that love; especially did he forget that to know his sad error could be no sin in his eldest son, though it might be a misfortune. With the perversity of a great sorrow, he widened the breach already so deep, by exaggerated coldness and severity. He stung Robert by his injustice, he alienated William and Edward by his harsh temper, and no one suspected that tenderness and jealousy were at the root of his harshness; least of all, that he was secretly proud of the son he was ever censuring. Miss Lavinia herself did not glory more in Robert's steadiness, sobriety, and sterling qualities, than did his seemingly harsh and unjust father.

"Are we going to get any dinner to-day?" angrily asked Mr. Ford, stopping suddenly short in the middle of the room.

He looked around him like one ready to quarrel, but his eye fell on Mab, who stood patiently waiting his return to a more peaceful mood, and it softened at once; he seemed ashamed of his roughness, and coughed gently by way of prelude to a better humour.

"What was it you were saying about Frederick Norton, pussy?" he asked, stretching out his arm to draw her to his side.

Mab laughed, and nestling her head on his shoulder, softly stroked his cheek.

"Oh! you want him here, do you!" continued

Mr. Ford, pinching her ear. "You and he used to be great friends; well, we shall see—we shall see; and now let us have dinner," he added, as the door opened and Miss Lavinia, followed by Lucy, entered the parlour.

The meal began. From her place by Mr. Ford, Mab glanced over at William, who smiled approval in his languid way; but she saw with concern that disapprobation, stern and strong, sat on Robert's straight, inflexible forehead. He evidently would not for one enjoy Frederick's presence in the house. Mab had not thought that he might not approve this plan, and, with some trepidation, she anticipated a lecture. In the meanwhile, Mr. Ford, determined to gratify his darling, prepared Miss Lavinia for her guest.

"Young Norton has come, Livy," he said to her, "I suppose we have a spare bed to give him?"

Miss Ford's knife and fork dropped on her plate at the suggestion. The bed was nothing, but to board a ravenous boy of twenty-one, without any increase to the two pounds a week, was not to be thought of.

"We have a spare bed," she said, faintly, "but—"

"Never mind about the rest," hastily interrupted Mr. Ford, who knew well enough what was coming; "when there's enough for eight there's enough for nine, and you are not going to make any difference for a young fellow who has been accustomed to roughing it in the bush and the diggings. I shall see him this evening, and tell him his room will be ready to-morrow. You need not wait for tea for me, Livy."

So saying, and, without giving Miss Ford time to demur, Mr. Ford rose from the table, and hastily left the room.

"Never mind, aunt," whispered Mab to Miss Lavinia, who sat a picture of dismay, "I shall manage about the money."

"I shall be glad to speak to you in the back parlour, Mab," solemnly said Robert.

"I must first go up to my room and water my plants," replied Mab.

"Very well."

He said this in the tone of a judge who agrees to delay an impending execution, but whose utmost kindness cannot possibly go beyond delay; and to show Mab that escape was impossible, he took up the newspaper and entered the back parlour, closing the door behind him, to read it there alone. At once Mab rose, and, going out by the other door, ran up to her room. Miss Lavinia remained alone with her two younger nephews. William languidly stretched himself on the sofa, and Edward beat the tune of "I'm afloat" on the window panes.

"I wish Mab had stayed," said William, "one never enjoys her unless when our brother Robert is out of the room."

"I wonder he does not put her in a cage!" indignantly said Edward.

Miss Lavinia gave each of the speakers as angry a look as the mildness of her nature allowed, but it fell harmless on William's shield of laziness, and Edward's high spirits were armour proof against looks. Moreover, neither was conscious of wrong. They did not care about their father; they cared but little for Miss Lavinia; they were fond and proud of Mab; devotedly attached to each other; and they looked up to Robert with a mixture of admiration and fear. They relied upon him in difficulties, but they grew silent when he was by, and were happiest in his absence. This feeling they unreservedly displayed in Miss Lavinia's presence—for, first of all, she was of no account, and, secondly, she would never betray them.

"I wish Mab had stayed," again said William. "Let us go and see Fred."

"Robert won't like it," replied Edward, evidently enjoying it all the more; "he can't bear Fred."

"Robert hates every one who contradicts him," said William, slowly.

"And Fred has a spirit of his own."

"Yes, but Robert was in the right, Ned."

"What about it?" warmly replied Ned; "Fred could not go back of what he had said; a man must stand by what he says—but Robert is domineering."

"I am surprised," indignantly began Miss Lavinia; but, before she could get through the rest, a "Come on" of Edward had roused the languid William.

They left the room, where Miss Lavinia remained alone in the growing twilight—alone with her indignation at their ingratitude to dear Robert.

"And I believe he is coming to me," she thought, as she heard him rise in the next room; but Robert had only got up to ring the bell, and all he said, when Lucy answered it, was,

"Ask Miss Mab to come down, if you please;" for strict politeness to servants was one of Robert's good qualities.

"So like him!" admiringly thought Miss Ford, and admiration of his perfections made her forget her solitude; "but Mab ought really to know better than to keep dear Robert waiting."

No doubt Mab ought to have known better; but Mab was in her room—a small but bright apartment, a little girlish world framed in by white curtains, where Mab found it very pleasant to sit and dream alone. It was a pleasant place. Books, flowers, and birds showed Mab's tastes.

The perfect neatness of everything around did credit to the habits of order and care Miss Livinia had inculcated on her adopted niece. In this sanctuary were spent Mab's happiest hours; to it she retreated whenever the mood of reverie, a frequent one, came on.

It was on her now. Through the open window she saw the summits of trees and a clear blue sky; the backs of other houses, and the chimney-tops, which were also included in her prospect, Mab ignored. She was at the happy age when the eye sees only that which the mind delights in. Just now it pleased her to let the book she was reading drop on her lap, and to lose herself in a sunlit forest, and to wander alone in its green and silent paths.

For some days past there had wakened in Mab vague yearnings towards unknown spots, often blending with remembrances, still more vague, of other places. Now, there arose a scene before her, one which she was sure she had beheld, when or where she knew not, but in that past which had preceded her arrival in Queen Square. It was a spot where three roads met, all overarched with stately trees that scarcely allowed a ray of sun to pierce their boughs, and that rarely opened their heavy foliage to let in a glimpse of sky. She sat on the last step of an old stone cross, defaced with age, and in her lap was a heap of wild-flowers, white daisies, tipped with red, buttercups, violets, and many more—a plenteous store.

So far the picture was so distinct, that Mab felt as if she could have painted it: the rest was confusion and mystery; there was a wild sound and a great terror, and she wakened in the arms of a stranger, who said, "She is not hurt." And the stranger was that "he" about whom Robert had so often taunted and questioned her—and that was all.

"I wonder I never thought of it before," thought Mab; and then followed another question, one which always jarred with pride, "Who and what was she?"

But on this subject Mab would not and did not linger; it was too bitter. She knit her smooth forehead into a frown, rebellious and indignant, and took up her book once more.

She was a great reader. And reading, which had taught her much, had made her dogmatic and modest. She had strong opinions, but she kept them to herself; ardent feelings, but no one suspected them, perhaps because she was not selfish; and that with an excellent opinion of her person and understanding, she thought very little about either. Mr. Ford's tenderness she never abused, Miss Lavinia's partiality for Robert she never resented, and Robert's assumption of superior knowledge and authority she submitted to good-humouredly. So they were all pleased, Mab was happy. At the same time, Mab now and then took a fancy to live for herself, to dream alone, to read the books she liked, and to have her own way. Her own way she would have this evening; and, though Robert was waiting below, Mab, after watering her plants, indulged in a reverie, and now coolly took up the life of Napoleon she was reading, and which she commented on as she read:

"Robert may say what he likes," thought Mab, "there never was so grand a creature as Napoleon Bonaparte—never!"

For there was war between Robert and Mab; part of his tuition she had received with ardour, part she had tacitly rejected. Robert wanted his rosy, smiling pupil to be a Robert Ford in petticoats, and Mab wanted to be Mab, and no more. Whilst he resented her idleness, as he called it, Robert was, in reality, blind to the real groundwork of Mab's education and character—daring thought. He imagined her, femininely, averse to study, and he did not perceive in her the phenomenon which is daily getting less rare—the clear, vigorous mind and firm temper clothed in the graceful form of the girl. That open brow, those smiling eyes and dimpled cheeks, concealed many a bold speculation, the result of study, reading, and secret meditation. Mab might object to the ethics, and to many of the "ologies" Robert patronized—not that he loved them, but because the world around him did, for she was sincere, and only studied what she liked—but, in reality, she knew far more than did Robert, with all his fancied superiority; and what she knew, she knew, too, far better than he did. She was not without a certain consciousness of this, and, perhaps, it helped to make her rebellious.

Yet, when Lucy came, and knocked at her door, with Robert's message, Mab did not hesitate one moment, but went down at once. For, after all, he was Robert, her teacher, her friend, her more than brother—Robert, whom she was bound to obey, revere, and love.

She found Robert walking restlessly up and down the back parlour. He stopped short on seeing her. Mab was struck with his look, and exclaimed,

"Robert, something has happened!"

"Yes," he answered, trying to laugh, "something has happened; for I sent for you, and I am going out, and we can have no lesson, not even on ethics."

"Never mind," replied Mab, "it will do to-morrow."

"Yes, but do not leave me yet," said Robert; "I want to talk to you."

"Oh, don't scold!" implored Mab, looking alarmed, and thinking of Frederick.

"About what?" graciously answered Robert, who, though much displeased, had wisely resolved to keep his displeasure to himself. "Sit down," he added. Mab obeyed. Robert sat down facing her, but without looking at her. He began:

"Mab, you are now seventeen."

"I believe I am."

"Has anyone ever offered marriage to you?"

He raised his eyes suddenly to her as he spoke. Mab blushed a little, and answered,

"Never mind."

Robert rose, and seemed almost excited.

"Mab," he said, "do not jest—this is no jesting matter. You are young, inexperienced, and can rely on no one's advice or judgment save mine. I may have put an ill-timed question with regard to the past, but, for the future, I must warn you. Mab, I am your best friend; and you must promise me that, until you are some years older, you will not listen to any proposal of marriage.

"He wants me for himself," thought Mab; "but why does he not say so?"

"Mab, you do not promise."

Mab's rosy mouth became very grave, and very demurely she said,

"I promise it, Robert."

"Well, but don't go away," he said, in high good-humour, "I have something more to say to you."

"Oh! I hope he is not going to make love to me *now*," thought Mab. She liked Robert to be her admirer, and to feel uneasy and even jealous, but she did not want the actual love-making just yet. But Robert, whatever he might intend for the future, had no such thought for the present.

"Do you think William is looking well?" he asked. "I thought he was pale to-day."

"Indeed no, Robert. William has looked very well since his last illness."

Robert's face cleared, then clouded again.

"Poor lad!" he exclaimed, "if I could only push him on, and Neddy too, I should be free—you understand, Mab? But there are times when I do not know what to do with the boys. They cannot stay as they are, shabby clerks—can they, Mab?"

"Robert, I must be honest with you. I love them dearly; they are good, warm-hearted young men, but really I do not think them superior."

"Oh! you do not," said Robert, much nettled, and speaking with very unloverlike sharpness; "and pray what can you know about it?"

"I certainly ought to know better than to disagree with you about your darling brothers," good-humouredly replied Mab.

"Their being my brothers has nothing to do

with it," shortly said Robert; "I see them as impartially as if they were strangers. You may smile, Queen Mab, it is so. I am sure my family feelings have nothing to do with my opinion of those two boys. I should think just the same of them if they were any one else's brothers."

As Robert was evidently excited, Mab would not contradict him by word or look, but remained listening patiently.

"And I say this," continued Robert warmly, "that William will make as fine a fellow as a brother need be proud of. Only, what can I do for him?"

"Good old Robert," said Mab, gently stroking his arm.

"And there is Neddy," continued Robert, musing, "not so intelligent as William, but so honest, so steady, such sense, with his high spirits. Mab, he would make a great merchant—one of those men who rise to anything, whose word is better than the bond of other men—only where is the first start?"

Mab shook her head and looked grave.

"And what can I do for them?" exclaimed Robert, with an impatient sigh; "nothing—I do nothing."

"Why, Robert, you do everything for them," warmly answered Mab. "You stint yourself for them. You deny yourself a long holiday to take a short one with them. Why, you are not a brother—you are a father to them."

But vanity is a strange passion. Robert had his share of it; he was weakly vain of his precocious steadiness; he assumed more gravity than he really felt, more knowledge than he really possessed, but he was neither proud nor vain of the daily sacrifices he made for his young brothers. These flowed without effort from the fulness of his heart, and he kept no reckoning of them.

"No, I do nothing," said Robert again, "and all my talk and all my plans end, as this conversation is going to end, in nothing. Time alone can help us all. Eh! Mab."

Mab understood his meaning now. He could not ask her to marry him; he wanted time, and in the meanwhile she was to marry no one else. Mab could not help being amused at the transparency of his plans, and she had a vague consciousness that Frederick Norton's presence in the house might have caused this declaration; but she kept her surmises to herself, and, as Robert's look was watching her face for a reply, she said demurely enough, "that time alone could do it." With this answer Robert seemed quite satisfied. He looked at his watch, saw it was time to go and keep his appointment with his employer, Mr. James George; and, bidding Mab a good evening, he left her.

CHAPTER IV.

LITTLE did Mab suspect on what errand Robert had left the house. The scheme he had been maturing years was now, he thought, drawing to a close, and, with some of his father's temper, he had no doubt of success. In all that was practical and straightforward, Robert was a man of business. Mr. James George often said of him, "That young Ford will be rich; he will be rich, sir." But there is a higher and other wisdom than that which is needed to make money, and in that Robert failed. He was a better judge of event and circumstance than of the human heart. Affection blinded him with his brothers, and self-esteem with himself. He had almost unlimited confidence in his own powers of achieving his own ends. The silent fear in which his father held him, Mab's gratitude, Miss Lavinia's adoration, the respect of his brothers, and the careful regard of his employer, Mr. James George, all combined to impress Robert with the conviction that he was destined to be a successful man. And being young and inexperienced, and sanguine, he forgot that success has her limits.

His heart had for years been set on a project in which Mab unconsciously held the first part. By dint of thought, by connecting many little broken links of the one chain, he knew as well as Mr. Ford who and what she was. He knew why she had been left at his father's door, with five hundred pounds; and whom that father, unconsciously at first, with full and guilty knowledge in the end, had abetted. Ay, Mab was rich, in right at least; she was dead to the world, and the two Georges had divided her inheritance; but if by one it had been rapidly squandered, carefully had the other hoarded his share.

Mr. James George was a wealthy man, and if gold was his ruling passion, disgrace was also the ruling fear of his life. It was that fear which had made him choose the weak Mr. Ford for an accomplice; it was that fear which had made him take Mr. Ford's eldest son into his office; and it was that fear still which had made him keep the young man, whom he secretly feared and hated; for Robert, though careful, had not kept his secret so well that Mr. George did not know it. Mr. George indeed knew that he was proof against detection, but no one is proof against suspicion. Now, though his name was not good, though it was connected with some strange transactions, yet, as he had slipped through them, as he still stood his ground, he clung to his fragment of reputation, such as it was. He clung to it with a desperate tenacity, which was the foundation of Robert's secret hopes; for on that, and on that alone, he could work.

Robert was ambitious for himself and his brothers; he saw no harm in deriving benefit from his father's great error, and in Mab he hoped to find the girl he liked, and the fortune he required. The double motive acted powerfully on a narrow, but tenacious mind. Robert loved Mab, but he loved her as the gardener loves the plant his care and labour have fostered into being—for its value first, next for its beauty. She was precisely, as he thought, the girl he ought to marry, on her own merits; but he also thought that she would be rich one day, and, without that conviction, Robert would never have loved her. These two convictions, that Mab was the very person who ought to become Mrs. Robert Ford, and that she would bring wealth to her husband, had blended so long and so closely in Robert's mind, that he himself could have given them no separate and distinct existence. To do him justice, he did not strive to do so; his was not an analytic mind; he loved her, and she would be rich—this much he knew, or thought he knew, and he sought for no more.

As he left Queen Square and walked slowly towards Oxford Street, Robert, who had a business appointment with Mr. James George in his private residence, at Bayswater, meditated how best he could manage to turn that interview to his own purpose.

"It must be done some time or other," he thought, "and it shall be done this evening. Mab is growing up. I will not wait any longer."

The young man was absorbed in these thoughts, but not so much so as not to perceive, with some surprise, that his father and Captain George were walking slowly before him. He was now in Bloomsbury Square, and it was quiet and lonely on that mild summer evening. There was no mistaking his father's stooping back, and Captain George's erect though most shabbily clothed figure. They suddenly came to a stand-still near the railings, and Robert, reluctant to pass them, stood still also.

"Make it ten shillings more," urged Captain George. "Remember how down-hill you were when the little thing sat at your door——"

"Say that again!" excitedly interrupted Mr. Ford's voice—"say that again!"

"Come, come, old fellow, we'll drop it. You are better, at least, than that shabby James, who will not give his own brother one shilling. But he'll quake for it yet, he will."

Something else Captain George added, but his words were lost in a resentful growl, and the pair walking on turned into a neighbouring street and vanished.

Robert went on his way, trying to make out something of what he had heard—something especially which he might turn to account that evening; but though he weighed the matter carefully, nothing came of it, and, wearied of the fruitless exertion, he dismissed it utterly from his mind.

It was dusk when he reached Mr. James George's house, one of the quietest and most sober-looking houses in Bayswater, by no means the house of a wealthy man.

Robert had never seen it before, for his intercourse with his employer was of the most limited nature; he scanned it with a curious and approving eye: so much the better that Mr. George was saving, that he was not extravagant and reckless like the spendthrift he had just seen; so much the better for Mab in the end. But for the present how tenacious a hold this saving spoke of Mr. George's ill-gotten wealth!

A demure-looking footman answered Robert's

double knock. In the gaslit hall behind him appeared a woman of thirty-five or so, fair and freckled, with auburn hair, and with a pale, worn face, that might have been pretty once, and the saddest look Robert had ever seen. She wore a black silk dress that had seen better days, and her cap had the same look of decayed smartness.

"Mr. George," said Robert, "I come by appointment."

"I know, sir," answered the woman, who seemed to be an upper servant or housekeeper; "this way, please."

She shewed him into a plain parlour, where sat Mr. George, surrounded by papers and books.

Mr. George had altered little during the last ten years. He was still a cold, grey, respectable looking man, but some lines in his face had deepened, and to a close observer they would not have seemed pleasant lines. There was a more covetous eagerness than of yore in the small grey eyes, veiled by the heavy and drooping lids; there was more will in the thin lips, and the fearfulness of the retreating chin was, at least, no less than it had been. But will ruled all. It is said that Frederick the Great was constitutionally a coward, but will made him brave and a great commander. Mr. George's temperament would have kept him from daring actions, but avidity and will ruled fear, and made him venture—rarely, it is true, but often enough for danger. Peril, however, Mr. George did not apprehend now, as the door opened and let in his clerk.

"Good evening to you, Ford," said Mr. George with a certain lofty kindness; "sit down here, Ford."

There are few of us without some characteristic manner or other: Mr. George's was pomposity. He was born lofty, dignified, and patronizing, and he never lost an opportunity of displaying those attributes.

"Now, Ford," he said, as Robert took a chair and prepared for business, "I will just give you an instance of human nature. It may be useful to you in your future career. You know, Ford, how I favoured young Slater. Well, Ford, he turned against me—he has turned against me—and I am compelled to ask you to come here and help me with this extra work—deplorable, is it not, Ford, deplorable?"

Robert was accustomed to such language. He said it was deplorable, and he looked at the papers, but Mr. George seemed in no hurry to begin.

"Now, could anything be fairer than my conduct?" he exclaimed with a sigh. "Young Slater wanted increase of salary. I felt disposed to favour him, but not just then; I told him so. 'Not now, Slater,' I said, 'not now; but you know how

I love to encourage rising merit, you know it, Slater. Well, then, there is Ford, who is above you, speak to him next Michaelmas; ask *him* to sound *me*, and then we shall see—then we shall see, Slater.' Now I put it to you, Ford, could anything be more fair, more candid; I will venture to add, more amiable? I actually forgot my own rank and position to advise my junior clerk to his own benefit. And now the ungrateful little vagabond, instead of waiting till next Michaelmas to ask you to sound *me*, goes off with himself, and leaves us all this extra trouble."

Robert looked up in his employer's face and said quietly enough:

"I suppose he got a good offer. His salary was but small."

Mr. George coughed and looked alarmed, but he said nothing.

"I was thinking," pursued Robert, "of asking you to raise my salary, sir. I am your only clerk now, and there is much work."

Mr. George did not refer Robert to some third person to sound him: he said sharply, and without taking any amiable views of the matter:

"Out of the question, Ford, out of the question. There are the papers. Let us go to work."

"I should like three hundred," coolly said Robert; "and with your recommendation I might help my two brothers to better berths than they have; I see, sir, you are but little inclined to favour me in this; but I am twenty-three, and I wish to marry, which I cannot do on a hundred a year."

Mr. George tightened his lips, and looked wary, but he said not one word.

"Or, perhaps," continued Robert, "it would make no difference to you to settle the amount on my future wife, Miss Winter. I should like that just as well."

Mr. George's hand shook a little as he scribbled with the pen he held, but he said calmly enough:

"Let us see about these papers first. After tea, Ford, after tea we will talk of your salary."

"We might manage it another way yet," pursued Robert; "you might make a will in favour of Miss Winter—or, if you liked it better, settle part of your property on her."

Mr. George put down his pen and looked at Robert, and his look might mean anything. It might mean the cool disdain of an upright man, or the steady insolence of a guilty one. Robert, by no means daunted, continued.

"Ten years ago Miss Winter was left at my father's door. Suppose she was then entitled to fifteen thousand pounds, which have been lying by since then. It is after all but a small part of your fortune, and the world knows your integrity, sir, there need be no unpleasant doubts either before or after your death. Miss Winter is probably the daughter of a friend or of a relative—the matter is one that defies scrutiny, and leaves your fair name untouched."

Still Mr. George did not reply. The blow that was falling on him had been expected for years, and Mr. George was in some measure prepared for this attack. Yet though he knew himself invulnerable in law, and almost invulnerable in opinion, he was too cautious to answer his audacious clerk without first maturing the matter.

"After tea," he said again, "after tea."

He pushed the papers to Robert, and, as if nothing had occurred, both went into the matter in hand, and worked amicably together. At eight Mr. George rang for tea.

To Robert's surprise, a little girl of ten or eleven, rather pretty, though she bore an unmistakeable likeness to Mr. George, came in, and behind her the sad-looking woman whom he had already seen. This person, whom Mr. George addressed as Mrs. Smith, made the tea. She was evidently an upper housekeeper.

The child, Miss Blanche Redmond, called Mr. George "guardian," and sat next him. He looked at her with a worshipping fondness that contrasted with the asperity of his tone when he addressed Mrs. Smith. That melancholy-looking person filled

Robert with pity. She was nervous, awkward, and committed blunder after blunder. In her agitation she spilled the tea she was pouring out. Little Blanche laughed and said pertly:

"How stupid you are, Mrs. Smith!"

Mr. George gave the unfortunate Mrs. Smith a withering look.

"I think you are not well, Mrs. Smith," he said austerely; "I think you had better go to your room."

"And I'll pour out the tea," cried Blanche, starting to her feet with great alacrity. "I like it."

"Mind you do not scald yourself, my dear," timidly said Mrs. Smith, rising to go.

Mr. George's breath seemed gone at the familiarity of the address.

"Mrs. Smith!" he cried—"you amaze me, you amaze me, Mrs. Smith!"

"Ay," thought Robert, "she has called her own child my dear." And he almost forgot the interest he had at stake in watching this domestic scene.

"Pour out the tea, my love," said Mr. George to the child; and in a less severe tone he added, "You may go, Mrs. Smith."

Mrs. Smith looked piteously at her master, then at the little girl who had already taken her place. She pressed her hand to her heart, as if she felt some strange pain there; then, not heeding Robert's compassionate look, she noiselessly left the room.

Blanche was in great glee at her new duties. She poured out the tea into the sugar basin; she mixed the cups, and did not know which was which; she transferred the contents of the slop-basin to Mr. George's cup, and Mr. George laughed with a low chuckle, he had not a word of reproof, and, to all appearance, too, he had not a care, not a thought on his mind.

Tea was over, the child had left, and Mr. George and his clerk were alone once more with the papers.

"And now, with regard to what we were saying," said Mr. George, entering at once on the matter, "here is my answer: the young lady you have just seen is my sole heiress. I will raise your salary fifty pounds and take no junior clerk; and the next time you mention to me the name of the young lady you wish to marry, I shall dismiss you on the spot."

Robert raised his eyes; they exchanged looks of mutual mistrust and defiance, but both felt that for the present there was no more to be done, and there the matter ended. At ten the business that had brought him was over, and Robert took his leave.

His thoughts as he walked home were bitter. He had not expected so complete a defeat of his ambitious hopes. He had laid a sure train, as he thought; for who better than he knew Mr. George's timorous sense of disgrace? The three hundred pounds salary was a mere blind to lead Mr. George to Robert's great object, the ultimate restoration of Mr. George's share of Mab's property. There he thought he was sure of him; for this plan combined everything—Mr. George's dislike of present expense, his hatred of his spendthrift brother, and his fear of leaving a disgraced name instead of that plausible reputation he had been at so much trouble to build up for himself. But he was supported, too, by a motive which Robert, who only knew that his employer was a childless widower, had never suspected; and the links which the young man had thought of iron were mere cobwebs to Mr. George's subtler mind. There was no proof against him, or Robert would at once have used it; all his proposals, therefore, were mere words, empty threats he could afford to defy, ay, and if need be, he could cast him off and dare him to do his worst. Still, it was better not to do that. Robert was worth a hundred and fifty pounds a year; the salary he earned was, Mr. George thought a fair bribe for his silence. "Let him talk, if he dare!" so cogitated Mr. George during tea-time; and after tea-time he spoke, and his words and his looks alike warned Robert that this resolve was final.

"And shall it end thus?" thought Robert as he

walked home. "Shall Mr. George's secret bring me in nothing but a hundred and fifty pounds a year—of my own earning, too?"

He turned the matter again and again, and could find no present issue favourable to his wishes. Ay, Mr. George was indeed invulnerable, and he knew it; but there was time yet, and as he entered Bloomsbury Square a sudden hope passed through Robert's mind. He remembered Captain George, dirty, shabby, needy, and embittered against his wealthy brother. Could he help, could he assist Robert in securing the immediate prize—one, too, that need not wait for Mr. George's death or good pleasure. The thought was too much for Robert's strength. He walked about the square restless, excited, and trembling like a criminal, till midnight struck. Then, feeling somewhat calmer, he proceeded to Queen Square. He found Miss Lavinia patiently sitting up for him.

"I am sorry, aunt, to have kept you waiting," kindly said Robert; "but Mr. George and I had to despatch a world of business. I came home as quickly as I could, for I knew you would sit up."

"Dear Robert, you are always so considerate," said Miss Lavinia, quite happy. And "dear Robert," who was accustomed to make his aunt happy at this cheap rate, smiled and went to bed with a peaceful conscience.

CHAPTER V.

ROBERT came down early the next morning. He had spent a sleepless night, meditating over his failure, and maturing his plans. He expected the parlour to be vacant, and he was surprised to find his father there before him.

Mr. Ford was sitting by the window reading the newspaper; he glanced up from its columns as Robert entered the room: and there was something strange and mistrustful in the looks father and son exchanged. Robert was wondering what could have passed between his father and Captain George after they went away together, and Mr. Ford, who on coming home had seen his eldest son walking about Bloomsbury Square in a state of much excitement, and a full hour before he entered the house, was perplexed to imagine what could have thus agitated the staid and sober Robert.

"You came home late last night," said Mr. Ford.

"Yes," answered Robert, calmly. "Mr. George kept me till half-past eleven. It must have been twelve when I got here."

Mr. Ford rubbed his chin, and looked meditatively at Robert. His son was not untruthful by habit, though he was plausible by nature. What made him tell that untruth now? There must be a motive. Robert, absorbed in his own desire to know something about Captain George, did not notice his father's bent brows and searching looks. He put on a careless air, whistled a while, then said negligently,

"Any news?"

"Funds flat," replied Mr. Ford.

"By-the-bye, what does that old captain do now?" exclaimed Robert, suddenly, as if that moment only he had remembered the captain's existence; "nothing, I suppose," he added, as his father did not answer him.

"What old captain?" asked Mr. Ford, who had not been able to repress a slight start.

"Oh! that old fellow—George—Georgey—who was here last night."

Mr. Ford gave another slight start—a very slight one, almost imperceptible. On it followed a dull, vacant look, well assumed, if it were not real—

a look which had often come over his face of late.

"I am sure I don't know," he said slowly—"something or other, I daresay;" and, taking up his newspaper, he read once more.

It was no use asking him where Captain George lived; yet that it was which Robert wanted to ascertain.

"Perhaps Aunt Lavinia knows," thought the young man.

He left the parlour, took a turn in the garden, then quietly walked upstairs to a housekeeper's room, which Miss Lavinia possessed, in the upper part of the house, and where she was to be found almost every morning before breakfast.

The door stood ajar, and through the opening Robert could see within.

Sunshine filled the small bright room; the morning breeze stirred the white curtains of the open window, showing a background of green trees and blue sky, and Mab attired in a pink morning gown—the sun shining on her golden hair and bent face—sat on a hassock, writing down in a ledger on her knees the items announced by Miss Lavinia. The careful lady was surveying the shelves on which the remains of last year's jams and preserves stood in broken rows with many gaps between.

"Wanting raspberry-jam," said Miss Lavinia.

"It is down, aunt."

"And, Mab, do not forget putting down the pickled onions—you know how fond Robert is of them."

"Thank you, aunt," said Robert, entering, and he gratefully kissed Miss Lavinia's pale cheek.

He was always kind and civil, but he did not always kiss her. Poor Miss Lavinia!—her eyes glistened, and her cheeks became all rosy again as she received this caress from her darling nephew.

"Good morning, Mr. Robert Ford," demurely said Mab, looking up from her ledger, and speaking with a pen between her rosy lips.

She looked so pretty a mockery of all grave business, that Robert could not resist the temptation of stooping and kissing her too. Mab offered no resistance, but she mischievously whisked her pen so that its contents remained imprinted on Robert's cheek. She expected a solemn reproof at the least, for Robert was not fond of such jests—but no, Robert only shook his fore-finger at her, and wiped his cheek, whilst Mab laughed to her heart's content.

Miss Lavinia's heart swelled. God bless them both!—they were handsome and good, and how fond they were of each other!—ay, that was true, innocent love, if there was any upon earth. It looked like it at least.

Robert, after wiping his cheek, had taken hold of Mab's two hands and compelled her to put down the ledger, and Mab was struggling silently, but wilfully, to regain her freedom. Robert did his best not to laugh, and Mab, half-amused, half-vexed, was trying to frown at him.

"What a pair of children!" said Miss Lavinia, shaking her head, and her eyes glistening with secret pleasure. "Oh! Robert! Robert! what brought you up here to my housekeeper's room this morning?"

The question sobered Robert.

"Aunt," he said, releasing Mab's hands, "I hope that old captain did not come again whilst you were alone?"

"No, thank heaven!" warmly replied Miss Lavinia. "I do not know what I should have done."

"If I only knew where he lived," exclaimed Robert, "I would see and prevent him from troubling you again."

"Oh! he told me where he and Mrs. George are living now," innocently answered Miss Lavinia; "they reside in some abominable court about the Seven Dials, and I hope, my dear Robert, you will not go near him. I would not enter that low neighbourhood on any account, and with your watch it would not be safe, it really would not. I should be frightened to death to think of your going on any such errand; and, indeed, I am very glad I have forgotten the rest of his direction, so now you cannot go."

Robert laughed.

"Thank you, aunt," he said. "Well, I am glad the old monster did not come again, and I shall now leave you to your pickled onions. Can you spare Mab? I should like to say a few words to her."

"Oh, yes; go, my dear, go with Robert at once," said Robert's over-yielding aunt. "I can do very well without you."

"But, aunt, how can you write?" demurred Mab, who liked a little housekeeping now and then, and who had her own pride in the ledger.

"Go, child. I tell you I can do without you."

Mab went, wondering what Rohert would say to her—a matter that perplexed Robert too, as he had only asked her to come with him in order that neither she nor his aunt might suspect the real motive of his morning visit to the housekeeper's room.

A useless precaution. Captain George was too little in their thoughts for a glimmering of the truth to enter the slow mind of Miss Lavinia, or for even the more penetrating Mab to have any such suspicions.

"Aunt will miss me," a little impatiently said Mab, as they went downstairs.

"I am sorry for it," composedly replied Robert, "but you see I want you."

He pushed open, as he spoke, the door that led to the garden.

Much altered and much improved was the garden at the back of the house in Queen Square. It was no longer a sandy waste dreary to the eye, but a nest of gay flowers and bright green grass. Its improved condition was all owing to Robert, who, if he had many faults, poor fellow, had, amongst other excellent qualities, an innate love of order and neatness, in which his more generous-hearted father had always failed. It was chiefly, however, to please his aunt and Mab that he had made the garden what it was now. Ivy still covered the walls, but it was kept in careful order. Neither smoke nor dust was allowed to defile its glossy leaves and their delicate white veins. Robert did his duty with artificial showers produced from the spout of the watering-pot, and the neighbours whose windows overlooked this little spot often saw Miss Lavinia doing hers on warm summer evenings, by dusting patiently the screen of verdure which hid the brown brick of the walls. Rows of bright flowers relieved the sombre green of the ivy. Scarlet geraniums, yellow calceolaria, red roses, shone there in all their splendour, and a neat edge of grass, sprinkled with daisies and buttercups, fenced them in from the shining gravel path. The jasmine arbour at the further end of this garden was in full bloom now, and nasturtiums and convolvuluses mingled with it. The old wooden bench had been replaced by a pretty rustic seat, and the very poplar trees that stood on either side of it had grown and improved and shot out new branches under Robert's fostering care. But the rockwork in the centre of the garden was Robert's masterpiece.

The rockwork in itself was a wonder. It had taken three years of walks in the country and by the seashore to collect those curiously formed stones of which it was composed. Robert's own hands had cemented them with plaster, and now and then helped the vagaries of nature. Robert's ingenuity it was that had contrived those sly little hiding places, moist and deep, whence ferns peeped out with the most innocent and natural look in the world—those recesses for creeping plants that hung about, throwing their long graceful tendrils over every bit of rock, mingling and parting again in a gay seemingly unsought-for confusion, that was in reality the acme of the gardener's art. But if the rockwork was the wonder of the garden, the fountain was the wonder of the rockwork. All Robert's mechanical skill had been called forth to produce that tiny jet of water, nearly one foot high, which sprang in the air clear, silvery, and bright from the summit and centre of the rocky pyramid, and fell again with a pretty little splash into its tin basin. It had its drawbacks—what that is earthly has not such? It had a trick of ceasing suddenly, and giving up playing, just when Miss Lavinia was pointing it out to a visitor, and it thereby so far provoked this gentle lady that she once impatiently exclaimed, "It did it on purpose." Its other error, of going all off one side was more excusable, and was leniently forgiven by Robert's aunt, whose pride in this masterpiece of her nephew was unbounded. Every one in the house, indeed, was proud of it. Edward and William boasted of it in their respective offices. Mab spoke of it frankly, as an extraordinary contrivance; and even Mr. Ford, whilst he affected to deride, secretly admired this result of his eldest son's ingenuity.

To this garden, on this sweet and balmy summer morning, Robert now took Mab. He made her sit down on the bench, and, sitting down by her, he looked at the rock-work and the fountain, and wondered what he should say. Suddenly a bright thought struck him. He turned to her, and looking full in her face he remarked, with unusual abruptness,

"Mab, do not wonder at the question—I have a motive for it: has it ever occurred to you to wonder who and what you are?"

A cloud came over Mab's sunny face.

"Oh! Robert!" she said, "what a question!"

"I am sorry it troubles you," replied Robert, in the tone in which he would have said "I am glad," "but it is an important matter. Your unknown parents——"

"I have none," impetuously interrupted the young girl; "a mother would not have left her child so many years without one token of remembrance. Robert, when I was left at the door of this house ten years ago, I was utterly forsaken. I belong to none."

"You belong to us," said Robert kindly; he was calculating, but he was fond of Mab.

"I have received the deepest kindness," answered Mab; "God knows how grateful I am; but for all that I have neither kith nor kin."

"Mab, I wonder you remember no more of your childhood than you do."

"What would it avail if I did? Yesterday there came back to me a forest scene, an old stone cross——"

"That must have been abroad."

"Perhaps it was—I know I crossed the sea in a steamboat; but, as I was saying, I remember myself sitting at the foot of a stone cross; then comes a blot. And I see a dark lad, younger than Ned, and it is all over."

"And who is that lad?"

"There it is, Robert—who is *he*?"

"But you used to talk of a place called *there*."

"Yes, where I was with a lady and Mary my maid."

A sudden thought flashed through Robert's mind. Were Mary and Mrs. Smith one person?

"What coloured hair had Mary?" he asked quickly.

"Red," answered Mab; "I am sure of that."

"Red—auburn you mean?"

"But, Robert, how can you know?" exclaimed Mab, surprised at his positive tone.

Robert did not answer her. Even if Mrs. Smith was the Mary who had helped to betray poor Mab, what availed him the knowledge? She would never turn against the father of her child. She would never help to rob that child of its destined inheritance. Still, all knowledge is useful, and that might be turned to good account yet.

"Robert, what is the matter?" asked Mab. "Robert," she added, rising and speaking with sudden warmth, "have you learned anything about me? Speak, Robert, speak!"

"My dear Mab, how you do go on! How could I learn anything? I may be trying to learn, which is a very different thing; and now, just answer this other question, and I will tease you no more. Do you think the lady, as you call her, was your mother?"

"I am sure she was not. I remember another woman very, very long ago, and she was my mother; but I cannot tell you what she was like. There is always a cloud on her face as it were, the cloud of my own oblivion. And now, Robert, this is all I know—tell me why you have questioned me?"

"Mab, I may be bent on a Quixotic errand, but I mean to try and discover who and what you are."

"You will fail, Robert."

"How do you know, Queen Mab?"

Mab's voice sank.

"Uncle has tried, Robert; he is trying, and he has failed, and you will fail too."

Robert had suspected as much, yet he seemed surprised, and asked on what Mab's belief rested.

"On his questions, on looks, and words, and broken speeches. I am sure he is trying, Robert—I am sure he has been trying these ten years."

Robert was sure of it too; suspicion became certainty, and certainty fired him. Ay, Mr. Ford was endeavouring to atone for the great wrong he had done Mab; he was trying to connect proofs and turn them into positive evidence. The vision dazzled Robert. What he had been attempting his father had been attempting too, but with far more chances of success than he had, for Mr. Ford knew well the story Robert only divined at. Where he, Robert, had failed, his father might succeed, and success was a fortune. That was why, then, he gave Captain George money, and still held intercourse with a man whom he despised and detested.

"Robert," said Mab, struck with his emotion, "what ails you?"

"Nothing," he answered, endeavouring to grow calm again, and fearing he had gone too far with Mab; "breakfast is ready, let us go in."

She stood up, and he followed her. As he passed by a rose-tree, Robert plucked the finest rose upon it, and put it in Mab's hair. She turned round with a surprised smile, for such attentions were not much in Robert's way. He looked down at her upraised face, and his look was secure, proud, and fond. She was pretty, she was good, and she would be rich.

"And I shall have her!" thought Robert.

The whole family was already seated around the breakfast-table when Mab and Robert entered the front parlour. Mab's rose at once attracted attention. Miss Lavinia nodded and smiled most significantly, and Mr. Ford asked, with some sharpness,

"Who has decorated you so, Mab?"

"I did," anwered Robert, pouring himself out some coffee, "and I meant it as a token of the victory I won last evening over Mr. George's inexorable stinginess—my salary is raised fifty pounds."

William and Edward at once fixed eager looks on their elder brother; he shook his head sadly.

"No, poor boys," he said, "I tried to get something for you, but I failed. Mr. George knows of nothing that would suit you—so he says."

Edward, who enjoyed a salary of thirty pounds a year, looked gloomy; and even the more phlegmatic William took his breakfast in sullen, disappointed silence.

"Then, my dear Robert, you now have a salary of one hundred and fifty pounds a-year!" exclaimed Miss Lavinia, full of fond admiration.

"I have, aunt, and I ought to have two hundred pounds, but Mr. George is all bent on economy. However, I am happy to have those extra fifty pounds. They will help me, I hope, to push on those two boys," he added, looking at his brothers.

"Dear Robert, just like him!" murmured Miss Lavinia, and even Mab looked kindly at Robert.

Mr. Ford said nothing. He went on drinking his tea, and wondering by what eloquence Robert had wrung the fifty pounds out of Mr. George. He was not far from guessing the truth, and the thoughts that suspicion suggested made him silent. Besides, he, too, had something to say, but he waited until his breakfast was over to say it. Pushing away his empty cup, he turned to his sister, and remarked carelessly.

"Livy, you have a carpet-bag you can lend me, have you not?"

"A carpet-bag!" repeated Miss Lavinia, much startled at so unexpected a question—"Yes, John, I have; but surely you are not going to travel?"

"Why not, Livy?"

"John, where are you going?" faltered Miss Lavinia.

The answer exceeded her wildest expectations.

"To America."

Miss Lavinia leaned back in her chair.

"My goodness!" was all she could say.

Mr. Ford did not heed her. He was looking at his children. For ten years he had not stirred from home. The boys had taken holidays; Mab and Miss Lavinia had twice gone to the seaside; but Mr. Ford had not left the house in Queen Square.

His sons, his sister, Mab herself felt convinced he remained at home out of that economy which had replaced his previous extravagance and become part of his character; but whatever his motive had been, he had remained, and now for the first time he spoke, not merely of ordinary travel, but of a long journey. He looked at his three sons, expecting, hoping to find signs of sorrow, or at least of concern in their faces. He saw none. He saw surprise, unequivocal and clear, but no regret. In all that family circle there was but one sad face—it was Mab's. Her cup stood half-full before her, her cheek rested on her hand, and her tears flowed silently, whilst her deep, earnest eyes were fixed full on his face. But though Mr. Ford saw this, it was not Mab he minded—not to her were directed those longing looks of his weary brown eyes, now soft as a woman's, and that implored in vain for some token of affectionate regret.

It is a strange feeling that parental love: a wonderful instinct—wonderful especially in its duration. What other love is there that passes not? This alone of all human feelings most resembles the divine tenderness of the Creator for his creatures, for it is patient, unwearied, and undying. Coldness, ingratitude can wound, but rarely destroy it. Its roots are in the very heart, and whilst that beats it lives; no virtue, no merit in man, but a perpetual miracle of God's goodness.

To all seeming, Mab was infinitely dearer to Mr. Ford than his own children; and yet she was not so. The love he bore her was the love of sorrow, repentance, and atonement. It sprang from the feeling that he could never do enough for one whom he had so wronged, and with it blended genuine tenderness and affection. But he loved his children, because they were his children—his real flesh and blood, born in sorrow, reared in adversity. William, Edward, and Robert were his boys—images of himself, part of his own being; for them he had sinned and suffered all these years, for them he would have died again and again. It smote his heart to see the coldness with which they could hear that he was leaving them for an unknown length of time, on a journey that might be dangerous. His lip quivered, his eyes grew dim, but he would not betray emotion which they did not share.

"Please to see about that carpet-bag, Livy," he said, and he rose and left the room.

CHAPTER VI.

A DEEP silence followed the closing of the parlour door. Miss Lavinia was still full of amazement, far too full to speak; Mab was crying; Robert was thinking, "He is going to America about Mab;" and Edward and William were exchanging glances of wonder and curiosity.

"What can papa be going to America for?" at length exclaimed Ned. No one answered this question.

"The governor looks a little cut up about it," slowly said William, who had more penetration and more feeling too than either of his brothers.

"What for?" petulantly exclaimed Edward. "I wish *I* could go to America; but there is no chance for me."

"I should prefer Australia," said William; "by far the newer country of the two, Neddy."

Neddy was fond of an argument, and this opportunity for one was not to be neglected.

"America is a democratic country," he said, warmly, "and I like republican institutions."

"Institutions fiddlestick," irreverently answered William; "can you tell me what an institution is? Just tell me that?"

Now, definition was not Edward's *forte;* he hesitated, and Mab, whose heart was very sore, and who felt no curiosity to hear the rest, rose and left the parlour. She went upstairs to go to her own room. As she passed the drawing-room door she saw that it was ajar, and conjecturing that Mr. Ford was within, she entered.

He was standing by one of the windows, looking out wistfully in the square. Mab approached him, and he never turned round. Mr. Ford was looking at his three sons, on whom the front door had just closed, and who were walking away together laughing and talking.

"Uncle," softly said Mab, who guessed his feelings, and she passed her arm within his and looked up in his face.

"Let them go, Mab," he replied, without turning round; "let them go away talking and laughing, though they do not know whether they shall ever see their old father again."

"Uncle, are you going to-day?" cried Mab.

"Oh! let me call them back." She wanted to open the window, but Mr. Ford held her fast.

"Hush!" he said, "call them back—what for? They are not children to hang about daddy, or cry because he is going! They are men, Mab; men grown up and ungrateful—men who do not want him, who have an elder brother that is more than a father to them! Provided the old man gives them board and lodging, they do not care where he is—in England or in America! What difference does it make to them! Do you think they will miss him! You cannot say you think it, Mab!"

Mab could not say she did; she felt mute and helpless.

"Oh! uncle, if they only knew how you love them!" she could not help saying.

"If they only knew it!" repeated Mr. Ford, shaking his white head; "if they only knew it! Am I not their father, Mab? Have I not well nigh sold my soul for these boys! and now they turn on me in my old age, when my hair is white as if I were eighty—they turn on me! Mab, never marry—never have children, Mab, to sting you with their ingratitude!"

"Uncle, they do love you, only you are often strict—"

"Say the word, Mab—I am harsh! To be sure, my life has not been cast on a bed of roses. I have had my trials—I have had a family to rear, and not always the wherewithal to do it; but I should be pleasant for all that. As to owing me any debt of gratitude, of course they do not! I have given them what shame, the world, the law itself compel every father to give his children—the shelter of his roof—a place at his table. Besides, of late Robert has paid full board, and Edward and William half. They owe me nothing, Mab, nothing—I keep a lodging-house, and they owe me nothing!"

Mr. Ford laughed as he said this, but it was a very dreary laugh, one that made Mab's heart ache. Anxious to change the subject, she leaned her head against his shoulder and said softly,

"Uncle, why are you going to America?"

Mr. Ford's brown eyes sparkled; a smile played around his sharp, irritable mouth; he drew Mab towards him, and kissed her fondly:

"It will end well for you, my pet," he said; "mind what I tell you, Mab, that journey will end well for you."

"But, uncle, what is it about?"

He smoothed her hair, and stroked her cheek, and called her "puss," but he would tell her no more. When she renewed her questions he gently put her away, and said with his abstracted look:

"I must see about that carpet-bag, child."

To see about the carpet-bag, proved, however, a

more serious undertaking than Mr. Ford anticipated. Miss Lavinia's mind had by no means recovered the shock her brother's extraordinary declaration had given it at breakfast. She was still too much agitated to remember where the carpet-bag was, and moreover she tried hard to convince the impatient Mr. Ford that he had better buy one than have hers.

"There is a trunk-dealer in Little Ormond Street, John," she said in her earnest way; "and I believe he has American trunks, or at least trunks for the overland route, which is just the thing for you—whereas my carpet-bag was only meant for England."

"I am not going to India, Livy," testily replied Mr. Ford; "and where is the use of buying a new trunk when an old thing will do? Come now, exert yourself, will you, and look for it."

"I think you had better ask Mab," said Miss Lavinia, sitting down, as she always did in cases of utter despair; "I feel unequal to it."

Mab, on being summoned, at once said that Miss Lavinia's carpet-bag was in a trunk under the clothes-basket in one of the attics, a piece of intelligence which so far roused Miss Lavinia as to make her do her best to convince her brother that, since the bag was in the trunk under the clothes-basket, it was expedient to leave it there.

But Mr. Ford was resolved on extracting it from its hiding-place, and his vehement obstinacy prevailed over Miss Ford's passive stubbornness. The packing, however, proved another field of battle. Miss Lavinia, in her eagerness to relieve Mr. Ford of all travelling anxieties, insisted on providing him with a hamper which she proposed filling with cold provisions.

"We had a joint yesterday, John," she said persuasively; "and cold lamb makes excellent sandwiches, and boiled eggs are a fine thing for travelling; and I always heard that the charges on board steamers are dreadfully high; sixpence for a cup of such bad tea! Now, if you take my Etna and some naphtha, you can manage very well for yourself."

"Livy, *will* you let me have my shirts, if you please?" asked Mr. Ford, with a desperate politeness which told of a coming storm; but still Miss Lavinia in her gentle obstinacy spoke of sandwiches and boiled eggs and the Etna, until Mr. Ford began to look wild, and Mab found it needful to interfere.

"Poor aunt is worried at your going, uncle," she said; "let me see about your linen—I know where it is kept; and let her have her way about the hamper," she whispered in his ear.

Mr. Ford muttered something which sounded very like an oath, though he had long given up swearing, and vowed, with much emphasis, "that he would settle the hamper—he would! Let her attempt it—that was all."

Mab, bent on conciliation, found means to make Miss Lavinia leave the room on some pressing business below, and, remaining upstairs with Mr. Ford, she helped to pack the carpet-bag under his directions. His mood softened as he saw her thus engaged.

"Pack away, my darling," he said with sparkling eyes; "pack away. I am an old fox—they have not done with me yet—I have many a doubling they don't think of, Mab—ha, ha! They have laughed at old John Ford, have they?—well, we shall see!"

And, smacking his lips with the gusto of an epicure, Mr. Ford whose hands were thrust into his pockets, with him a token of high good-humour, or of angry displeasure, began walking up and down his bedroom, where he and Mab were now alone. She was kneeling before the carpet-bag, with its future contents scattered on the floor around her. She looked up at Mr. Ford, surprised at his use of the word "they;" he could not be talking of his sons—of whom, then, was he speaking? But he did not heed her inquiring look; he was absorbed in his own thoughts, and, still walking up and down the room with a firm and elastic step, he muttered, laughing and shaking his head; but all Mab heard or understood was: "I have got my teeth yet. And they shall feel them—they shall feel them!"

"Uncle," quietly asked Mab, "how much linen will you take?"

Mr. Ford was at once by her side, and his instructions were cool, clear, precise, and collected. In less than an hour the carpet-bag was packed to his entire satisfaction; Lucy was sent for a cab, and he was ready to go.

"We shall see you on board, John," said Miss Lavinia.

John gave her a mistrustful look.

"I am not going on board," he said.

Miss Lavinia put only one construction on this speech: Mr. Ford intended going by rail to America; she gave him a bewildered look, until Mab relieved and enlightened her by saying:

"Are you going by Liverpool, uncle?"

"I don't know," he answered, almost as sharply as if he had spoken to his sister; "I can go by Southampton if I like."

"Then we shall see you to the station, John," said Miss Lavinia.

The cab was at the door, and Mr. Ford was on his way down. He turned round with his hand on the heavy wooden banisters, and said coolly:

"You and Mab had better stay within. I can see it will rain this afternoon."

"Why, there is not a cloud, John, and the sun is shining."

"Dear aunt," softly whispered Mab, "let him go alone. He wishes it, you see."

"Good-bye, Mab," said Mr. Ford, stretching out his arm, and gathering her to his heart. "Good-bye, darling—*you* will think of the old man, eh?"

Tears and kisses were Mab's only reply.

"Good-bye, Livy," said Mr. Ford, holding out his hand to his sister; "I have often been cross, I know, but I meant no harm—no harm, Livy."

"My dear John, you have been all goodness," said Miss Lavinia, much affected; "and I hope and trust you will soon come home to us safe and well. I only wish," she timidly added, "you would let us see you on board."

She stopped short, for Mr. Ford's irascible lips began to twitch, preliminary to a wrathful reply, which Mab checked with a kiss.

"Good-bye, uncle darling," she said, trying to laugh and seem cheerful; "make haste and go, or I shall get into the cab with you and be off to America."

"Tell the boys——" began Mr. Ford, but he checked himself.

"What?" asked Mab.

"Nothing."

She questioned him in vain. The fond remembrance of the father's heart was checked by the father's pride. He only shook his head when she spoke, and entered the cab without uttering another word.

Mab and Miss Lavinia stood on the door-step, and, with streaming eyes, watched the cab rolling away. Suddenly the door of the vehicle opened, and a dark object leaped out and bundled on the pavement; upon which the door was shut again, and the cabman, unconscious of what had happened, turned sharply the corner of the square.

"Good gracious!" faintly cried Miss Lavinia; "he has thrown it out. I told Lucy to put it in and he has thrown it out!"

It was the unfortunate hamper which Mr. Ford had thus violently expelled.

Miss Lavinia's next remark bore no reference to the hamper.

"I declare!" she exclaimed, "that John has gone away without leaving me a farthing of money."

She turned to Mab, but Mab had gone upstairs to cry in her room, and Miss Ford remained alone with her perplexity, wandering about the house and exclaiming, as she went, "What shall I do?"

Mr. Ford had been gone about a quarter of an hour, when the rattling of a cab was heard across Queen Square; it came nearer—it stopped at the door. Something had happened, Mr. Ford was coming back; before the cabman's knock had subsided at the door, Miss Lavinia had opened it herself, and breathlessly exclaimed,

"I am so glad, John! You forgot——"

She said no more: a stranger had alighted from the cab and stood before her.

"I am afraid Miss Ford has forgotten me," said the stranger with a smile.

He was young, good-looking, and he had dark hair, blue eyes, and very white teeth.

"I am afraid I have," stammered Miss Lavinia, who saw that the cab roof was covered with a formidable quantity of luggage.

"I am Frederick Norton," continued the stranger, "and I come by Mr. Ford's invitation."

Miss Lavinia was mute: the extent of the calamity overcame her. Her brother was gone, a guest had come, and she had no money!

Frederick Norton reddened.

"I am afraid my arrival is ill-timed," he said; "perhaps I was not expected."

He looked very much inclined to get back into the cab; but, delighted though Miss Lavinia would have been to see his visit end thus, she could not think of allowing it.

"Pray, come in, Mr. Norton," she cried eagerly; and, conscious of the coldness of her welcome, she added, "And pray excuse me. My brother went off a few minutes ago to America, and we are still rather upset about it. If the cabman will help to put your luggage in the hall, I shall see about having it conveyed to your room presently."

Frederick Norton bowed. He felt there was something odd in all this, but he could not very well withdraw from the invitation so freely given and so freely accepted, the preceding evening. He saw his luggage transferred to the hall, he entered the parlour, and then exchanged a few words with Miss Lavinia. But quickly perceiving her perturbation of mind, he begged that she would take no further trouble about him, and that she would leave him, if, as he could not help suspecting, her presence were required elsewhere.

"I shall send Mab to you," eagerly said Miss Lavinia.

"I shall be delighted to renew my acquaintance with Miss Winter," answered Frederick Norton smiling.

He took up a book, and Miss Lavinia hastened to leave the parlour.

In great distress she went up to Mab's room. The young girl's face was buried in the pillow of her bed. She had not heard the cab stopping at the door; she did not hear Miss Lavinia entering her room, until that lady said, in a most melancholy tone of voice,

"My dear, what shall we do? Young Mr. Norton has come to stay with us, and I have no room ready for him, and I have no money."

Mab raised her face still bathed in tears, and an expression of the deepest surprise passed over it.

"Young Mr. Norton has come, and I have no money," repeated Miss Lavinia; "do you think one could take a cab and overtake John, and ask him either to give us the extra money, or to tell Mr. Norton to come another time?"

"I have money, aunt," replied Mab, recovering from her astonishment. "Uncle left me plenty, and if you like to give Mr. Norton my room—pray do so. I can sleep with you."

"No, my dear," replied Miss Lavinia, looking fondly at Mab's little delicate white bower, "no, we shall have no young man in here. I shall give him my room and come and sleep with you; and, since you have the money," she added, brightening up, "I think it is almost as well John is not here. He would only worry about the expense."

"Poor uncle!" thought Mab, feeling a little sore at Miss Lavinia's frankness.

"My dear, will you go down and talk to that young man in the front parlour," timidly suggested Miss Lavinia, "whilst I get his room ready."

"Yes, aunt, if it will oblige you; besides, I must do it—I am the cause of his coming here."

Mab bathed her eyes, smoothed her hair, shook her skirts, and went down at once. She found Frederick Norton walking up and down the front parlour, and looking, as he felt, rather rueful. Very sincerely indeed did he regret having left his comfortable hotel for a house where he received so odd a welcome. He was almost meditating a sudden flight, when the door opened; he turned round and saw Mab standing on the threshold.

We have already said, that, though Mab was neither pretty nor beautiful, she was something beyond both, and that something is far more rare than beauty, and, unless when this is of the highest order, far more seducing. Mab, however, only vaguely knew that she was attractive; she had not as yet been in society, and had not received that test of admiration which envy itself must yield, and modesty perceive. She was certainly not prepared for Frederick Norton's amazed and dazzled look. He was taken by surprise, and betrayed more than he knew, the admiration he felt. She stood before him, her cheeks still flushed with recent tears, her deep, dark grey eyes half shyly veiled by white lids and long black lashes, a smile trembling on her parted lips, her whole countenance breathing a spirit and sweetness which made him forget that her features were not classical, and her outlines by no means faultless. He only saw that the pretty yellow-haired child now stood before him a lovely and blooming girl. He advanced towards her, and taking her extended hand, he said with slight though perceptible emotion,

"I hope you have not forgotten your old friend Fred, Miss Winter,"

"Friend and defender," replied Mab, with a smile which completed Frederick Norton's undoing. He fell in love that moment—deeply, desperately, and for the first time in his life. But he did not know it—the patients who suffer from that malady rarely do; he only thought Mab was the sweetest girl he had ever seen.

"I must give aunt time to get his room ready," thought Mab; and, with this praiseworthy object in view, she sat down and kept Frederick Norton in conversation.

She knew how to talk, and she talked very well, like a clever girl as she was. We are not sure, indeed, that Frederick Norton minded much what Mab was saying; she had a very sweet voice, he thought, lively and soft, and beautiful eyes, and the prettiest turn of the neck he had ever seen, and just the coloured hair he liked, golden and silky—and all these charms helped Mab's eloquence to such a degree, that, whilst the poor girl wondered if her aunt would ever come down to the rescue, Frederick thought Time never had had such nimble wings—or rather he did not think at all about it; he only sat and listened enchanted, and said little or nothing. Admiration silences some people, and it certainly made Frederick mute. If he was not a very brilliant, he was not either a very foolish young man. He had as much wisdom as many, and plenty of spirits and good humour. In business he was shrewd beyond his years or appearance; in every-day life he was generally found sensible, modest, and well-bred. But now, sense, spirits and politeness all forsook him. He found little or nothing to say, and the little he did say he said very badly. Mab learned from him that he liked Melbourne and disliked Sydney; that his aunt Mrs. Norton and his sister Ellen were in Ireland; that his father was doing capitally in Australia, but that he, Frederick, meant to settle in England. Beyond such discourse Mab could not lead him. Poor Frederick! he was in a delicious dream, in the sweetest of intoxication; he was conscious of neither time, nor sound, nor language; he knew nothing, save that Mab was sitting there, and that he was with her.

"I shall certainly die of exhaustion if aunt does not come down," thought Mab. Suddenly a bright thought struck her.

"You have not seen the garden. Will you come and look at it?" she said.

"I shall be delighted to visit it," replied Frederick, full of alacrity. And delighted he looked with this little square of grass and flowers. He admired the roses, the fountain, the arbour; above all, he admired Mab. Some women look well in gardens, girls always do; but a garden became Mab especially. That green background, the fresh flowers, were the natural set-off of her bright hair, and her blooming face. The nymphs of old knew well that secret of beauty. They were seen in forests, by crystal fountains, in Nature's own domain, wherever grass grew and trees gave shade, never in man's cold and garish dwellings. Armida knew it too, and Circe and all the perfidious enchantresses of the old world of song, and of the new, and Laura, Petrarch's Laura herself, did she not know it—she who showed the poet her angel face near the lonely fountain of Vaucluse? Mab had not known it before, but she learned it now, she learned it in the glances of Frederick Norton, who was drinking in love with alarming rapidity. He looked at the fountain, at the rustic seat, and the arbour, and he said with a half sigh:

"You sit and work here?"

"Sometimes."

Frederick's eyes seemed to say: Happy seat, happy arbour! Mab looked demure, and felt very much amused.

"You must think very little of an English garden now," she said.

Very warmly did Frederick Norton assure her that an English garden, such an English garden as this, was delightful in his eyes; and then the variety of the English climate was so delightful, too, and the singing birds! Of course she had singing birds.

"Yes, but I have no dog," replied Mab despondently.

"You wish for one?" cried Frederick, with sparkling eyes.

"I long for one, but cannot get it."

"A King Charles, perhaps—a Blenheim."

"No, nor yet a Scotch terrier. I want a small black and tan terrier; but the breed is extinct, I am sure, or Robert would not be so long about getting me one."

Tired with standing, and having fairly exhausted every subject of discourse, Mab sat down on the bench. At once Frederick sat down by her side. To her despair, he was evidently preparing for another delightful hour, and Mab was wondering if the laws of hospitality really forbade escape, when relief came from an unexpected quarter.

The back parlour window opened, and Robert, who had come home an hour earlier, for the express purpose of having some tender conversation with

Mab, appeared standing there in a rigid attitude, and looking at the pair on the bench with a solemn and severe countenance.

Mab saw him first.

She rose, and Frederick Norton, looking up, perceived Robert's gloomy and forbidding countenance. But Frederick was in a delightful mood; he forgot that he had always disliked Robert, and that they had nearly fallen out the day before. He left the bench, and went towards Mr. Ford's eldest son with a friendly face and a hand frankly extended, which Robert could not well refuse to press. They shook hands through the open window, but Mab saw that the cloud had not left Robert's brow, and she was shrewd enough to guess what had brought it there. She smiled and nodded at him, however, with a look of perfect innocence, and saying significantly,

"I dare say aunt wants me; I shall leave you and Mr. Norton together."

She left the garden, and entered the house.

Frederick's looks followed her until the hem of her garment had vanished; then turning to Robert, he said, with more frankness than good-breeding allows,

"What a charming creature your sister has grown up!"

"Miss Winter is not my sister," drily replied Robert.

"Ay, true: has that mystery never been cleared up?"

"Never."

But Frederick seemed unconscious of Robert's short replies; he was in that dreamland where neither politeness nor impertinence can reach the happy wanderer, and it was plain that politeness only made him talk at all. Talk he did, however, leaning on the sill of the parlour window, and listening for the sound of Mab's voice in the house; and, secretly exasperated though he felt, Robert was compelled, by all the laws of hospitality, to keep him in conversation.

No sooner was Mab free, than she ran up to her aunt's room. She found Miss Lavinia sitting on a chair in the deepest mental distress, and the room as little ready for Frederick Norton as when he arrived an hour before.

"Oh! Mab," she said, "why did you not come?"

"I was with Mr. Norton."

"And what did he want with you all this time? Could you not have sent him into the Square? I do not think Robert will like it."

Mab, though innocent, blushed, and asked what she should do.

"Do go and ask Mr. Norton if he will have the chest of drawers so, near the door or between the two windows."

But Mab refused to do this, and entreated that they might get on.

"But Mab, do tell me about the chest of drawers. Do you think Mr. Norton would object to our leaving matters as they are?"

"I am sure he would not."

"Are you really?"

"Indeed I am, aunt."

"Well then," said Miss Lavinia, rising, "that chest of drawers was a weight on my mind, and now I feel relieved, and we can see about the rest."

The rest meant everything, for, in her anxiety about the chest of drawers, Miss Ford had forgotten the dinner.

"You know," she faltered, "that John went away without——"

"I have money, aunt; what shall we get for dinner?"

"We had lamb yesterday, but I cut it up for sandwiches——"

"Aunt, we cannot give Mr. Norton sandwiches."

"I am sorry I cut it up."

It was useless to argue with her. Mab ran downstairs, ordered a couple of fowls, a tart, vegetables, and wine and fruit for the dessert. She had Mr. Norton's luggage transferred from the hall to his room, and, after giving the kitchen a last look, and seeing the cloth laid in the parlour, she ran up to her own room and dressed for dinner. Through her open window she could hear Robert and their guest talking in the garden below, in tones that sounded cordial enough. Mab laughed to herself and thought:

"Old Robert, you must get accustomed to seeing me admired—indeed you must."

Mab had too much good taste to make herself fine, but there was no harm in putting on a very becoming pale blue muslin dress. None, indeed; and she looked as fresh and fair as is "the pleasant month of May," when she joined the two young men in the garden. Was not Robert there, and were not William and Edward coming? There they are indeed! That is their knock, they have learned the news from Lucy, and they rush into the garden, gleeful and joyous. They do not know their father has left; and if they knew it, what then? Frederick, the new friend, the new pleasure, is there. There is a warm shaking of hands, as if years had passed since their meeting; during that ceremony Mab and Robert stand apart, Robert reproachfully looking at Mab, who bends over a flower, apparently unconscious of the gaze. She feels it, however, and she knows it is her muslin dress is the cause; and Robert is very tiresome and despotic, and Mab will not yield to him in this. She will look pretty—ay, and as pretty as she can.

Across these thoughts comes one tender and remorseful. Mr. Ford is away ; the friend, the more than father. He is away, is this a day for rejoicing? He is sailing on a sea which may be stormy, for clouds are gathering in the mild evening sky, and the wind is rising—is this a day for merry-making, for muslin dresses that make Frederick Norton's looks ever wander towards her with increasing admiration!

Robert saw the tears in her eyes.

"What is the matter?" he whispered.

"Uncle is gone," she replied.

William turned round full of surprise.

"Yes," resumed Mab, addressing him and his brother in a tone of some reproach, "he left this afternoon, and you never bade him good-bye."

She felt she had said too much, and left the garden. As she entered the house, she met Miss Lavinia, attired in her best cap and her grey silk, and unusually fluttered. Mab, forgetting her own muslin, felt virtuously indignant.

"Oh! aunt," she exclaimed, "you too do not care about poor uncle being gone—no one cares about him. What would he think if he came back and found us all so gay?"

"My goodness! I hope he will not come," cried Miss Lavinia, distracted at the mere prospect; "he would never forgive me, the fowls and the tart—never, Mab!"

"Yes he would, aunt, for I am to blame, not you. Well, I suppose we cannot help it, with a stranger and a guest in the house," she added in a less remorseful tone; "and is dinner ready, aunt?"

"Yes, my dear, quite ready."

The tidings that dinner was ready reached the garden. The young men came in; each took his place, and Mab found herself next Frederick, and opposite Robert. Miss Ford said grace in the absence of her brother; this, and his vacant place filled by Robert, recalled to Mr. Ford's sons the fact that he was no longer with them. Robert looked thoughtful for many reasons, and there was just a touch of regret in the otherwise happy faces of his younger brothers. But it could not last. Frederick's presence, the good cheer on the table, the roast fowls, the delicate vegetables, the tart—it stood on a side-board awaiting its fate—the sparkling wines banished all melancholy thoughts. Robert, indeed, sat silent and dark, for, with growing displeasure, he saw how Frederick's eyes were ever seeking Mab's; but William and Edward had not a thought, not a care. Miss Lavinia herself felt pleasurably excited. The roast fowls, "just as they used to be at her godmother's," had roused her into a sort of joy and liveliness. Oh! how pleasant it would be to have money, and spend it and see company, and live daintily as do the rich!

And she does not think of Mr. Ford! How should she? when to think of him is to think of keeping house for eight on two pounds a week, and not daring to call one's soul one's own.

But Mr. Ford is not forgotten. There is one—not his child—on whose plate the dainty fare lies scarcely tasted. There is one whom neither Frederick's adoring though shy glances, nor Robert's jealous looks, can move this evening; one whose heart would leap with joy if he were to appear suddenly. Ay, Mr. Ford, you were right: it is not the beings whom we most love, for whom we sacrifice most, that return that love—the wronged one is often the truest.

END OF VOL. I.

CPSIA information can be obtained
at www.ICGtesting.com
Printed in the USA
LVHW040339110522
718423LV00001B/288

9 783375 001643